FRAGILE SPIRITS

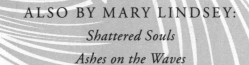

ALSO BY MARY LINDSEY:

Shattered Souls

Ashes on the Waves

Fragile Spirits

Mary Lindsey

PHILOMEL BOOKS
An Imprint of Penguin Group (USA)

PHILOMEL BOOKS
Published by The Penguin Group
Penguin Group (USA) LLC
375 Hudson Street, New York, NY 10014

USA | Canada | UK | Ireland | Australia | New Zealand | India | South Africa | China
penguin.com
A Penguin Random House Company

Library of Congress Cataloging-in-Publication Data
Lindsey, Mary, 1963–
Fragile spirits / Mary Lindsey.
pages cm
Companion book to: Shattered souls.
Summary: "Paul has been training his whole life to be a Protector. Together he
and his assigned Speaker will help lingering souls move from our world to the next.
But no amount of training has prepared him for Vivienne—a Speaker with hot pink
hair, piercings, and a blatant disregard for rules"—Provided by publisher.
[1. Ghosts—Fiction. 2. Future life—Fiction. 3. Supernatural—Fiction. 4. Love—
Fiction.] I. Title. PZ7.L6613Fr 2014 [Fic]—dc23 2013012761

Printed in the United States of America.
ISBN 978-0-399-16186-5
1 3 5 7 9 10 8 6 4 2

Edited by Jill Santopolo. Design by Siobhán Gallagher.
Text set in 11.5-point Adobe Garamond Pro.

TO EMILY LINDSEY

Don't worry.
I didn't take my eyes off you.
Not even for a second.

He died as he had lived, with unmentionable
wickedness on his lips—
a sad spectacle of depravity, unwept and
unregretted by all!
              Thomas North on Nicaragua Smith from
                        Five Years in Texas, 1871

ONE

21st-Century Cycle, Journal Entry 1:

I have been instructed to keep a journal of my Speaker's progress for this cycle in order to track her/his preferences and trends to carry over into our future lifetimes together. I await my assignment with great excitement.

Paul Blackwell—Protector 993

D o you know the answer, Mr. Blackwell?" Ms. Mueller tapped her pencil on the grade book laid open on her podium.

I didn't know the answer. I hadn't even heard the question. Ever since Charles had told me I'd meet my Speaker tomorrow, I couldn't concentrate. I cleared my throat. "I'm sorry. No."

Lenzi shot me a sympathetic look over her shoulder as Ms. Mueller smirked and marked her grade book. This was the second time this class period she'd caught me not paying attention. I'd always been an exceptional student, but the thought of being paired up at last with my Speaker made it impossible to focus. Charles would be furious if I made a bad grade after he'd fought so hard to get me into this exclusive private school in the middle of the year. More than that, *I* would be furious if I made a bad grade.

"Mr. Thomas?" Ms. Mueller crooned. She loved Alden. He always knew the answers to her questions about the American Civil War.

I fought the urge to roll my eyes. Of *course* he knew the answers. He'd lived one of his past lives during the Civil War. It hardly seemed fair.

It was strange to see Alden in a regular classroom. Instead of his usual black, he wore a preppy school uniform complete with starched white shirt and navy blue blazer. I was used to seeing him in his role as Protector 438. We'd trained together at Wilkingham Academy since we were ten or so until two years ago, when I turned fifteen and Charles pulled me out to be his apprentice.

Lenzi slumped in her desk while, to Ms. Mueller's delight, Alden described what events had led to the Battle of Whateverberg with perfect accuracy and in excruciating detail.

As if the air had been charged with electric current, my

body came alive, causing the back of my neck to prickle. I gasped as fear crashed through me.

Lenzi's fear.

Alden stiffened and turned to face her.

From her podium, Ms. Mueller droned on to the class, unaware of the invisible danger that had entered her room.

Lenzi sat rigid in her chair, giving no physical indication of what was going on, but her emotions were a jumble of terror and confusion. She was under attack. Alden and I couldn't hear it, but being Protectors, we could feel her reaction as if her emotions were our own.

A spirit was communicating with her, and unable to reveal her special abilities to "normal" people, she was hiding the event as best she could from our classmates.

This wasn't an ordinary dead person she was dealing with. It was more than just a Hindered seeking her help for resolution. Her level of fear indicated it was a demon—a Malevolent.

She hissed a breath of air through her teeth and gripped the side of her desk like she was in pain. Alden slid sideways in his chair, preparing to rise. She jerked her arm down to her side, and crimson drops of blood splattered the beige linoleum floor. Terror still emanating from her, she grabbed her navy blazer from the back of her chair and slipped it on. She pressed her arm to her body and met Alden's eyes. He rose.

"Mr. Thomas? Is something wrong?" Ms. Mueller asked.

He shot me a look as Lenzi stood. Her face paled, and she

shook all over. Something was terribly wrong. Neither of us would be able to soul-share with her in front of so many people, so all I could do was wait for Alden's cue. I'd been assigned to shadow the pair in case of an incident like this—in case he needed a second Protector to keep her alive.

"Mr. Thomas?" Ms. Mueller's voice was shrill, but Alden's eyes never left Lenzi's face.

The bell rang, and our classmates scrambled to the door—the last-period-of-the-day-on-Friday excitement drowning out the bell and Ms. Mueller.

"Follow us, Paul," Alden ordered, grabbing Lenzi's backpack. He put his hand against the small of her back and guided her to the door, pressing into the mass of students and away from Ms. Mueller's curious stare. Once clear and in the hallway, he pitched the backpack to me and scooped Lenzi up in his arms as if she weighed nothing. "Is it—"

"Yes," she answered. "Smith is back."

T W O

Alden buckled Lenzi into the center of the backseat of his car, slid in next to her, and tossed me the keys. "Your place is closest, Paul."

I ran around the front of Alden's Audi and started it without hesitation. This was what I'd been trained to do since I was ten: serve and protect the Speaker.

Before I could back out of the parking place, Lenzi's fear spiked and shot through me, heightening my alertness.

"Is he here now?" Alden asked, shoving Lenzi's backpack into his little sister's empty toddler seat, which was on the other side of her.

"No," Lenzi said, trembling. "I just freaked out because I didn't expect him to come back so soon. You told me he wouldn't. You said he couldn't get this far away from where he died."

"I didn't think he could," Alden replied. "He's one tough demon." He met my eyes in the rearview mirror as he snapped his seat belt. "I'm going to soul-share just to be safe. Get us to your house quick, Paul."

Foot still on the brake, I held my breath as Alden whispered, "Out." His body went still, and his eyes glazed over. Lenzi shuddered and grabbed the back of my seat. His soul was in her body now, preventing the demon from possessing her.

Two souls in one body. As accustomed as I was to the concept, it still amazed me. I put the car in gear and backed out. "Are you okay, Lenzi?"

Still clutching the seat, she took a deep breath. "Yeah. I'm good. Alden wants me to tell you to call Race and step on it."

Once I was away from the school and on the main road, I grabbed my phone from where I'd tossed it on the seat. Race was second on my list of "favorites," though I couldn't actually say he was one of my favorite people. He rubbed me the wrong way most of the time.

"What's up, Junior?" he answered.

"You need to meet us at Charles's house. Lenzi's been hurt," I said.

"How bad?" he asked.

"I don't know. She's bleeding from her arm." I turned right and pulled up to the guard station at the entrance of my neighborhood.

"Where's Alden?"

"Sharing the Vessel," I said, waving at the security guard, who stepped out of his station. He looked to be a billion years old and had never missed a day of work in the two years I'd lived here. I put the phone in my lap and lowered the window several inches, hoping he'd just wave me on once he knew it was me.

"New car, Paul?" he asked, taking off his cap to wipe his forehead with his sleeve.

Dang. He was going to be chatty. "No, sir. Belongs to a friend. And I have a visitor coming in a few minutes. His name is Race McLain. Please let him in." I forced a smile and raised the window before he noticed Alden's lifeless body buckled in the backseat. The windows of Alden's car weren't as tinted as mine, but at least the guy wouldn't have a clear view. Part of our charge from the Intercessor Council was to not reveal our mission to people outside our world.

After giving me a thumbs-up, the guard returned to the station and the metal gates drew open.

"Hey, Junior," Race's voice called from my lap.

"What?" I shouted, raising the phone to my ear.

"Oooh. So aggressive. What's the matter?"

"When you call me that, it makes me want to kick your ass."

He laughed. "Why do you think I do it? See you in a few."

"Really?" Lenzi said. "You're worried about me getting blood on the seat?" Obviously, she was having a conversation with Alden who could talk to her when his soul was in her body. "Well, if it was really a joke, it wasn't funny. And yeah, the bogeyman's gone, so get out."

Alden's body reanimated as I pulled into the circular drive in front of the mansion. "What, no Batcave?" he asked, unbuckling.

"The garage opener is in my car back at the school." Charles had had a spectacular garage added on to the house with a wall of high-tech surveillance gadgets fit for the king of geeks—or a first-class spy—whichever fit his mood that day. "We'll have to enter like plebeians. Sorry."

"Plebeians." Lenzi snorted as we entered the double-height marble foyer, with its massive chandelier. "Someone's been studying for the SAT. If I hadn't just been hacked up by a bogeyman, I'd laugh."

"Let's do this in the kitchen," I suggested, squeamish at the thought of getting blood on the white marble in the bathroom. Blood was not my thing. The kitchen counters were stainless steel and much easier to clean up. I led them out of the foyer into the first room on the left.

"Do you have supplies for stitches?" Alden asked as we passed through the dining room with its highly polished table that seated probably twenty people. I'd never seen this room used in the two years I'd lived here. "Mine are in my locker at school."

"Stitches?" Lenzi squeaked.

I held the kitchen door open for them. "We're supposed to use your supplies, since she's your assigned Speaker."

Alden guided Lenzi to a stool at the island in the middle of the kitchen. "I'm going to be your assigned nightmare if you start quoting the rule book to me right now, Paul." He helped Lenzi out of her jacket and laid it on the stool next to her. "Rules are necessary to a point, but then they become impractical. Keep in mind, your supplies are much easier to replace than your teeth."

I'd never seen Alden this intense. And he'd certainly never threatened me before, even when we were sparring partners at Wilkingham Academy. But his Speaker was hurt—that would explain it.

I nearly threw up when he turned Lenzi's arm to where the wound was visible. It looked like letters were carved under the smeared blood covering her skin.

"It's not deep," Alden said. "But you need a couple of stitches up here." He indicated the area near the inside of the elbow. Tears pooled in Lenzi's eyes, and a wave of panic rushed from her and shot through me. I closed my eyes and caught my breath.

"Supplies now, Paul. I don't care where you get them." Alden's eyes never left Lenzi's arm.

I was just about to break the bad news that my medical kit was in my car back at the school when Race's voice came from the front of the house: "Hey! Where's the party?"

"Here," Alden called.

To my relief, Race had a medical bag in his hand. Wearing

faded blue jeans, a plaid flannel shirt with a western yoke, and snakeskin cowboy boots, he looked out of place in the elegant stainless and mahogany kitchen.

"We have to quit meeting like this, Lenzi," Race said, kissing her on the cheek.

"Yeah, let's," she groaned.

Race placed the bag on the kitchen counter and pulled out several sealed containers of instruments and supplies.

Lenzi's fear skyrocketed, racing like flames through my extremities. Being able to feel her emotions was distracting. For Alden, it would be much worse, because he was her bound Protector and their souls were linked together with a marking the IC called a soul brand.

"Whoa. Take it down a notch there, sugar," Race said. "A guy's gotta think if he's going to do something like this."

Lenzi covered her face with her free hand. "I hate medical stuff. You know that."

"We need a pillow and a couple of towels, Paul," Alden said, looking around the kitchen. "This island is perfect because of those lights above it." He indicated the halogen pendant lights with chrome accents above his head with a nod.

"Oh, God," Lenzi groaned.

When I returned with the pillow and towels, Lenzi was seated on the kitchen island. Alden took the pillow, and I set the towels near Race's supplies on the counter near the door, feeling totally useless. Race wore surgical gloves and had made a makeshift surgical tray on a sterile towel from his kit spread over a cookie sheet.

My mind kept wandering to my own Speaker. I wondered if I would be as calm and controlled as Alden if my Speaker were injured.

Lenzi's fear spiked again as Alden laid her down on the counter with her head on the pillow. "Bring me a towel, please, Paul," he said, brushing hair out of her face. He placed his hand on her neck, and her fear subsided. He was transmitting calm to her through his hands, a beneficial power of Protectors for times when the Speaker needed to relax. Alden placed the towel under Lenzi's arm.

When Race picked up the syringe of local anesthesia, Lenzi panicked. The jolt of fear was so extreme, it took my breath away. She jerked her arm out of Race's grip and tried to sit up.

Alden held her in place. "It has to be done. There's no other way. We can't go to the hospital with a wound like that. They'd ask unanswerable questions. You know this."

She stared at the needle in Race's hand, brown eyes huge, fear thrumming from her into all of us.

I stared at the hypodermic needle too, t hen braced myself against the surprise assault of uninvited images pounding my brain. I'd never seen them outside of childhood nightmares until now. My own terror blended with Lenzi's fear in a para-lyzing concoction that seemed to stop time. I could envision the whole scene as if it had happened yesterday: The woman's black hair was a mass of snarls and knots, her head cocked at an unnatural angle, her mouth gaping open like one of the culverts under the highway near the apartment. The tourniquet still bound her emaciated upper arm, the syringe jutting out where she had last jabbed it into her bruised flesh. And I felt . . . nothing. No loss, no sadness, nothing—until the man came in. Then I felt fear.

"Hey, Junior. You okay?" Race asked, syringe still in hand.

I pulled myself back to the present, giving myself an internal shake. "Yeah."

"You looked strange for a minute," he said.

I shrugged. "I'm fine."

"I'll do the stitches if you prefer, Lenzi," Alden said, taking her good arm and lacing his fingers through hers, "but Race is much better at it than I am."

She took a gulp of air.

"Paul could do it too. Tell me what you want." His gray eyes locked on her face.

Not me, not me, not me, I chanted in my head. I'd never sewn up a real person before, only a practice dummy, but that's what my mentorship with Alden was for—to get hands-on training. *Just not now.* Not when I was freaked out, and not on Lenzi when she was so scared.

"Go ahead, Race," she whispered. I almost collapsed from relief.

"Don't watch." Alden turned her face away.

"I can't help it," she said, her panic welling and surging through me again.

Race crossed his arms over his chest and shook his head. "The bleeding is not stopping, and I've got to clean it off again before I numb her." He gave Alden a pointed look, lifting an eyebrow that matched his red hair. "A distraction maybe?"

Alden walked to the back side of the island and placed his hands on either side of Lenzi's face. He closed his eyes, concentrating on transmitting calm.

"The Zen vibe thing you do is not going to cut it," Lenzi said. "Nice try, tho—"

Her words were cut short by Alden's mouth covering hers.

"Hold her arm still, Junior," Race instructed, wiping the fresh blood away.

I didn't know where to look. The blood made me queasy, and watching Alden make out with Lenzi was wrong on every level, so I ended up staring at stainless-steel cabinet doorknobs, ineffectively trying to ignore the crazy emotions radiating from Lenzi.

"There," Race said, capping the syringe and putting it in a red sharps disposal bag. "The local anesthetic needs time to work. Come on, Junior, let's give the lovebirds some privacy."

I couldn't get out of the kitchen fast enough.

THREE

Race flipped channels between a biography of a serial killer and a trashy reality show. "You've gotta give it to Charles; he lives well. I mean, look at this place." He gestured around him and switched channels on the enormous flat-screen TV again, putting his feet on the coffee table.

I cringed inwardly at his boots on the fine, polished wood.

He was right; the mansion was amazing. It was built by the finest artisans money could buy. It wasn't only high-class, it was high-tech, especially this media room with its state-of-the-art electronics. Charles was one of the oldest Speakers in the world. As IC regional director, he held a lot of power, but he no longer interceded on behalf of the Hindered. The older a Speaker got, the more difficult it was to soul-share—not only was it hard on the body, it taxed the soul as well. Most retired in their fifties, relaxing until the next lifetime. Not Charles. Every cycle, his Protector, who was considerably older, had died before him, and he spent the remainder of his cycle training new interns. I was lucky to have been chosen for this position two years ago. I lived in luxury most people only dreamed of. Over his many lifetimes—heck, maybe thousands of years—he'd amassed a fortune, kept safe by the IC between cycles. My good luck at his favor still baffled me, but I'd learned at a very early age that when opportunity knocked, you answered the door, took its hand, and held on.

"So any idea of when you'll be assigned a Speaker?" Race asked.

"Soon—tomorrow, actually."

He grinned. "It's about time." The reality show went to a commercial break, so he switched back to the serial killer bio. "What do you suppose took the Council so long to decide?"

I hadn't realized it had taken a long time. I shifted in my chair, trying to sound like his news didn't bother me. "I've no idea."

"Yeah, my contact in administration says they've been debating your assignment for months."

Race's contact was undoubtedly his assigned Speaker, Beatrice, who worked in the statistics office—his estranged Speaker, actually. They hadn't worked together in lifetimes, but no one had ever told me why. All I knew was that she hated him, which I could understand. Race had a way of really getting on people's nerves, and if he were my partner, I'd insist on a desk job too. I shrugged. "Whatever."

Race looked at his watch. "Anesthesia has taken effect by now. Let's do this."

Back in the kitchen, I couldn't bring myself to look at Lenzi's wound and instead handed Race things he needed as he stitched her up, closing my mind to the brutal images that had taken me by surprise earlier.

"You need to do this next time, Paul," Alden said.

"Yeah! He wants to do your part, Alden, and distract the Speaker," Race said. "Don't ya, Junior?"

"I'd rather not volunteer to get sewed up again," Lenzi said as Race wrapped her forearm in white gauze.

Race winked at her. "How are you feeling? Did Alden make it all better?"

She blushed and sat up. "Yeah. Thanks for sewing me up. Sorry I was a baby about it."

Alden helped her off the counter and then picked up a glass of ice water from near the fridge. Lenzi seemed fine as she walked in front of us back to the media room.

Race plopped down on the far end of the sofa, grabbed the remote, and muted the volume on the TV. "You're welcome, Lenzi. Stitches are no biggy. So, did you guys know that Paul's getting his Speaker assignment tomorrow?"

Lenzi grinned and sat on the other end of the sofa, practically on top of Alden. "That's fantastic! Do you know anything about her . . . or him yet?"

I shook my head and slid a coaster under the drink Alden had placed next to Race's boots on the coffee table.

"Where will it happen?" Alden asked. "They usually do it at headquarters in Galveston. Since Lenzi's and my reinstatement hearing is tomorrow, maybe we can be there for it."

"That would be great!" Lenzi said. She picked up Alden's glass and took a sip.

It was hard to believe it had been a month since Alden's discontinuance hearing. I closed my eyes and took a deep breath. I wondered if my Speaker would be like Lenzi, willing to stand by me no matter what awful things happened. I opened my eyes to find them all staring.

"You okay?" Lenzi asked, setting the glass back on the coaster.

I nodded. "My car is still at school. Can you guys drop me off there to get it?"

"I'll take you," Race offered, turning the volume back up on the serial killer show.

Great. Just what I needed: alone time with Race.

"I wonder if it will be an experienced Speaker, since this is Paul's first cycle," Lenzi said.

The TV screen flickered, and white streaks washed across it in horizontal waves. Race pushed some buttons on the remote, but nothing changed. He slapped it against his palm.

"It's probably a signal problem." I took the remote from Race before he broke it.

"No, it's a bogeyman problem," Lenzi said, rolling her eyes. There was no fear emanating from her, so whatever spirit she was dealing with was not posing a threat. "Beat it. I'm not open for business right now."

The TV brightened, and what appeared to be human silhouettes writhed behind the glass.

Lenzi sighed. "Yeah, nice freak show, but I'm not helping you right now. Get lost." She took the remote from me and pushed the power button with no result. With a huff, she strode to the TV and reached behind it, then straightened and held up the plug she had pulled from the outlet. The TV didn't respond; the figures still undulated in the white static. Lenzi stared at the plug and then back at the TV. "Show-offs," she grumbled. "Nice try, but no. Not today. Begone!"

The screen went black. Without plugging the TV back in, Lenzi placed the remote on the coffee table and plopped down on the sofa next to Alden. "Sorry. Just not up to it."

Alden draped his arm over her shoulder. "I understand completely. We don't need the points anyway. We're still leading the region this month."

Lenzi sighed, closed her eyes, and leaned her head on his shoulder. Their intimate, comfortable trust was evident in everything they did. When I looked over at Race, he was studying me. "What?" I asked.

A sly grin crept across his face. "Nothing."

But I knew there was something. Maybe he had information concerning my Speaker, since he knew about the unusual length of time my assignment had been under consideration.

"Beatrice told you something about my Speaker assignment."

He sat back and put his arms behind his head in nonchalance.

Lenzi reached over and punched his shoulder. "Come on, Race. If you know something, spill."

He shrugged. "I really don't. I just know the pairing was controversial, and the guys at the top argued over it a lot. Bea said it got ugly a few times."

My stomach dropped to my feet. Why would my assignment cause the elders to argue? Perhaps they thought I wasn't ready. No. That seemed impossible. I'd fulfilled every requirement. Excelled at my Wilkingham education with almost perfect scores in all areas of my training. "I'll go clean up the kitchen," I said, anxious to get away from them.

After pitching the towels from the kitchen counter into a hamper in the laundry room, I returned to find Lenzi leaning against the refrigerator.

"It's okay to be nervous. Being assigned a partner is a really big deal," she said.

"Do you remember meeting Alden for the first time?" I opened a plastic bag next to Race's kit and placed the medical instruments inside.

"You know I have no memory of my past lives." She didn't sound angry, but I wouldn't have blamed her if she were. Lenzi's lack of past-life memories was the reason for the reinstatement hearing tomorrow. Alden and Lenzi's efforts to hide her past-life amnesia had almost resulted in his discontinuance and her resignation from the Intercessor Council.

"Sorry. I spoke without thinking."

She shrugged. "It's cool. I'm getting little bits and pieces of memories every now and then, but no, I don't remember meeting Alden for the first time. I've been told I trained him, though, and my number is pretty low. Much lower than his, so my soul has cycled more times than his. I'm Speaker 102, and he's Protector 438."

That didn't necessarily translate directly, because Protectors were lost more often than Speakers, so Protectors of comparable age would have higher numbers, but not that far apart—usually fewer than one hundred. She was many cycles older than Alden. It must have been unnerving to not remember any of her lifetimes.

"I wonder if my Speaker will be cycles older and have experience." I hoped so.

Lenzi shrugged. "I would assume so. The IC usually pairs new members up with someone who has been left solo by discontinuance of a partner or by choice."

"By choice like Race's Speaker," I said.

She nodded. "Yeah. Beatrice ditched him after only one cycle."

"Why would she do that?" It probably wasn't any of my business, but I knew Race would never tell me.

"Race made a mistake lifetimes ago, and she couldn't forgive him." She paused as if considering her words carefully. "The IC discourages romantic involvement between pairings to prevent what happened between them."

I wanted to point out that she and Alden had obviously not

heeded the IC's advice, but decided against it. Obviously, my thoughts were transparent.

"Alden and I had worked together for lifetimes as business partners only before we made that change to our relationship. Race and Bea jumped right in, hot and heavy, and then he . . ." She fiddled with the edge of her bandage. "Well, he did what Race does. He flirts with everyone, and Bea took it personally. She filed for a desk job and has worked in the statistics office for three cycles. She's still so mad, she hasn't given him a release to be assigned a new Speaker."

The cabinet door seemed as loud as a gunshot as I pushed it shut with my foot after pulling out a cleaning rag and spray cleanser. I couldn't recall being this edgy since childhood. I wondered if my nervousness had brought on the unexpected flashback earlier. I spritzed the counter where Race had stitched Lenzi.

"You want me to do that? You shouldn't have to clean up after us."

"No. I've got this." I was glad to have something to do. Putting things in order was calming.

I heard footsteps behind me. They were too quiet for Race and his clunky cowboy boots. It wasn't until a blast of emotion, concern maybe, hit me that I realized it was a Speaker. It was only a short burst that ended as quickly as it came. By the time I spun around, Charles, my boss and foster father of sorts, had masked all emotion and greeted me with his usual placid demeanor.

"Rough day?" he asked, eyes skimming Lenzi's bandage.

Charles was well into his seventies—balding and gray—but his carriage was that of a much younger man. A powerful man.

"Smith is back," Lenzi answered, getting right to the point. "He cut me up again."

He nodded. "Any witnesses?"

She shook her head. "No . . . well, yes. It happened during class, but nobody knew what was going on. The bell rang right after he hurt me."

"You are certain it was Smith?"

"Absolutely."

He pulled a glass from the cabinet. "It's highly unusual that he would venture this far from his place of death—and unexpected. I'd hoped he would be too weak to come back this cycle after his last encounter with you."

"Yeah. Alden said the same thing." Lenzi moved away from the refrigerator so that he could open the door.

Charles filled his glass with iced tea. "I was going to pull Paul off your case and move him and Vivienne elsewhere, but I think it best they stick with you until we know what Smith is up to."

Vivienne. My Speaker's name was Vivienne! The name alone gave me chills. "Vivienne," I tried the name out loud.

Charles turned to me and smiled. "She's here."

Here? In the same house? My knees almost buckled. She was here.

Lenzi squeezed my hand. "This is awesome!"

"Well, it's a bit irregular, but the circumstances are out of the ordinary." He placed the glass on the counter. "I have to warn you, Paul. She's not happy about this right now."

Perhaps she didn't consider me experienced enough. Maybe she had lost her Protector and didn't want to be reassigned. I closed my eyes and took a deep breath. I would simply have to try my hardest to show her I was a quick learner and had studied and trained hard to be the best Protector possible. I would earn her respect.

"Would you like to meet her?" Charles asked.

From the minute I had understood what I was, I'd dreamed of this moment. I'd never tried to imagine her face or even her hair color, but I had always envisioned someone as eager to excel and achieve as I was. Someone funny and easy to work with like Lenzi. I nodded, trying not to look too eager.

Lenzi took the cleaner and rag from me and set them on the counter. "Should Alden and I leave, Charles, or can we meet her too?"

"It's up to Paul."

The fact my Speaker was here in the house threw me. This was not in accordance with the IC manual.

Charles's wise eyes seemed to miss nothing as he studied me. What was I supposed to say? I shrugged. "Sure." My voice cracked, betraying my alarm. I'd waited for this moment forever, it seemed, and now that it was here, nothing was going as I had expected.

"She's in my office. I'll go get her now, and she can meet all of you at once. That might be best as you'll be working as a team until we determine how strong Smith is and what he intends."

Smith again. I knew he was a Malevolent based in Galveston that stalked Lenzi and had for lifetimes, but that was the extent of my knowledge. "Okay."

From what I'd read, new partners were customarily introduced in front of the full Council, so an audience was not a huge departure. It might even be better. At least Lenzi, Alden, and Race were my friends. The Council members were all ancient souls, and they scared me a little. And were I to meet her alone, I might do something silly, like reveal how excited I was to finally be assigned.

Charles gestured to the door from the kitchen, and I took a deep breath. This was it.

When I returned to the media room, the TV had been plugged back in and Race was flipping channels while Alden typed something up on his phone.

"Hey, Lenzi," Alden said as she sat next to him on the sofa. "I've typed up the report for today's attack. See if this fits what happened from your point of view." He handed her the phone.

"Not now." Her grin was huge.

"Is something up?" He took his phone back.

"Yeah. Something cool."

I felt Vivienne before I saw her. Her anger slammed into me

in continuous, oppressive waves. Alden and Race, being Protectors, felt it too.

"Uh-oh," Race whispered.

Uh-oh was right. My excitement melted away and was replaced by dread that knotted my stomach. My Speaker was furious. I closed my eyes against the torrent of aggression transmitting from her.

Lenzi reached over and took my hand. I could feel flashes of her compassion, but it was drowned out by my Speaker's anger.

Lenzi's concern switched to alarm, and I opened my eyes.

"Paul, this is Vivienne Thibideaux, Speaker 961," Charles said in a calm, level voice.

Standing next to him, chin up, was my partner—my partner for an indeterminate number of future lifetimes—and judging by the emotions blasting from her, and the narrowed eyes, it was clear she hated me already.

I sensed Race, Alden, and Lenzi staring at me, but I couldn't take my eyes off Vivienne. She was not what I'd expected. Neon pink hair framed what would have otherwise been a classically beautiful face with high cheekbones and large green eyes, were it not for the overdone eyeliner, unnaturally pale skin, and black lipstick.

Race was the first to respond with a whispered half laugh. While my stomach churned with a sickening dread, Race appeared amused and completely at ease. He lowered himself into a chair facing her as if he were preparing to watch a movie.

"Are you Paul?" she asked him.

"No. I wish I were, sugar," he said with a cocky grin.

"Call me sugar again, and you won't be calling anyone anything for a long time," she said, devoid of any expression. Her flare of anger indicated she wasn't kidding.

"Whoa, there," Race said, palms up in surrender. "I was just being friendly."

Her metal and leather spiked bracelets clicked together as she crossed her arms over her chest. "Well, I wasn't. And I'm *not*."

"Fair enough." Race winked, and fury surged from her.

Charles stepped away from her and took the TV remote from Race, turning the screen off.

She watched his every move, then settled her eyes on Alden. Her anger subsided slightly as she raked her eyes from his feet up to his too-long blond hair.

"I'm Alden Thomas, Protector 438, and this is Lenzi Anderson, Speaker 102." He stepped forward and held out his hand. She didn't take it and instead turned her attention to me.

"That leaves you, then."

Since leaving my home so many years ago, I'd never felt insufficient or unworthy. All those horrible feelings of inadequacy from my childhood reemerged, making me want to flee the room. Pulling strength from down deep, I crossed to her and held out my hand. She stared from my fingers to my face, but made no move to shake my hand.

She spun to face Charles, who had crossed to the bookcase

behind her. Her anger shifted to hurt and fear. "You lied to me. You said I'd be safe." She gestured to me with her thumb over her shoulder. "He can't protect me. I'll end up just like my aunt."

From the back, her appearance wasn't quite as shocking. She wore knee-high lace-up combat-style boots. Her net tights had huge holes in them—probably deliberate—that made the skin of her pale legs seem to glow through the openings. The conservative green and black plaid school uniform-style skirt was out of place with the black skintight tank top tied in a knot at her waist.

Charles met my eyes over her shoulder and then turned his attention back to her. "I would caution everyone in this room to consider the adage 'don't judge a book by its cover.'" To my amazement, he took her hand, and her emotions dialed down.

She surveyed me from head to toe before looking back up at Charles's face. "You said he was powerful. That he was the most promising new Protector you had discovered in lifetimes."

"That I did," he responded calmly.

Before I could enjoy a heady rush from the fact he'd said such a thing about me, her next words slapped me back down. She pulled her hand away from Charles. "He doesn't look it."

Charles took a long pause and straightened his tie before he answered, masking all his emotions as usual. "Sometimes the most placid river surface hides tremendous depth and power, just as the opposite is true—under a stormy sea can lie peaceful waters."

"You sound like a fortune cookie." She rolled her eyes and

then tilted her head as she studied me. I forced myself to stand perfectly still, affecting a calm I didn't feel. She turned her attention back to Charles. "You said I could try it out for a while before I commit to a forever kind of thing."

He nodded. "Indeed I did."

I couldn't read her emotions clearly. She was a jumble of confusion, frustration, and something else . . . resignation, perhaps. Interpreting other people's emotions when they were conflicted was difficult, and this girl's turmoil was intense and all over the place, like a fireworks show.

"Okay." Her green eyes bored into mine. "You've got some time to prove you're not a loser." And with that, she left the room, Charles following.

Loser! I was top of my Protector training class—chosen for an internship by Charles MacAllen, the Intercessor Council Gulf Coast regional director, because he believed I was a prodigy and showed the most promise of my cycle of Protectors. What did she mean, *loser?*

I hadn't been angry in a very long time, and the heat surging under my skin was uncomfortable. It pissed me off that this girl, with her bad attitude, pink hair, and creepy Goth (or whatever they were) clothes, had given me an ultimatum about not being a loser!

"Wow," Lenzi said.

Race whistled. "Mercy, Paul. What are you going to do with that?"

I wanted to tell "that" to get lost, that's what I wanted, but I couldn't. I was born for this, and I had to trust the Council's decision. They must have had information that made them believe we would be well suited . . . maybe. The heat under my skin cooled, leaving prickles on the back of my neck and arms.

I sat on the edge of the coffee table—something completely out of character for me, but I didn't think I could stand upright one more second.

Alden sat on the sofa. "Sorry, man."

"Can't Paul do something?" Lenzi asked, sitting next to him. She put her hand on his knee. "He can't really be stuck with her forever, can he? Can't he refuse?"

Race shook his head. "The Speaker holds the power, Lenzi. You know that." He sat on the arm of the sofa. "All you can hope for now, Junior, is that she rejects you." He gave a half smile. "Which looks pretty likely."

Race calling me Junior didn't even make me twitch. Somehow it seemed insignificant. This was a nightmare. *She* was a nightmare. And all I wanted to do was wake up and end it.

The doorbell rang. We never had unexpected guests. Because of the guard station, we always got a call first. Visitors were either from inside the business and expected, or they came in with Charles. The bell rang again.

"Expecting someone?" Alden asked, standing.

"No."

"Do you think it's Smith up to something?" Race asked.

Lenzi remained seated. "No. I don't feel or hear him."

Alden strode to the door of the media room. "You wouldn't feel or hear him if he's possessed someone. He's done it before."

Race jumped up to join him. I caught up just as they had made it through the foyer to the front double doors.

Ding-dong.

I looked through the peephole. I could only see the top half of a girl's head. From the bit of her I could see, she appeared younger than me. Fifteen maybe.

"Can I help you?" I called through the thick wood.

She shifted uncomfortably. "Um . . . I'm here to see Paul."

Race patted me on the back so hard I almost coughed. "Ha! You've got 'em coming atcha from all directions, Junior!"

"What do you want?" I called to the girl on the other side of the door.

Alden looked through the peephole. "She's tiny," he whispered. "If Smith possessed her to get to Lenzi, he chose poorly. She's not a challenge unless she has a weapon. Let her in."

I turned the key in the dead bolt.

"I'll grab her," Race whispered. "You guys search her for weapons."

"Keep your hands in the right places, Race," Alden warned. "You tend to get carried away."

Race's blue eyes flew wide and an astonished expression washed across his freckled face. "Me?"

"Yes," Alden said as I unlatched the second lock. "Some things never change. *You* are one of those things."

When I pulled the door open, Race reached around me and grabbed the girl by the upper arm, dragging her inside and pinning her against him, facing out. She screamed, and Race put his hand over her mouth, muffling her shrieks while Alden did a quick pat down for weapons. "Calm down, sugar," Race said. "We're not going to hurt you."

She made a growling sound, and Race jerked his hand away from her mouth. "Ouch! Shit! She bit me."

She wriggled free from his grip. "Darn right, I bit you. What are you doing? Charles told me to come here and deliver Paul's car. I didn't expect to get jumped."

Fear and rage trickled in bursts from her. Her transmissions were weak, but could only mean one thing. "She's a Speaker," I said. "Just coming into her abilities."

Race turned his hand over and stared at his palm. "Dang, girl. You drew blood."

"And I'll do it again too," she threatened, straightening out her T-shirt.

"I'm really sorry," I said. "I'm Paul. This is Alden, and that's Race."

She pulled my keys out of her front jeans pocket and handed them to me. "I'm—"

"You're Hannibal Lecter!" Race cut in. "Check out what you did." He turned his bloody palm toward her, and she smiled and shrugged.

"I'm Cinda Weatherly. Charles's new intern."

The world seeped away from under my feet, and the floor seemed to shift. I braced myself against the wall. *Charles's new intern.* I'd been replaced.

After meeting Vivienne, I'd been certain things couldn't get worse. Man, oh, man, had I been wrong.

Cinda wasn't nearly as young as she looked. It turned out she was actually eighteen and worked part-time at an upscale clothing boutique. She and Lenzi talked shoes while Alden and I tried to appear interested in women's fashion and Race flipped channels.

"Thanks for bringing my car back," I said during a rare pause in their conversation.

"Sure." Cinda ran a hand through her short, silky black hair. "Nice car, by the way."

It *was* a nice car. Too nice. The Mercedes had been a gift from Charles.

"Well, we'd better be going," Alden said. "I still have to finish the report about today's attack before the reinstatement hearing tomorrow."

Lenzi stood and laced her fingers through his. "Bye, Race. We'll see you in Galveston tomorrow, Paul."

"Um . . . no. Paul won't be at the hearing," Cinda said. "I'll be there, and Race will act as a second Protector for you. Paul and Vivienne have been assigned a civilian oversight mission."

Lenzi grinned. "Your first official assignment, Paul! Cool."

Yeah. Cool. I'd been replaced as Charles's intern and would have to spend the day with a girl who hated me. So very cool.

"The file is on the seat of your car," Cinda said.

"That's against code." I hadn't intended to sound so pissy, but it just came out that way. "You're never allowed to leave IC documents in public view."

"Junior is all about the rules. He'll get over that in a few lifetimes." Race's condescending tone sounded like he was making excuses for a naughty toddler.

I needed to get out of the room before I either punched Race or my head exploded. "I'm going to go park my car in the garage and get the file."

"Thanks for letting us come here to take care of Lenzi." Alden shook my hand. "And good luck with your new Speaker tomorrow."

Race remained seated on the sofa, which didn't bode well for the rest of my evening. "He's gonna need luck. That one's a handful—a couple of them, actually." He winked at Cinda, who looked awkward and uncomfortable standing in the middle of the room.

"Charles told me to wait here for him." She lowered down to sit on the edge of the chair farthest from Race.

I nodded and headed to the door, eager to be alone with my raging emotions. I hated feeling out of control, and it was as if every ounce of control had been sucked away the minute I met Vivienne.

I held the door for Alden and Lenzi, who got into his car, parked in front of mine in the circular drive. Once inside my own car, I took a deep breath through my nose, letting the familiar smell of leather drown out everything. I leaned back against the headrest and closed my eyes, trying to untangle the turmoil knotted up in my brain. I glared over at Race's truck, parked at the curb. Maybe if I stayed in my car long enough, Race would leave and I wouldn't have to deal with him again today.

I pulled into the vast garage next to Charles's silver Bentley and killed the motor. He must have already come back from returning Vivienne to whatever Circle of Hell she came from. I usually heard him come in, but I'd been a little distracted with my replacement and all.

I pushed my remote, and the garage door shut behind me, plunging me into welcome darkness. I simply couldn't face Race again today. I groaned and flipped on the radio. A popular pop song I couldn't stand screeched from the speakers at full volume, nearly making me launch from my seat. Before I could switch the channel, the banging started. I looked over to find Vivienne pounding on my window. *Ugh.* I thought she was gone. I turned the radio off and opened the window.

She smirked, hands on hips. "If you're out here trying to kill yourself by carbon monoxide poisoning, you have to leave the car *running* in a closed garage." She crossed her arms over her chest and cocked her head. "But then, maybe you're trying to commit suicide by bad music. I know it would certainly kill *me* to listen to that."

"I—"

"Charles sent me to find you. He wants you in the room with the TV."

Before I could raise my window and get out of the car, she strode away and disappeared through the door to the house.

"I don't listen to Justin Bieber!" I shouted after her. When I skidded into the side hallway of the house, she was waiting for me.

"Don't worry. I won't tell anyone. Your secret is safe with me."

"Seriously, I—"

She pushed open the door to the media room. "I found him. He was jamming to the Biebster in his car."

"I was n—"

"I love Justin Bieber," Cinda said, swiveling in her chair to face us. "Your car has a great stereo. I rocked out the whole way here."

I gestured toward Cinda and waited for the apology from Vivienne that never came. She simply clomped over to the other side of the sofa from Race and sprawled out on it, putting her boots up on the upholstery.

Charles cleared his throat. "I'm leaving town after the hearing in the morning. Cinda will help me tomorrow, while the two of you"—he nodded to each of us—"handle the ghost hunter television shoot."

Vivienne sat up. "Television sh—"

Charles held up his hand to silence her. "Paul has the file and will fill you in over dinner."

Dinner! No. I wanted time alone. I loosened my grip on the file so I didn't bend it.

Charles turned his attention back to Cinda. "Race can help you get your things out of my car and carry them to your bedroom. You'll be next to Paul. Second door on the left up the stairs."

I was certain my heart had stopped. My replacement was moving in to the room next to me. Well, at least I hadn't been kicked out yet.

"And Vivienne, dear, you will stay in the room at the end of that hallway for now."

Her too! My heart *had* stopped, because right then, it kicked back on so hard it hurt.

"I'm not going to stay here," she said. "The deal was I would live with my grandmother, not in this place . . . with *him*." It felt as though her eyes burned me, but it was just her emotions that stung as she fired them my way.

Charles slid his hands in his pockets. As usual, he revealed no emotion whatsoever. Even though he was a Speaker, centuries of practice had made him a master at hiding not only visual signals, but transmissions of emotions as well. "Her shop is almost built out. She will arrive tomorrow or the next day."

She didn't pull her eyes from mine. "And if I decide that this isn't going to work out?"

Charles shrugged. "You and your grandmother keep the shop and quarters courtesy of the Intercessor Council."

Finally, she looked away from me toward him. "That easy?"

Charles took a deep, suffering breath before he answered. "You of all people know that nothing is ever easy, Vivienne."

She rolled her eyes. "Typical answer."

Nothing with Charles was ever typical. I was shocked she spoke to him that way—like a petulant child—and got away with it.

"Let's go get your stuff," Race said to Cinda as he stood and stretched. After they left, Charles moved toward the door.

"Make this pairing work, you two," he said. "It's been a tremendous struggle for me to make this happen. Don't prove me wrong."

Charles was the one who did this? *On purpose?* Silently, we watched him leave before I finally dared to meet Vivienne's eyes.

I studied her face, trying to read her emotions. They were jumbled, but fear played a large part of it. The instinctual need to protect my Speaker kicked in. Well, it would have happened with any Speaker, I told myself. It's how I was made. "Do you have a preference for dinner?"

She sat up. "Something quick." She stood. "And this isn't a date. Don't get any weird ideas."

"Don't worry. Weird isn't my thing," I said before I could stop myself. I felt her anger flare.

"Don't knock something you've never tried," she shot over her shoulder on her way out the media room door.

"I don't try things unless they appeal."

She stopped in the white marble foyer and faced me. She arched an eyebrow. "You're quicker than I expected."

Her compliment gave me an unanticipated rush. "I'm a lot of things you don't expect."

The other eyebrow rose. "That'd be a nice surprise."

"Don't get any weird ideas."

She laughed, and suddenly something in me shifted. Just the sound of an honest laugh, coupled with the happiness her soul transmitted, caught me completely off guard. If nothing else, she was genuine . . . and prickly, harsh, obnoxious, and an overall pain in the butt.

FIVE

I opened the car door for Vivienne. "Any preference for food? Italian, American, Chinese, Mexican?"

"Something spicy. I miss New Orleans." She got in the car and pulled the door shut before I could close it for her.

New Orleans. That explained the business with her grandmother; they must have just moved to Houston.

I started the motor and she reached over and turned on the stereo. An electronic-sounding dance mix was playing on the channel Cinda had left up. Vivienne wrinkled her nose as if something smelled bad.

I changed presets by pushing the button on my steering wheel and stopped on an oldies rock station. She relaxed and leaned back in her seat.

I had a million questions I wanted to ask her—this girl, my Speaker, whom I'd waited on for years. But the timing seemed wrong. We were having a moment of calm, and I didn't want to blow it.

"Mexican okay?" It was the spiciest of the choices nearby. I opened the garage door with the remote.

She nodded and closed her eyes. Her brow wrinkled and then she shook her head.

"Is that a yes or a no?"

She didn't answer, but her brow creased further and her emotions jumbled into something that felt like agitation or impatience.

"Are you okay, Vivienne?"

"Ghosts suck." Her fear spiked and zapped through me, causing my heart to pound.

I held my breath and waited to see what she would do. Protectors are trained to remain silent and observe until the Speaker makes his or her needs clear. Vivienne folded up into a ball on her seat and for a moment, it was hard to imagine this fragile-looking girl with her knees tucked to her chest being the obnoxious beast I'd witnessed only a short while before.

"Let me know if you need me."

She snorted. "I've never needed you before now, and I've dealt with this my whole life, Pauly."

So much for fragile.

I turned the motor off and waited. After many long minutes of her silent blasts of emotion, I couldn't stay quiet any longer.

"If you tell Hindered to go away, they evidently do."

She didn't open her eyes. "Just drive."

"The dead can't be outrun."

In the dim light of the garage, her green eyes seemed unnaturally bright. "Shut up, and get us out of here."

I restarted the car and backed out of the driveway. She turned the radio louder and covered her ears. And then it dawned on me what she was doing: She was ignoring the calls of the Hindered—tuning them out—rather than confronting them directly and asking them to leave her alone. *Why?* I wondered. She certainly had no problem confronting live people.

She'd said she'd heard the Hindered her whole life. That was unusual. Speakers usually grew into their powers and only heard the calls of the dead when they were of age or at least mature enough to deal with it effectively. It must have terrified her as a child to hear them.

By the time we reached the restaurant, her emotions were under control. Her tactic to rid herself of the voices must have worked.

The hostess showed us to a booth in the corner. Vivienne immediately took the seat with her back to the wall.

"Please let me sit there," I said.

She crossed her arms over her chest and said nothing.

"Please, Vivienne. It's best if I have a view of the room if I'm going to effectively protect you. It's harder if I can only see the wall behind you."

"You can't protect me. You can't see them."

"No, but I can see if one has possessed a human and is coming after you."

She slid out of the booth and glared, eyes level with mine. "Fine. Lot of good that did my aunt."

Her aunt. She'd mentioned her to Charles back at the house.

"Hi. Can I get you something to drink?" I hadn't heard the guy arrive, so his sudden appearance startled me, and I flinched.

Vivienne laughed. "Some big, bad Protector you are." She flopped into the opposite seat, facing the wall. "I'll have a Dr Pepper."

I slid into the booth facing her. "Just water, thanks."

"Your waiter's name is Jim, and he'll be here to take your order in a minute." He placed chips and salsa on the table and took off.

"What happened to your aunt?" I asked.

She picked up her menu and held it up high enough to cover her face. "Ask the old man. He thinks he has all the answers."

"If you're talking about Charles, he pretty much does."

The menu stayed in place, so I studied her hands. She had long, slender fingers tipped in short, black nails. Silver rings adorned every finger. The most notable were a fleur-de-lis, a snake, and a skull on her thumb. The creepy, heavy jewelry seemed out of place on her delicate hands. They reminded me of ornamental brass knuckles—defensive like the rest of her.

"Hey, Paul. Good to see you again," my favorite waiter said, placing our drinks on the table.

"Hi, Jim. This is my friend Vivienne. She's new to Houston."

Jim extended a huge tattooed arm to shake her hand. "Great to meet you, Vivienne. Have we decided on dinner yet?"

I couldn't take my eyes off of Vivienne as she ordered. Her neon pink hair against her skin accentuated her paleness, and the thick black eyeliner made her eyes appear the color of emeralds. She didn't fit my image of pretty, necessarily, but she was fascinating and striking . . . and certainly drew attention, which was obvious from the curious faces of people watching us from nearby tables.

Because the Intercessor Council was secret, we were supposed to blend in and not draw attention to ourselves. It would be impossible to not notice Vivienne.

As I watched her order her meal, I realized it would probably be impossible not to notice her even if her hair were a natural color and she wore more conventional clothes. There was something about her that drew the eye.

"So, Paul, do you want your usual?" Jim tapped his pencil on his pad. "Paul?"

"Oh, sorry. Yeah, that would be great. Thanks."

Jim snapped his notebook shut and wandered off to the kitchen.

"So, you obviously come here a lot." She stared up at the ceiling, which was covered with brightly painted wooden fish hanging to look like they were swimming in a school.

"I do."

She gestured to the gaudy velvet paintings on the wall displayed in heavy gold carved frames as if they were precious museum art. "I'm surprised."

"Why?"

She shrugged. "No reason."

"That's not fair. You can't just dump that and run." I knew I wouldn't like her answer, but I was dying to know what she thought of me and why.

She scooped a chip in the hot sauce. "Because this place is fun. You don't strike me as fun."

I mulled over her words. *Fun.* I'd never thought about whether I was fun or not. Honestly, she was probably right, and it bothered me for some reason. It shouldn't have. Being a Protector was not about fun.

"Fair enough," I said.

She smiled, well, more like smirked, and dipped another chip. "I'm really good at reading people. It comes from living with my grandmother. She taught me how."

"Here ya go," Jim said, placing chicken enchiladas in front of each of us. "Plates are hot. Be careful."

She eyed my enchiladas and then hers. Her surprise almost made me laugh.

"You ordered my regular." I took a bite. "The 911 enchilada dinner is the best thing on the menu. Habanero peppers. Yum."

She tilted her head.

"What else do you think you know about me?" I asked.

"Nah." She cut off a bite of enchilada. "Too easy."

"You think?"

"I know." She took a bite.

I picked up my fork. "You're very certain of yourself."

"You're very judgmental."

"Am I?"

She pointed at me with her fork. "Why don't you tell me what you think you know about *me*?"

With my knife, I separated my beans away from my rice, dividing them in a straight line. "I wouldn't begin to assume I knew you."

She leaned closer across the table. Close enough for her scent to override the smell of my food. "Ah, but it's human nature to formulate opinions and judge based on first impressions."

She smelled amazing. Like one of those stores in the mall that sells candles. She leaned back, and I almost had to shake my head to pull myself together. It must have been my Protector instincts kicking in. Nothing about her really appealed to me, so it made no sense for her to affect me outside of that.

"What do I get if I guess right?" I asked.

"Ah, reward-based, are you?" She took another bite. "Figures."

"If I get three things about you right, you'll answer a question honestly for me," I said.

She grinned. "Game on. Go."

"Based on the way you interact with people your own age, you've lived only among adults and have no brothers or sisters."

Chewing, she arched a brow. "Very good."

I searched for something I knew I could get right. Losing wasn't an option. "Your grandmother is your only living immediate family."

She picked up her drink and lifted it in toast. "That's two."

I needed a sure bet, but I'd only known her a few hours, tops. She gave me an off-putting smirk and stared me straight in the eye. Such calculated hostility. I took a bite of my enchilada, then leaned back and studied her appearance. The hot pink hair was the most striking color possible—clearly intended to draw attention—yet, her attitude and dress were intended to repulse and keep people distant. She wanted to be noticed, but left alone. I hadn't known her long enough to make a personality judgment, but I was fairly certain I'd put a piece of the puzzle in place. My concern was how she would react.

I met her heavily lined eyes directly. "Your appearance is a defense mechanism rather than a fashion choice. You're like one of those plants in the rain forest that's brilliantly colored as a warning. It's toxic so animals won't eat it." Her eyes widened. I leaned closer and whispered, "Only I think you're bluffing. I don't think you're really toxic. I believe you're using your unconventional appearance and harsh attitude to hide your vulnerability." I held my breath. I might have crossed a line with that one.

She leaned back in her booth and crossed her arms over her chest. She stared at me for an eternity before she finally spoke. "What's your question?"

"Why are you doing this? Joining the IC?" I knew it wasn't because she wanted to. Something or someone was forcing her.

Her brow furrowed. "It's none of your business."

"Everything okay here?" Jim asked.

Not really. Nothing was okay here. "Yeah. We just need the bill," I said.

He dropped it on the table. "Done!"

I handed him my credit card and he left.

"Why you are doing this is absolutely my business. Your motivation affects me, and will affect me for lifetimes." I smoothed the folded napkin in my lap while she finished her enchiladas.

She leaned back in her booth. "Only if I decide to go through with this Speaker crap. Why don't I guess three things about you now? If I'm right, you answer *my* question."

"You owe me an answer," I said.

She held up a finger. "Number one: From your bossy, take-charge manner, I can tell you are used to getting your way. You've always gotten your way and will do whatever it takes to keep it like that."

She could not have been more wrong. I sat back and gave no indication she had missed the mark.

A second finger joined the first. "Two: You have perfect manners and dress like a politician. From that, and the fact you

are used to getting your way, I've deduced that you are the oldest child from a rich family—one step short of a spoiled brat."

I almost laughed.

And another finger. "Three: Everything to you is black and
white. Good or bad. Right or wrong. You can't see in shades of
gray, and you're going to be a nightmare to work with."

"That is far more opinion than fact," I said, "but I'll answer
your question anyway."

She placed her elbows on the table and her chin in her
hands. "Why are *you* doing this?"

"Because I want to. Because it gives me a sense of accom-
plishment and is a solid living. It's difficult, dangerous, and
serves a higher purpose."

She rolled her eyes. "It has nothing to do with immortality,
huh?"

"I would do it even if that weren't part of the bargain."

She leaned back and crossed her arms over her chest.
"Riiiiiiight."

"Then I take it that's why you're doing it. So that you can
return in subsequent lifetimes."

"Um, yeah. Immortality has a certain appeal, don't you
think?" She stood. "Let's go. I've had enough."

And so, just like that, I'd been dismissed.

She was silent the entire way home, staring out the window
and never looking at me. Her emotions ebbed and flowed from
anger to what felt like remorse and then anxiety.

She finally spoke when I pulled back into the garage, the door closing silently behind us. "A toxic plant, huh?"

She was staring at me with those unusual green eyes. "A spoiled brat?" I answered.

She unbuckled and stepped out of the car. "This is going to suck so bad."

No kidding.

SIX

21st-Century Cycle, Journal Entry 2:

*I have met Vivienne Thibideaux, Speaker 962.
We have received and look forward to our first
assignment together.*

Paul Blackwell—Protector 993

I didn't see Vivienne again until the following morning, when I found her in the kitchen guzzling coffee, oblivious to everything but her electronic reader.

I stood in the doorway and watched her for a moment. Her pink hair was tied back in a braid. She wore a long gray shirt covered in skulls and crossbones over tattered black tights and the same boots she'd worn yesterday.

I felt her anger surge when she realized I was there. She wasn't happy to see me, of course. She turned to say something, most likely something nasty, but Cinda entered the kitchen before Vivienne could get the words out.

Cinda's voice was musical and pleasant. "Hey, guys! Are you ready for your first assignment?"

"It's not my first assignment," I said. It sounded grumpier and more childish than I'd intended, but for some reason, I wanted them to know I wasn't completely new at this. I'd been Charles's apprentice for two years, after all. I was qualified and well trained.

Cinda shifted from foot to foot uncomfortably. "I meant your first assignment as a team."

"We're not a team," Vivienne snapped, sounding equally childish.

I took a step closer. "Yet."

She spun on her stool to face me. "Ever!"

"Well, y'all have a great time today," Cinda said. "I'm off to Galveston." She scurried from the room as if a battle were about to erupt. Maybe it was.

"Good morning," I said, sliding onto a stool next to Vivienne.

She pushed a button on her e-reader, changing pages. I placed the file on the bar and opened it. I'd studied it last night, but I'd had trouble concentrating because my mind kept turning over our conversation from the restaurant.

She shifted on her stool, turning away and cutting me off a bit more. I wasn't getting any good emotional readings from her. Hopefully the IC manual was correct and the soul branding would make her easier for me to read, because multiple lifetimes of this—heck, even one lifetime of trying to decode this complex girl—would drive me crazy.

"Do you want me to brief you on the case?" I asked.

She pushed the page turn button again and didn't look up. "No."

"It won't go as well if you—"

"It's not going to go at all." She turned the power off on her reader. "Look, Paul, I don't need any more time to know that we can't work together. I don't like you, and you don't like me. I wouldn't commit to a day with you, much less multiple lifetimes. Deal's off." She slid off her stool.

"We don't know each other well enough to dislike each other," I said.

"I know enough." She picked up her reader and stomped out.

"You're scared!" I shouted after her. "You're running away scared."

She stuck her head around the door. "Nothing scares me. Not the voices I've heard since childhood, not this job, and certainly not *you*."

And she was gone. I buried my face in my hands. Talking to her was like trying to hold a rational conversation with someone from another planet. We just didn't speak the same language. What was I supposed to do now? I'd been replaced by Cinda, I'd let Charles down, and I'd probably be assigned a desk job. Vivienne might not have been scared, but *I* certainly was.

I grabbed a glass and poured some orange juice. There had to be a way to solve this—to find some kind of peace with Vivienne so that we could at least try to resolve one case together. We might work out if she'd only give us a chance. I couldn't figure out what I'd done to make her so angry. Obviously, the toxic plant comparison had made her mad, but it was true. Maybe that was it. Perhaps I'd hit the nail on the head, and it pissed her off.

She might have been taught how to read people as a fun trick by her grandmother, but from the time I was a small child, I'd been reading people in order to stay alive, and I was pretty sure I was correct about why she was so abrasive.

"Good morning, Paul," Charles said.

I almost dropped my glass of OJ. "Good morning, sir."

He remained in the kitchen doorway, dressed in his usual business suit. "How was dinner last night?"

"Great." My voice sounded strained. I hoped he didn't notice.

One gray eyebrow cocked up. "So everything is good between you and your Speaker, then?"

I ran my finger down the condensation on the outside of my glass. "Um, yes. It's fine."

He smiled. "But you wouldn't tell me if things *weren't* fine, would you, Paul?"

I took a deep breath. "No, sir."

"Good for you. And good luck today. I'm leaving town right after Alden and Lenzi's reinstatement hearing. Cinda will keep you posted if something comes up."

"Thank you." I fought the urge to ask him where he was going and how long he'd be away, but after working with him for two years, I understood my place and knew he'd tell me if it was important. He wasn't my father. He was my boss, and at that moment, the distinction was painfully clear. "Have a good trip."

He nodded and had to turn sideways as Vivienne burst through the door. She pointed a finger at me, eyes narrowed. "You did this, didn't you? You're so set on always getting your way, you involved my grandmother."

"I . . ."

Charles saluted me and headed out the door. I couldn't believe he was going to just leave me in this mess.

"I have no idea what you're talking about," I said.

She pointed her thumb in the direction Charles had taken his exit. "He pulled the plug on her shop unless I go with you today. What did you do, run and tattle that I wasn't playing nice?"

"It doesn't take a genius to figure out you're bailing on this. He must've overheard your little temper tantrum when you huffed out." I took several steps toward her. "I'm a lot of things, but a snitch isn't one of them. I'm on your side. I'll *always* take your side."

No problem reading her at that point. She was so angry, it was hard to catch my breath.

"Why?" she almost yelled.

I took several deep breaths and ran my hands through my

hair. "Because it's what I do. I'm trained to protect and serve my Speaker. My only function is to facilitate your success."

She stared at me and caught her breath. Her anger ebbed, but I couldn't read her emotions well enough to tell what had replaced it. She leaned against the counter by the stove. "Sucks for you, huh?"

"Pretty much."

Her eyes shifted to the open file on the kitchen island. "Well, I don't really have a choice, do I? What do I need to know?"

Now she was speaking my language. Work. "It's a TV show filming." I picked up the file. "The new homeowner called GhostHunters, Inc., to come rid her house of what she calls 'an evil spirit.' The owner of the ghost hunter business thinks the house is legitimately haunted and wants us there just in case."

She took the file from me and thumbed through the top pages. "Is this for the show *Spirit Seekers*? 'Cause if it is, it's totally bogus."

"Yes, but they call us in all the time because even though they can't get rid of ghosts themselves, they know ghosts are legit sometimes and are dangerous." I took my place back on my stool. "Usually, the IC just resolves the ghost quietly during breaks or after shootings so that nobody's the wiser and nobody gets hurt."

"Why?" She closed the file and set it on the counter, then she got back on her stool.

"To help out and to earn money. Not only do we help the Hindered move on, we get paid for it. Lots of entities hire the IC. Police, FBI, even churches. We quietly and invisibly rid the world of hindered spirits and sometimes even help solve crimes using the information given to us by the Hindered."

She rolled her eyes. "Because you're just so awesome."

"*We* are."

She slipped off her stool. "Don't count me in just yet, Pauly. I'm being blackmailed into this."

Dread crept up my throat. She was being blackmailed into it. Who would force her? Certainly not someone inside the IC. I knew that was impossible . . . or was it? Everything I thought I knew had flown out the window when I met Vivienne. What used to be simple now seemed impossibly complex.

I finished off my orange juice and put the glass in the sink. "Are you ready?"

"One sec."

I followed her out of the kitchen and watched as she bolted up the stairs two at a time. She was graceful and quick, even in her clunky boots. Moments later, she returned wearing a silver-spike-studded black leather jacket.

On the way to the resolution site, I briefed Vivienne on the case. Although she had been given a copy of the IC manual, she said she hadn't read much of it, so I recited the finer points of a Speaker's duties in a case like this. She didn't act interested at all. Hopefully, this would be a simple case that didn't involve soul-sharing. By all accounts, the spirit haunting the house was simply a powerful Hindered and not a Malevolent.

"What would happen if the IC weren't around to help the dead guys move on?" she asked, toying with one of the studs on her jacket.

I turned onto a narrow county road. "After being stuck long enough, the Hindered would all become Malevolents and would eventually gain enough power to harm humans." The pavement ended and I slowed down as the road surface became loose dirt and rocks. "It could mean the end of the living if it went on long enough and the Malevolents became too numerous and powerful."

"So Hindered go away when we help them out with what's bugging them. What about Malevolents?"

I slowed and pulled to the side of the narrow road to let an oncoming car pass. "Well, they ordinarily can't be given what they want because it's often an evil intent that holds them here. They have to be weakened until they no longer have the energy to remain Earth-bound. The Speaker wears them down, and the Protector pushes them out when they are sufficiently weakened for resolution."

She shuddered and remained silent the rest of the way.

The address in the file led us to a farmhouse that stood on several acres on the outskirts of the city. Several vans with the *Spirit Seekers* logo and a few cars lined the dirt road leading to it. The gate to the house was closed, so I pulled up in front of a neighbor's mailbox and parked.

Vivienne was already out of the car and over the gate by the time I had locked the car. "Don't get dirty, pretty boy," she taunted from the gravel walk to the house.

The gate was secured with a padlock and chain, so I climbed over as well. "Shhh," I hissed. "We don't want to disturb the shoot. We're here at the request of the film company. We have to stay out of the way."

She rolled her eyes. "Like I said, the show is totally bogus. I can't believe people pay these crooks to come to their houses to do this. It's a total scam."

The door opened as she reached the first porch step. A tall, skinny guy in a black shirt stepped out and pushed his glasses up on his nose. He looked right past Vivienne to me as if she weren't even there. "Hey. Are you the IC guy?"

I nodded.

"Great, I'm Steve Jacobs, owner of GhostHunters, Inc. Thanks for coming."

"I'm Paul Blackwell." I shook his hand and gestured to Vivienne. "This is Vivienne Thibideaux, my associate."

He shook her hand. "Hi, Viv."

"Vivienne," she said, pulling her hand away.

He put an arm around my shoulder and led me away from Vivienne to the edge of the porch farthest from the door. "So, we kind of have a situation here. Usually, people call us with ghost stories, and they are just that—stories. This one seems to be credible. We'd just love it if you and your chick could rid the place of this ghost for us before we begin."

I was beginning to share Vivienne's obvious dislike for this guy. "She's not my 'chick,' she's my business partner."

He shrugged. "I've told the homeowner you're a medium. In the past, you guys have just come in and taken the ghost out with you. Can you do that?"

I looked over my shoulder straight into Vivienne's eyes. She'd followed us and was only a foot or so behind.

"Vivienne is the one who hears the voices of the dead, not me," I said, positioning so that she was included in the conversation. "And we'll try. When do you start the shoot?"

"Twenty minutes. The homeowner is really skittish. She paid us to rid the house of the ghost, and we talked her into letting us film it for an episode of *Spirit Seekers*. She didn't like the idea at first, but we convinced her finally." He winked. "Gotta make a living, you know."

"Yeah," Vivienne said. "Gaff the poor haunted people while you lie to them, then sell that lie to a TV show and make even more money off their misfortune. Well played."

I groaned inwardly. She was going to blow the whole deal. Charles would never forgive me.

Before I could say anything, Steve jumped in to his own defense. "Look, sweetheart—"

The rage rolling from Vivienne caused me to hold my breath. Clearly, she didn't like endearments.

"In most cases," he continued, "there's no ghost and we give the people peace of mind. And in cases where they really are haunted, we do the right thing and call you guys." He gave a nonchalant shrug. "We perform a public service both ways."

Vivienne put her hands on her hips and glared at him until he squirmed. "So either way you slice it, you're scam artists."

Steve's face went red, and he shoved his glasses up his nose. He opened his mouth to say something, but Vivienne cut him off.

"S'okay, Stevie, *sweetheart.* My grandmother is a fortune-teller. And even though our clients weren't terrified, I grew up doing the same thing—tell some lies, make them feel good, and take their money—no harm done." She leaned casually against the porch railing. "I'm right there with you. I just don't pretend to be a philanthropist."

"Excuse us a moment." I took her hand and led her down the porch steps with me. "What are you doing? You are going to blow this whole deal," I whispered.

She jerked from my grasp. "So?"

"So, it matters. That guy isn't hurting anyone, and we can help this woman and that Hindered in there. That's what you are called to do. Help the Hindered pass over."

She met my eyes directly. "Ah, so now being an entrepreneur has a higher calling?"

"Yes. It's not about money at all."

"Says a guy who drives a Mercedes and lives in a mansion."

I paced in a small circle and glanced at my watch. This was

a nightmare. "We have fifteen minutes left to get in there and resolve this case."

"Rolex?" Her smirk was maddening.

I stopped very close to her, about a foot away, and kept my voice low so that Steve could not hear it. "Why do you have to do this? Why do you piss off everyone around you? What is it about 'I'm on your side' that you don't understand?"

"No one is ever on my side. Ever." She headed for the gate.

"Vivienne, please," I called. "Then be on *my* side. Help me out. Please."

To my relief and surprise, she stopped and her shoulders relaxed. Maybe that was the key; she didn't want to receive help, she needed control.

I stayed planted in place for fear she'd bolt if I got closer. "It would mean a lot to me if you'd cooperate just this one time and help me resolve this case. I agree that the guy is a jerk. We can't fix that, but we can help the homeowner. Let's just go in, find out what the Hindered wants, help it, and get out. It should be simple."

She came closer until she stood toe-to-toe with me and stared directly into my eyes as if looking for something there. Honesty? Trust perhaps? I held my breath and waited for her answer.

"Your eyes kick ass. They're almost purple," she said.

I stared in stunned silence as she tromped up the steps and into the house. No one could ever accuse her of being predictable.

The small farmhouse was in chaos. Crew members crowded together talking. Light cables snaked across the living room floor. A small camera was mounted on a tripod in the corner, and a man held a larger camera on his shoulder.

A tiny woman who looked to be in her early fifties, dressed in jeans and a striped shirt, sat on the sofa next to another guy wearing the same black shirt as Steve.

"I just want it gone," the woman whined. "I didn't want all this to-do and hassle."

The man patted her hand. "We'll get it out very soon. We appreciate your letting us film it."

A man laying cables in the corner bumped an end table with his knee, and a vase fell to the floor with a thud. The woman on the couch screamed.

I looked across the room to Vivienne, who was wandering the perimeter, appearing to study pictures hanging on the wood paneling. She met my eyes and shook her head. She couldn't hear the Hindered.

"Sorry," the woman said to the man next to her. "It kept me up all night knocking things over. I'm a little jumpy."

The man patted her shoulder and said something in a comforting tone.

"So, did you get your chick in line?" Steve said from behind me.

My desire to punch him surprised me. "No." Vivienne didn't need to be kept in line, she needed to be freed to relax and be herself. I just had to find what made her tick. "My job is to assist her, not control her."

He whacked me on the back. "Yeah, good luck with that, buddy."

I looked across the room to find Vivienne studying me. She looked from my clenched fists back up to my face, then to Steve. Because there was so much going on in the room, I couldn't feel her emotions. Again, she shook her head.

"She hasn't heard anything yet," I whispered to Steve.

The woman on the sofa blew her nose into a Kleenex. "The ghost only comes out at night. I don't know why we have to make such a fuss during the day. I really wish all of these people weren't here."

"Sometimes apparitions respond to activity," the man next to her on the couch said.

"Time!" Steve called. The people in the room scattered and manned their various posts. Two behind cameras, two with reflective boards, and a guy who looked to be dressed as a Native American all stood at the ready.

The woman on the sofa sat up straight and dabbed her eyes with another Kleenex. Vivienne signaled me to come to her from an archway leading to the back of the house. I tiptoed around behind the lights and joined her. "There's nothing here," she said. "Maybe the TV jerks are wrong."

"Maybe, but the woman is honestly shaken. She believes something is here. Have you called it or tried to communicate?"

She rolled her eyes. "Here's how it works: Dead guys talk to *me,* I don't talk to them."

She was wrong. Speakers reached out to the Hindered all the time. But I knew enough about her now to know that telling her she was mistaken would backfire. "Have you tried? Sometimes it works."

"Like, try to get it to talk to me?"

I nodded.

Her fear spiked. "On *purpose?*"

I had been right. She was afraid. "Yes. It won't hurt you. I'll be here. If it possesses you, I'll shove it out if you don't want it to share your body."

"Let's get this straight here and now. The dead guys can just tell me what they want, and that's that. I don't do the soul-sharing garbage or possession. Nope. No way." She crossed her arms over her chest and leaned against the wall. "Seen it, and it's not gonna happen."

She'd seen a soul-sharing. "Your aunt?"

She nodded. "Her partner was the one who could do it."

"Your aunt was a Protector."

She shivered. "It's freezing in here."

It wasn't. The lights had made it hot. Scorching, in fact. I pulled her farther into the hallway with me. Her skin was cold to the touch. Terror shot through her and into me, causing a thrill and an adrenaline dump.

"It's here," she whispered, clutching my sleeve. "Oh,

God." Her fingers twisted in the fabric. "It's really pissed off."

I pulled her trembling body next to mine and rubbed my hands down her back to warm her up. "Shhh. It's okay. I'm right here. Ask it what it wants."

She shook her head and plugged her ears. "No. I want it to leave me alone."

"You need to help it. It only wants help. Please, Vivienne." I took her face in my hands, focusing on transmitting as much calm through my palms as possible. The ends of my fingers felt tingly.

She looked dazed for a moment, probably because of my transmission, then she nodded, stood up straight, and took a deep breath. "What do you want?"

The single lightbulb in the hallway flickered and went out. Flooded with Vivienne's fear, I pulled her against me even tighter. "He wants them to leave," she whispered.

A loud pop came from the living room, followed by shouting. Still holding Vivienne, I moved to the archway and peered into the room. It appeared a large stage light had exploded, stopping the shoot. The guy dressed as a Native American was standing closest to us, holding an abalone shell with something burning in it with one hand and a feather in the other. "I only brought enough sage for one shot," he told the guy next to him.

The homeowner sobbed on the sofa as several crew members swept up glass.

Vivienne's fear shifted to anger.

"Just hang in there, Mrs. Nelson." Steve told her. "We'll be up and running again soon. We'll start over with the history of the murder that took place in the house and then you telling us about the first time you heard the man in your hallway, then we'll burn sage in all four corners of the room again."

"Burning sage?" Vivienne's voice was a low growl. "She's terrified, and they are screwing with her. I hate this."

The woman sobbed loudly from the couch. "Please don't make me go through this again."

"Better hurry," the guy with the abalone shell said, "or we'll have to cut my part. I'm almost out of smoke."

Vivienne pulled away. "Enough!" she shouted. "That's enough. This woman needs help. She doesn't need to be exploited."

Steve crossed to us and spoke very low. My adrenaline spiked and my body immediately prepped for a confrontation, because for a moment he acted like he was going to get physical, but he kept his cool. "Get her out of here right now, or I'll go public about the IC. I'll go to every media outlet I know and tell them all about you. I know how important it is for you guys to remain invisible. I can fix all of that. Now get out."

He was evidently satisfied with his threat, because his facial expression could only be described as a gloat. As quickly as it came, it left, replaced by wide-eyed terror.

"Under the boards," he croaked in a gravelly voice. Steve grabbed his throat and gasped. "Help me," he said, sounding like himself again. He staggered forward and grabbed Vivienne by the shoulders. "Please."

Vivienne's anger shifted to amusement. "Now, isn't this something? So, if I help you, you won't out us, right, Stevie boy?"

He nodded, eyes so huge the white was exposed all the way around them. "Right. Absolutely. Get it out. Make it leave me alone!"

"And you'll pack up and leave this woman in peace."

He nodded. "Yes, yes."

Vivienne placed her hands on her hips. "And you'll give her all of her money back."

He paused, then his body trembled all over. "Floorboards," the gravelly voice growled through his mouth.

"Refund, Steve?" She knocked gently on the side of his head as if it were a door. "Can you hear me in there? Can you answer, or does the ghost have your tongue? Are you going to give this woman her money back?"

"Yes!" he shouted in his own voice.

Vivienne cupped her hand to his ear and whispered something. Steve cried out and crumpled to the floor in a heap. Obviously, she'd gotten the spirit out of his body with her words. Two of the techies ran over and crouched next to him.

"Mrs. Nelson," Steve said as the guys helped him to his feet. "We can't help you with your case. We're going to have to refund you your money."

"But—" the woman said.

"Sorry." He straightened his collar. "Pack up, guys."

Vivienne crooked her finger, and he came over. "You'll pay the IC its fee anyway."

Steve's face grew bright red. "I'll do no such thing. You ruined this episode. I lost a ton of money today."

"You pay the IC to get rid of ghosts. Well, once things calm down around here, I'm going to get rid of it. You'll pay for services rendered."

He shook his head. "No way."

She shrugged. "I hope you like having ghoul dude in there with you, then, because if you renege, I'm going to tell him to have at it and jump back in. You'll be shouting about floorboards until he shoves you out and *you* become the ghost."

Steve's eyes opened wide.

She put her mouth right next to his ear. "Because, you see, Steve, ghosts are real. They're not imaginary TV gimmicks to make you money. And they're dangerous. I don't think you're up to playing with them. Do you?" She stepped away. "Go back to your scamming, and let the 'chick' handle the dead guys, okay?"

She walked over to the homeowner on the couch. "I really want to help you get rid of this ghost, Mrs. Nelson."

"I-I just want to be left alone," the woman said. "I want everyone to leave. I want to—"

Vivienne took her hand. "I totally understand. But I can come back later after everything has calmed down."

The woman shot a glance at me and then turned her attention back to Vivienne. "Just you. None of these men. Only you."

Vivienne nodded. I stepped forward to explain that was impossible, but Vivienne silenced me with a glare.

"Just me. Do you want me to stay and do it now?"

She shook her head. "No. I need get out of here for a while. I'm going to go see my daughter for a few hours."

Vivienne grabbed a ballpoint pen out of a techie's pocket and wrote something on the woman's hand. "Here's my number. You give me a call when you're ready, and I'll come get rid of the ghost without any lights, cameras, or action, okay?"

The woman wiped a tear and nodded. "Thank you. I'll call you when I'm on my way back."

Vivienne spun and met Steve's eyes. "You're going to leave now. Floorboards forever. Think about it."

"Pack up," Steve ordered his crew. Vivienne grinned and strode out the front door. Somehow, even though I should have been mortified, I wanted to applaud. What a scene.

SEVEN

There were lots of better ways to handle that," I said, unlocking and opening the car door for her.

She slid in. "You mean *your* way. The way described in that idiotic manual."

"Precisely." I closed her door and walked around the car. "There are rules," I said, getting into the car. "We have to follow them."

"Or what?" she said, slumping in her seat. "What'll they do? Kill us?"

I snapped my seat belt buckle. "If we screw up badly enough, that's possible." Her jaw dropped. *Good.* I had her attention finally. "You need to read the manual."

Several guys came out carrying metal trunks full of film equipment.

"That poor woman," Vivienne said. "I hope she calls me. That was a pissed-off ghost, and I got it to leave that guy's body by promising I'd clear everyone out. He was as freaked by all that activity as the woman was."

"What did he want?"

"I don't know. He kept yelling at me about floorboards. Scared the crap out of me at first."

She admitted fear. That was a step forward. "And then?"

"Then, I just realized he wanted something and if we helped him, he'd be cool."

I put my head against the headrest and closed my eyes, concentrating on her emotions.

"What are you doing?" she asked. "Are you sick?"

"No. I'm feeling you."

She laughed, and I opened my eyes. "If that was going on, I wouldn't ask what you were doing."

"You really need to read the manual. Protectors can feel Speakers' emotions."

"No way!"

"True fact."

She crossed her arms over her chest. "Not so sure I like that. It's pretty intrusive."

"Yeah, but it helps keep you safe. I feel your fear right when it spikes, and I'm ready to help before you can articulate it."

"So you know when I'm afraid."

I nodded. "Yep. Your tough-girl routine is pretty transparent."

"I *am* tough." She sat back in her seat and stared out the windshield.

"You are. Ghosts are scary. Anyone and everyone is right to experience fear when dealing with them."

"So, you don't think I'm a wimp."

I turned the key in the ignition. "That's the last word I'd use to describe you."

"What words would you use?"

I put the car in gear and pulled out onto the dirt road. "*Irritating* and *impulsive*."

"That's better than *stuffy* and *predictable*."

"Not if you want to stay alive. Read the manual, Vivienne."

"Whatever."

I turned around in a neighbor's driveway and turned back out toward the highway. I reached into my console and pulled out my copy of the IC manual. "Here. Dig in."

She took the book, but grabbed my hand before I could pull it away. Her touch made concentration difficult. "I can read palms, you know," she said, turning my hand palm up.

I blinked hard and focused on the narrow dirt road.

She chuckled.

I almost gasped when she ran her fingers across my palm. "You have a very long lifeline, Paul. Really long, like you'll live forever." Her gentle touch was driving me mad.

I pulled my hand away. "It will be a very short life if I don't pay attention to the road."

"In all seriousness, you have great hands."

I pulled to the side of the road and stopped. "I don't get you. You clearly can't stand me, but then, you pull crap like this. I'm not a Ping-Pong ball you can bounce around."

One side of her mouth quirked up. "Well, now you've gone and surprised me, Mr. Predictable. The fact you speak your mind to me doesn't jibe with how you act around the others."

I put the car in park. "What others?"

"The people that were at Charles's house last night. I thought you were weak."

"But you don't now."

"No. I think there's a lot more to you than I originally thought."

Her emotions were unreadable, but she seemed sincere. A strange pinching sensation seized my chest for a moment. For the first time since I'd met her, I had a glimmer of hope this could work out.

I put the car in gear and pulled back onto the road. "Don't get any weird ideas."

"All my ideas are weird," she said, tucking some escaped strands of hot pink hair behind her ear as she opened the IC manual to the rules section.

We drove through a burger place on the way home and I didn't see her after that until evening, when she came barging into Charles's office while I wrote up our report for the morning's fiasco.

"The haunted woman called!"

I set the pen down on the desk and enjoyed the excitement flowing from her.

"She's ready. She's leaving her daughter's house and wants me to come get rid of the ghost tonight." Her smile was contagious.

"What time do we leave?"

"Oh, no. Not us, me only. She was adamant."

I closed my file. "That's not how it works. You can't go alone under any circumstance. It's why pairs are designated. The Vessel can't be unattended."

She put her hands on her hips. "English, please."

"Did you read the manual?"

She shuffled from foot to foot. "I'm working on it. I kinda fell asleep."

I turned in the desk chair to face her. "There are three kinds of bodies: open, single-souled, and closed. Being a Speaker means you are an open Vessel. You can accommodate more than one soul in the same body. The Hindered know this and use your body to resolve the issues holding them here."

She sat on the arm of a leather wing chair. "So I don't let it in."

"It's not that simple. Sometimes they force their way. That's where I come in. I have the ability to split my soul and put part of it in a Speaker's body in order to shove the second soul out."

"So why wouldn't it bounce into your body?"

"I'm a closed Vessel. My body will accommodate no soul but my own. I can't be possessed."

"But regular people can. I've seen it."

I nodded. "Yes, they are single-soul Vessels. The stronger soul wins after a very short time. They can't comfortably accommodate a second soul for an extended period like you can."

She sighed. "Okay. So what do you suggest?"

I was stunned she had asked my opinion. "You talk her into letting me come with you."

"Okay, well, she wants me to come right now, so I'll call her from the car."

I grabbed my jacket from the back of the desk chair. "At your service."

She smiled. "I could get used to that kind of talk."

A strange, unfamiliar emotion bounced from her, but only for a moment. "I hope so."

She stood. "Why?"

"Because I've wanted to do this my whole life. It's all I've ever wanted to do." An entirely different emotion transmitted from her. It felt like disappointment or low-level pain. I slid my jacket on. "You okay?"

"Never been better," she said over her shoulder as she stomped out the office door.

When we arrived at the farmhouse, the gate was locked. I parked just outside of it and waited for Vivienne to finish her phone conversation with Mrs. Nelson, who was still insistent that she come alone.

"I have a solution," I said after she hung up. "I can go with you while inside your body. She won't know I'm there, and I can prevent the ghost from possessing you that way."

"Can't you just come along as a bodiless soul, like a ghost or something? Can't we do it without the soul-sharing business?"

"No. It's dangerous and painful for me, and I have to get clearance ahead of time for my soul to be detached for any period of time."

She unbuckled her seat belt. "Or what?"

"Or I could be discontinued."

"What does that mean?"

I made a cutting sign across my throat.

"Yeah, well, let's not let that happen."

"Agreed."

"Okay, we'll soul-share. Let's get on it."

I started the car.

"Wait! What are you doing?"

"I'm going to leave my body at home, where it will be safe."

"Nuh-uh." She reached over and turned the car off. "The woman is freaking out. The ghost is throwing stuff around."

"Well, either I come in with you, or we leave my body in a safe place and we soul-share."

"The locked car is safe."

I took a deep breath. "It's not. There are too many variables involved. I need to leave it at home."

Her phone rang. "Hey, Mrs. Nelson. I'll be there in just a minute. I really want to bring my . . ." She stared at me a moment. "My associate, Paul, with me. Yeah. The guy with me this morning." Her eyes closed. "Okay. Just me."

She disconnected the call. "She's serious about it only being me. She thought you were on Steve's side, and she's figured out he's a crook."

I shook my head. "You can't go in alone."

"Paul, please. What harm can come of it? We're in the middle of nowhere. What could happen?"

I shook my head. "The rules are clear."

"Screw the rules. That woman's freaking out."

"It's a bad idea." Worse than bad. Terrible.

"Look, I read enough of that book to know I'm in charge. You kind of have to do what I say when a ghost is around." Dread filled me in a sickening wave as I realized I was about to be outmaneuvered. She put her hand on my arm. "Well, a ghost is around, and I say we leave your body here and go on in."

"Vivienne—"

She withdrew her hand. "Now, Paul. As your Speaker, I'm asking you to soul-share right now in order to facilitate this resolution."

Shit. Straight from the book. She *had* read the manual. I had no choice, really. "Have you soul-shared before?"

She shook her head, and a spike of fear came from her. "What do I do?"

"Nothing. I do all the work."

She rolled her eyes. "I could give you such a hard time about that statement, you know."

I'm sure I blushed, but it was too dark for her to see, fortunately. "Touch me."

"Oh, look who's getting weird ideas."

"No. Really. Soul-sharing kind of hurts at first, and contact helps."

She studied me with narrowed eyes.

"I'm not kidding you. It hurts less."

"Pain doesn't bug me."

I glared at her. "Well, it bugs me. Touch me."

"Why don't you touch *me?*"

"Why does everything with you have to be a challenge? The touch is consent. It has to come from you. Touch me, please, Vivienne."

"I love it when you beg."

I reached up to crank the key to start the car, and she took my hand between hers.

"Do it, Paul."

This was it. My first soul-share with my Speaker. I faced front and closed my eyes. "Out," I whispered to my soul. Beginning with my chest, a burning, ripping sensation filled my body and worked its way out to my extremities. The peculiar feeling of my soul ripping apart and breaking free of my body sort of defies words. It's nothing that my familiar human body had experienced and is singular to the Protector. "In," I commanded my noncorporeal form. Much faster than my soul had exited my own body, it entered Vivienne's.

"Ow! Son of a . . . Ow!" she gasped. "Dang, Paul."

It's okay. It's over now, I said from inside her body. I couldn't hear her thoughts, but she could hear mine, just like she could hear Hindered. I could feel her emotions, though, and she was as excited as I was. I felt no fear at all from her. *Are you okay?*

"Whoa. Cool. You're in my head!"

I am. Please take my keys with us and lock the door to the car.

She pulled the keys out. "So how much control do you have in there? Can you make my body do things like the Hindered can?"

Someone has been reading the manual.

"I told you I would. I just didn't finish it."

No. I'm only a partial soul. A tendril of my soul is left in my body to keep it alive. Not enough to animate it, though. It takes a complete soul to animate a body. You've got the conn, Captain.

She locked the car, and through her eyes, I could see my body buckled into the driver's seat, looking like it was peacefully asleep.

The resolution began the second Vivienne entered the house. The ghost tried to barge into her body several times without invitation, but my presence kept it out. The average Hindered waited for an invitation, but this one turned out to be a borderline Malevolent and was sick of waiting around. The good news was that he didn't seem to be looking for revenge, which was what most Malevolents craved.

"Floorboard!" he said for the billionth time.

"Yeah, I've got that," Vivienne said. "Which floorboard?"

He made groaning sounds, and a lamp flew across the room, smashing against the wall and landing in pieces on the floor, causing poor Mrs. Nelson to scream yet again.

"Now, listen to me," Vivienne said. "What's your name to start with?"

"Ethan Hollister Jr.," he wailed.

"Does the name Ethan Hollister Jr. ring a bell?" Vivienne asked Mrs. Nelson, who was cowering in a corner.

She shuddered. "He was the previous homeowner. He died

last year. It was his wife who was murdered in this house." She covered her face and wept.

"No!" the ghost screamed. *"Floorboard!"*

Vivienne took several steps closer to Mrs. Nelson. "How was the wife murdered?"

"According to the articles I've read, her head was smashed in," Mrs. Nelson said. "With some type of blunt object. The son is on death row, awaiting execution for the murder."

"He didn't do it!" Ethan moaned. *"Floorboard."*

"And her finger was cut off." Mrs. Nelson slumped into a chair in the corner. "They never found the murder weapon or the finger." She began to sob again. "My real estate agent told me about the murder and the rumors that the house was haunted. I just didn't believe her. I thought it was all nonsense and was glad to have such a cheap price on the home because of silly superstition. My daughter and her husband told me not to buy this house. She won't even set foot inside it."

Vivienne jumped and a surge of surprise ran through her when Ethan yelled, *"Floorboard!"* She spun around to face the direction of his voice.

"Okay, Ethan. Here's how it's going to go. You're going to show me the floorboard. I want you to tell me when I'm close. Is it in this room?"

"No!" he screamed.

"Lower your voice, or I'm leaving." She walked to the kitchen. "How about here?"

"No!" He was not as loud this time.

The hallway, I said. *It's where the homeowner first encountered him.*

"Two invisible people talking to me is over-the-top, Paul. Just felt the need to share that." She stopped in the dark hallway. "How about here, Ethan?"

"Here, yes! Here. Dig. Dig!"

"Too loud, dude. Keep it down."

I marveled at her ability to remain calm and keep the spirit calm as well.

"I'm not liking the idea of ripping out the entire floor. How about we play a game of hot and cold. You tell me when I'm standing over it, okay, Ethan?"

"I'll do it. I want to dig it up!" he shouted. It felt like I'd been gut punched when he tried to enter her body to soul-share. I pushed back at him and he exited.

"Why won't you let me in? I need your body," he wailed.

Vivienne took a few more steps down the hallway. "Yeah, well, I need it too, and you seem a little unstable to me. I'm afraid you'd get carried away if you had a real body."

She was even up-front and honest with ghosts. More than that, it worked.

"There," Ethan moaned when a floorboard creaked under Vivienne's boot.

"Got a crowbar or something to take up this wood?" Vivienne asked Mrs. Nelson.

"Now you've gotta stop being so cryptic and come clean

with me, Ethan," Vivienne said after Mrs. Nelson scurried to go fetch tools. "Exactly what's under that floor? Because if it's a body or something creepy, you need to tell me now so I don't lose it when I see it, okay?"

"Letter. Letter for son."

A flood of relief washed through her. "A letter I can deal with."

"Exonerate! Clear his name! ME!" His screams were so loud, Vivienne covered her ears.

"Shut it, Ethan, or that board stays right where it is. Got it? I'm not in the mood for this." She leaned against the wall. "Are they always this loud and pushy, Paul?"

They're all different. This one is pretty agitated. It sounds like he killed his wife and his son was prosecuted for it. I was glad Ethan couldn't hear me talking to her from inside her body, or he would have probably gone nuts. *Since this one keeps trying to barge into your body, I think it's actually a Malevolent and not simply a Hindered. The fact he wants to clear his son's name, rather than seek revenge, makes it unusual. It's good we're catching him now, because after a while, they lose sight of what can be done to help them. We'll know if he's turned when you resolve it.*

"What does it matter?"

We are kind of graded. We get more points for resolving a Malevolent.

"Graded like school? This sucks."

Mrs. Nelson returned with a crowbar and other garden tools. Vivienne reached for the crowbar.

No, I said. *It's best that she tear up her own house.*

Before long, Mrs. Nelson had pried up the creaky board.

"There's nothing here," she said, dropping the crowbar with a clang.

Having my soul in Vivienne's body made reading her emotions easy. Disappointment flooded through her.

"Further south!" The ghost yelled. *"Idiot girl. Go further south."*

Vivienne spun in the direction of his voice. "You start calling me names, Ethan, and you'll be haunting this house forever, you hear me?"

"Let me in! Let me do it!"

"No. Freaking. Way." She picked up the crowbar. "Which way is south, Mrs. Nelson?"

The poor woman pointed toward the entrance to the living room, tears streaming down her face. "Is he here? Are you really talking to him?"

Vivienne nodded.

"Why is he doing this to me?"

"It has nothing to do with you, really. He's just trying to get something cleared up." Vivienne shoved the end of the crowbar under the next plank closest to the living room and pulled up. After several tries, she had an end of the board loose. She reached under and yanked the board out.

"There! Yes, there!" The spirit yelled. *"Clear his name. Condemn me to hell where I belong."*

Vivienne set the board against the wall. "Whoa, there, crazy dead guy. I don't condemn anyone to anywhere. You're on your own there. I'm just digging up floorboards and talking to you. That's all."

Mrs. Nelson leaned over to pull out what looked like a rolled-up newspaper. When she tugged on the end, it unrolled and several items fell back into the empty space under the floor with a thud.

"Crap," Vivienne said, kneeling down. "What is it? That didn't sound like a letter, Ethan."

Don't touch it! I shouted.

"Don't you start screaming too, Paul."

Mrs. Nelson huddled against the wall. "Who is Paul? Are there two of them?"

Sorry. Just don't touch anything until we know what it is, I said.

"It's evidence!" Ethan wailed. *"Proof I killed her."*

"Oh, man," Vivienne said. "Now what?"

We need to see it.

"Do you have a flashlight?"

Mrs. Nelson nodded. "Yes, in the kitchen. I'll be right back."

Ethan continued to moan and wail about justice and exonerating someone named Wayne while Vivienne paced the hallway.

Once we check it out, we need to have the homeowner call the cops. She needs to tell them she found it because she was suspicious of the loose floorboard. If it's possible, she should not mention us. She should not mention the ghost at all, or she'll come off as crazy.

Mrs. Nelson shone the flashlight in the hollow in the floor

and gasped. She covered her mouth and backed away, dropping the flashlight with a bang. It rolled under a bench against the wall.

"What is it?" Vivienne asked, kneeling to retrieve the flashlight.

Mrs. Nelson remained speechless, a look of wide-eyed horror frozen on her face.

Through Vivienne's eyes, I stared down into the gap between the bottom of the wooden floor and the concrete slab below. A hammer, a bloodstained piece of paper, and what appeared to be a shriveled, severed human finger lay in the flashlight's beam.

"Clear his name!" Ethan shouted.

"Oh, God. That's hair and dried gunk on the hammer," Vivienne gasped. "And that other thing is a . . . Is that a . . . ?" Because I had no physical sensation in a Speaker's body, I could only feel her emotions—the panic and revulsion—but I could tell by her rapid breaths she was about to throw up.

Stay together, Vivienne. I'm here. You're okay. Keep calm and help Mrs. Nelson.

"Clear his name. He didn't do it. I did!"

"You did this, Ethan? Why?"

Why doesn't matter, Vivienne. Find out what he needs done in order to release him.

"Yes, I did it, but they blamed him."

"Who?"

"My son! He's innocent. I let him go down for something I did. Give me your body. I must make it right."

She stood and set the flashlight on the bench. "No way! You think I'm letting your sorry, murdering self into my body, you've got another thing coming."

Ethan howled, and the bench slid to the end of the hallway, crashing into the wall. Mrs. Nelson covered her ears, screamed, and flattened against the wall.

He's turning demonic, I said. *You've got to help him before it's too late. Find out what he wants.*

"Why would I help him? He obviously murdered his wife."

We can't let them linger here. You've seen the damage he's done already. He's strong enough to move things. If they have evil intent, the longer they're here, the stronger they get. Find out what he wants and free him.

She took several deep breaths, and her heart rate slowed. "So, I uncovered your dirty secret, Ethan. What do you want me to do about it?"

"What is he saying?" Mrs. Nelson whined.

"Call the police. Clear Wayne," Ethan howled.

"Now what?" Vivienne said.

"I beg your pardon?" Mrs. Nelson asked.

Have her call the police. Then we need to leave. IC involvement needs to be minimized.

Vivienne turned to face her. "So, Mrs. Nelson. I'm not really supposed to be here, and you probably shouldn't tell the cops about me or the ghost, okay?"

Trembling, she darted glances down the hallway. "Is he gone?"

Vivienne placed her hand on the woman's shoulder. "Not yet. Will you please call the police right now and tell them you found what looks like evidence of a murder under your floor. Tell them the board creaked, so you wanted to check it out and found the stuff."

Mrs. Nelson pulled a phone out of her jeans pocket and dialed 911.

"Promise me!" Ethan shouted.

"Sure. What?"

"Clear his name. I feel like I have to leave. Can't . . . stay."

"Yeah, no problem. We'll take care of it."

"Promise!" His voice had become weak. Almost a whisper.

"Consider it done. The cops will come and clear this up, and he'll be free as a bird."

"Over."

"Yep. Done. Take off now, okay?"

As I watched through Vivienne's eyes, an elderly man in overalls appeared standing over the gap in the floor. He glowed luminescent blue, like a hologram.

This is it, Vivienne. He's about to move on. That's the only time they're visible.

"It'll be all right, Ethan. I'll be sure the cops set it straight."

"Be sure Wayne reads my note."

"You bet. Done."

"It's finally over."

"Over and out. You can go on now."

He opened his mouth to speak again, but before a word came out, a black cloud surrounded him and then dissipated into nothing.

I felt the turmoil of sorrow and relief welling up in Vivienne's chest. We didn't have time to hang around. *We've gotta get out of here before the cops arrive.*

Sirens wailed in the distance.

"Crap," Vivienne said, panic rising.

"Go out the back door," Mrs. Nelson said. "And thank you. Thank you so much."

Go, Vivienne!

She ran to the back, winding through the kitchen, out the back door, around the hedge line on the side of the house, and to the dirt road where we had left my car. A spot that was now empty.

"Oh, great. Where's your car? How are we going to get back?"

We had a much worse problem than trying to get home. *Where's my body?*

EIGHT

A Protector losing his body is one of the worst mistakes possible. Charles was going to kill me. Actually, the Intercessor Council would probably take care of that for him.

"What are we going to do?" Vivienne asked.

I have no idea.

She laughed. It was a high-pitched, awkward sound. "Well, this certainly sucks. We're stuck here, I guess."

Headlights winked from down the road.

"The cops could help us find it," she said.

No. We can't be conspicuous.

She took several steps closer to the road and waved her arms. "Okay, we'll just ask for a ride, then. We'll run it by the old man when we get back to your place and figure out where your body is."

No! I shouted.

"Ouch!" Vivienne said, covering her ears. "Well, covering

my ears won't help much, considering you're inside my head. Keep it down."

Hide. Now.

"What? You're kidding, right?"

No. I'm dead serious. Hide in the bushes. Quick.

"I—"

For once, Vivienne, don't argue. It's really important. Trust me.

She headed back toward the house and crouched behind a bush off the side of the porch.

Thank you, I said.

A spike of adrenaline ran through her body when the cruiser pulled up to the gate. She remained silent until the two police officers were inside the house with Mrs. Nelson.

"Now what?" she asked. "I don't know anyone in Houston and don't have anyone to call to help us. Do you know any of your buddies' numbers? Couldn't that tall blond guy come get us?"

I was so reliant on technology, I hadn't bothered to commit anyone's number to memory except Charles's and the IC's, neither of which I could use without compromising us. Cabs probably didn't come out this far from the city. And if by some miracle, one did, it would take forever, and my wallet was on my body . . . wherever that was. *We wait for the police to leave, then we ask Mrs. Nelson for a ride home.*

She rolled back from her crouching position and sat, head in hands. "God, this sucks. I've got stuff to do, you know."

So did I, like find my body before the IC found out I'd lost it. It felt like forever before the cops finally left, taking Mrs. Nelson with them.

"Crap. Crap. Crap. She went with them, and I have an appointment," Vivienne muttered, feet crunching in the gravel on the front walk of the house. "We could take her car and return it later."

Take her car? Did your grandmother teach you to hot-wire cars between telling fortunes?

"I have lots of hidden talents," she said. "But no, I saw her keys hanging on the hook inside the door."

We'd lost my body, and now we were preparing to steal a car. Perfect. *It's a terrible idea,* I said.

"Why?" She tugged on the front door. It was locked. She walked around to the back of the house and tried that door. "Locked."

Let's just wait for Mrs. Nelson to come back. They're probably just taking her statement or something.

"Nope. I've gotta be somewhere. Can't hang out here all night." She pulled up on a window. "Ha! We're in."

Great. Add breaking and entering to jacking a car and top it off with losing my body. Perfect first resolution.

She climbed through the window and headed straight to the hook by the back door. "Got it."

Stop! I said. *We can't just steal her car.*

"We're only borrowing it."

Without permission. That's theft.

"You are the most uptight person I've ever met. I need to be somewhere soon." Her frustration was like a live current blasting through the part of my soul in her body.

Where do you need to go so badly that you'd steal a car to get there?

"Someplace important. Okay. I'll leave her a note and my phone number. Does that make you happy?" she said.

Not really.

"Close enough." She grabbed a pen and paper and scrawled a note, then stabbed it onto the key hook at the door.

Mrs. Nelson had an old pickup truck that rumbled to life after several failed attempts to start it. Then there was the matter of the locked gate. Fortunately, the key to the padlock was on the ring with the truck keys. Vivienne was so determined to get wherever she needed to be, she'd have probably busted down the fence to get out.

"Ha. I wonder what the old man will say when he sees this hunk of junk in the driveway of his humongous house," she said when she finally pulled onto the dirt road.

He can't know this happened, I said. *We have to find my body and make everything right before he ever finds out.*

She pulled onto the highway. "Exactly how do you propose we do that?"

I have no idea. I didn't even know who had taken my car and body. *Maybe we should start calling hospitals to see if I'm in any of them.*

"We?" She changed lanes and passed a slow-moving RV.

"You mean *me*, because you're pretty much useless right now."

Useless. Yep. No disputing that. No body. No plan. No car. Possibly no future, unless I figured something out quick.

She glanced at her phone long enough to see the home screen. "Ugh. I'm going to be late."

What is it you have to do that is so important? We're in real trouble here.

She put her phone in her lap and rolled her eyes. "You are such a worrier. Loosen up. It'll all work out."

You don't understand.

As she turned off of the country highway onto Interstate 10, her phone rang. A quick glance at the screen revealed the number was unknown.

Answer it, I said.

"Nope. I don't answer calls from people I don't know."

Answer it. It could be the IC.

"They don't have my number."

Don't kid yourself.

She kept driving, and the phone call went unanswered. Her emotions were level, as opposed to mine, which bordered on frantic.

Pull over.

"What?"

Pull over. I need to show you something.

She took the first exit and pulled into a closed windshield repair company parking lot. "What?" she asked, irritation rising.

I'm going to give you a memory. I think it will help put this in perspective. Are you ready?

"What do I do?"

Just watch.

I accessed the memory, careful to recall every detail. I started it as the hearing was dismissed. The first out of the room was Ophelia, one of the elders who commonly sat on discontinuance panels. Then a middle-aged man, who appeared visibly shaken. He tapped Ophelia on the shoulder. "I honestly had no idea she was allowing that," he said.

Ophelia turned and glared at him. "I'm aware of that. Otherwise, you would be meeting the same fate as your Protector."

He gave a quick nod and scurried up the stairs at the end of the hall.

Ophelia stared right at me. I put my pen down and folded my hands in my lap to keep from fidgeting. "I trust you are learning and taking lessons away from this. Being a Protector is an honor. If Charles ever approves you for duty, don't abuse the privilege."

I'd never liked Ophelia and was relieved when she climbed the stairs out of view.

From inside Vivienne's body, it was easy to feel her anger as the memory played. She didn't like Ophelia either. "What a condescending hag," she said.

Wait. It's not over.

Another Speaker from the board of elders emerged from

the room, holding the arm of a weeping woman. My heart ached for her. I stared down at my papers until the couple disappeared from view. A file was slid onto the desk before me. Charles's gold and ruby ring glinted in the halogen spot from above.

"Please delete her from the system and then destroy this file," he said. He sounded tired. When I met his eyes, he stared at me for a long time. He took a deep breath. "Being a part of this system is harder every lifetime. It used to be so simple. There are so many variables now. Just . . ." He shook his head. "Just be careful."

When his footsteps reached the top of the stairs, I stared down at the standard black IC file. When I opened it, my heart stopped. In huge red letters, "Discontinued" was scrawled across the black-and-white photo of the woman who had left before Charles came out. The woman who was weeping. Now I knew why. I turned the page and found the grounds for the hearing: Sharing the body of a human outside of an exorcism.

"Is that it?" Vivienne said.

No.

I focused on a particular memory from the next day. I was sitting at the kitchen counter reading the newspaper. When I turned to the local news page, a picture of the woman I had seen the day before stared back at me. "Local Florist Dies in Car Accident."

"Oh, my God. They killed her?"

Yes, they did.

Vivienne was quiet for a long time. The only noise was the rumble of the old truck engine. "So, she'll come back again, though."

No. Her soul brand was erased. She was discontinued, body and soul.

"But, that's murder, just like Ethan committed." Her anger was raging.

No, Vivienne. Protectors are told from the start what's at stake. We go through intensive training, as opposed to Speakers. We are held to tight scrutiny and accept the rules and punishments assigned by the IC. She knew what could happen when she entered the body of a human.

"Why would she do it?"

Well, in this case, she was floating around the casino card tables and then entering the body of her boyfriend to tell him what the other players were holding. They made a lot of money cheating at cards.

"She had a guy outside of her Speaker?"

Many do. Pairing up with your partner is sort of discouraged, but it happens more than the IC would like. Conversely, it's a hard lifestyle for the average person to accept. Speaker-Protector pairs spend almost every waking hour together, so outside affairs are usually shallow and limited.

"The blond guy and the brunette girl at your house appear to be together."

Yes, but it's recent. Alden and Lenzi went lifetimes as only business partners.

"Whew," she said. "It'd be hard not to be his partner in every way possible. Just sayin'."

My jolt of jealousy surprised me. *Lenzi's remarkable as well.*

"Remarkable, huh?"

The phone rang. "Unknown" popped up on the screen.

Please answer it this time.

She sighed and pressed answer. "Hello?"

"Vivienne. Where are you?"

She pressed the phone to her chest. "It's Charles," she whispered.

I know. I can hear through your ears.

"Oh. Duh. What do I say?"

I'll coach you from inside. Say only what I tell you to say, okay?

"Okay."

Tell him where we are. Wait to see why he called. He may not know. This was a false hope. Charles seemed to know everything.

"Hi, Charles. I'm on I-10 on my way back from the resolution."

"Is Protector 993 in the Vessel?"

She put the phone to her chest. "What the heck does that mean?"

Tell him yes. He knows. Be honest no matter what, or we're doomed. We were probably doomed anyway. He had used my Protector number rather than my name, which didn't bode well at all.

"Yeah."

"Get to Mercy Hospital West immediately. Meet me in the ER. Do not answer any questions or say anything to anybody. Is that clear?"

"Yeah, got it."

Yeah, got it? She just answered him with "Yeah, got it." We didn't stand a chance.

NINE

The drive to the hospital was silent except for my repeated instructions that Vivienne tell only the truth and not contradict me, no matter what I said.

"What's the old man like when he's mad?" she asked, pulling into the parking garage outside the ER.

I've never seen him mad.

"I bet the top of his little bald head gets red." She snickered. I found nothing in the conversation funny whatsoever.

The ER seemed unnecessarily bright and harsh. I could see what Vivienne saw and heard through her ears, but I had no sense of smell at all. She headed to the counter, but I urged her to stop. *We should just wait. He'll know we're here.*

"How?" she whispered.

He'll have a Protector with him who will have felt you arrive.

She moved to the side of the waiting room near a large aquarium full of tiny fish.

"There you are. I must have missed you coming in," Race said, emerging through the set of stainless-steel double doors between us and the reception desk. "You're in some fierce trouble, my friends."

"I'm not your friend," Vivienne said.

"You're going to wish I were, sweetheart. It's hittin' the fan around here." He tilted his head. "You in there, Junior?"

Tell him yes.

She nodded.

"Follow me," he said, heading back to the doors. He nodded at the woman behind the counter, who buzzed them open.

It was the longest walk I'd ever made—well, that I'd ever been a part of. Finally, Race turned into a room at the end of the hallway.

And there I was. My body lay in a bed with an IV and machines all around. It wasn't hooked up to any of them, but it was scary anyway.

Vivienne scanned the room and found Charles sitting in a pink plastic chair in the corner.

"Put him back," Charles ordered, gesturing to my body. I was instantly alarmed because his words were accusatory, as if she had taken me out of my body in the first place.

Touch my body, I said.

She looked back at Charles, and I could tell she was going to say something rude.

Remember the memory I showed you? That could be us. Touch my body, and let's get this over with.

She pressed her palm to my ankle. "Out," I whispered to my soul. For a moment, I hovered over my body on the bed. I wanted to zip away without entering. To just run away from everything, but it was not feasible . . . or right. I had always done what was right. "In," I commanded my spirit, focusing on my sleeping form on the narrow hospital bed.

My body gasped to life. I took several breaths before I opened my eyes.

Charles remained in the chair in the corner. "Your body was discovered by Mrs. Nelson's neighbor, who called an ambulance. Your car was towed to a lot downtown. How did you and Vivienne get to the hospital?"

Vivienne took a position near the bed, as if to put herself between Charles and me. "Well, when his car was gone, I decided—"

I cut her off. "I convinced Vivienne to borrow Mrs. Nelson's car."

He leaned forward. "I assume you have a good reason why your body was left in an unsecure place unattended, Paul?"

Vivienne took a step even closer. "I—"

Again, I cut her off. "It was my fault entirely. I should have been more careful. I apologize . . . and I apologize to you, Vivienne. I put us both in jeopardy."

Vivienne opened and closed her mouth several times while

I gave her a pointed look. Surely she would pick up on my lead and stay quiet. There was no need for both of us to go down.

Race cleared his throat. "Are you through with me here, sir?"

Charles turned to Race. "Follow Vivienne back and return the car. Then take her to the house."

Vivienne shuffled foot to foot. "I have somewhere I need to go."

Charles's eyes narrowed.

"It's really important."

He sighed. "Take her wherever she needs to go, then deliver her to the house, please, Horace."

Race nodded and strode out the door. Vivienne cast me a look before following. A blast of worry washed over me. Was her concern for herself or me? I wondered.

Long moments passed with no sound except the gentle, high-pitched beeping from one of the machines.

"I'm really sorry, sir," I said.

He nodded. "I know." He reached over and pushed a red button on the wall.

After a few moments, a nurse entered. "Well, hello there! Your father said you'd wake up soon."

My father?

I tried to smile. "I'm fine. Can I go now?"

She pulled a blood pressure cuff off the wall and wrapped it around my arm. "No. Not until the doctor discharges you, which won't be until tomorrow morning at the earliest. They are going to transfer you to a regular room for observation." She puffed the cuff up on my arm and put a stethoscope in her ears. She smiled and made an entry on the computer on her cart. "Any pain, dizziness, nausea?"

"No. I'm fine."

Charles shifted to the front of his chair. "I told you he's done this before. I gave the doctor his neurologist's number. She can chat with him on Monday, but I'd like to take him home."

"I'll call the doctor and get back to you, okay?" she said sweetly. It was obvious I wasn't going anywhere without a scene, and there was no way Charles would make a scene. I settled in and pulled the sheet higher over the hospital gown.

After she left, Charles stood and paced the room. "You've put me in an awkward situation."

"I'm sorry, sir. I made a huge mistake."

"You certainly did. You've forced me to step outside my job as regional director for a personal role." He stopped pacing and met my eyes directly. "It won't happen again. Do you understand?"

My heart thumped so hard in my chest, I was sure the sheet was moving with it. "Yes, sir."

"The IC has many reasons for avoiding hospitals, records being one of them. I'll have one of the IC doctors make up a story to cover for your temporary coma." He scrubbed a hand over his bald head. "I had to answer lots of questions about your scars."

I fiddled with the rough sheet. Charles and I had never touched on this subject before.

He leaned closer from his chair. "I didn't know how extensive they were. Your file from Wilkingham didn't mention it in detail. You should have told me."

Still unable to meet his eyes, I folded the top of the sheet over in a neat pleat. "Some things don't warrant discussion."

"Fair enough." He stood and collected his jacket from the chair. "The doctor will most certainly ask you about them. I suggest you relay that you have no recollection of how they happened."

"I don't."

He paused in folding his jacket over his arm. A blast of concern emanated from him, which surprised me, since he was so good about keeping his guard up and not letting his feelings transmit. As quickly as the emotions came, he masked them. "None at all?"

"I only remember the last one. The others . . . ?" I shrugged. "Nothing."

He reached out as if he were going to place his hand on my shoulder, but stopped just short of touching me. Silently, he studied me for a moment, then headed for the door. "Please don't put me in a position like this again."

He paused in the doorway but didn't turn to face me. "Race will come get you in the morning. Your things are in the closet."

And with that, he exited the room, leaving me in absolute chaos—completely alone to battle not only my current mistakes, but the demons of my past as well.

TEN

21st-Century Cycle, Journal Entry 3:

*Our assignment as a team was a great success.
The newly turned Malevolent was resolved in a
routine manner with no injury, incident, or
issue.*

Paul Blackwell—Protector 993

I 've been sent to bust you out of here, sleeping beauty. Look alive!" Race's voice startled me awake with a jolt. My knees slammed into the metal rolling tray pulled over my hospital bed, nearly launching the Styrofoam plate of cold scrambled eggs into my lap. He ran a hand over his hair and chuckled. "The doc called Charles and said your discharge should happen this morning."

I rolled the tray away. "The doctor was here about two hours ago."

"And?"

I rubbed the back of my neck to alleviate what felt like a sunburn. "I'll be surprised if she doesn't transfer me to the psych floor. She thinks I'm nuts."

"You're not?"

My situation surely was. "How's Vivienne?"

He laughed and flopped into the vinyl recliner in the corner. I'd been moved from the ER to this room sometime in the middle of the night for observation.

"Vivienne's fine. Really fine, if you know what I mean."

I ignored his clumsy innuendo and pushed a button that put the top of my bed upright. "Where did she have to go after she left here?"

He popped the footstool up, which caused the whole chair to tilt back in a rapid jerk. "Whoa! It's like a mechanical bull! Yippeekaiyay!" He swung his arm over his head as if balancing on a bucking bull.

I sat up straight. "Where'd she go?"

"She had me drop her off at some row houses in the ward."

"Why?" The sunburn feeling on my neck was really bugging me. I hadn't been in the sun recently, though. I placed my hand over it, and it felt hot to the touch.

He shrugged. "Honestly, Junior, I didn't ask. Seemed like something I didn't want to know, if you know what I mean. It was a sketchy place."

"Why would she go there?" I hadn't realized I'd asked it out loud until he answered me.

"By the way she dresses and acts, the possibilities are endless."

I narrowed my eyes. "Watch it."

"Or what, Junior? You gonna hop out of that bed in your little cotton gown and kick my ass?" He pushed on the wooden handle on the side of the recliner, but nothing happened. He struggled with it again and then laughed. "You'd have to give me a head start, though, because this thing has me trapped." Then he really laughed. "That'd be awesome, you with a bare butt and me with mine stuck in this chair. All we'd need is a cute nurse, and it would be a YouTube sensation."

I sat back and sighed. What was Vivienne doing in the ward at night in a row house? "Can we just leave?" I asked.

"Nah. The big guy told me not to make a fuss. I'll go check with the nurses' station, though. Might find a cutie while I'm there." He yanked the handle and shoved his booted feet hard on the footrest, and the footstool finally slipped down into place at the front of the chair, bringing it upright with a slam. "Free at last!" he said, standing.

"Where is she now?" I asked.

"Who, the cute nurse?"

I rolled my eyes. "No. Vivienne."

He shrugged. "Who knows? Cinda was taking her to some meeting in Galveston when I dropped by to talk to Charles this morning. He wouldn't discuss this over the phone. Guess he's covering your ass this time, huh?"

"What kind of meeting?" I pushed on the bed rail, but it wouldn't come down. "What meeting did Cinda take her to?"

I was getting frantic. Were they questioning her about last night? Charles had seemed accusatory when he spoke to her. He may have been covering for me, but letting her take the hit for breaking the rules—I couldn't let that happen. "You've gotta get me to Galveston. I have to stop it."

"Stop what?"

I scooted to the end of the bed and threw my legs over the edge. "Stop the hearing."

"Nobody said anything about a hearing."

"But—"

"Calm down, Junior. Nobody's going to get discontinued. Not today, anyway." He looked me up and down. "Might want to put on some clothes." Then he left.

She was in a meeting at headquarters in Galveston, but it wasn't a hearing. My mind tried to run through the possibilities, but came up blank.

I pulled my clothes out of the closet and changed in the bathroom. I didn't even have her phone number, I realized. I took a deep breath. I needed to get my act together and start operating on logic. I ran some cold water over my hand and put it over my burning neck.

"Hey, you're good to go," Race said, waving a pink paper over his head. "Ready to get out of here?"

He didn't need to ask twice. I grabbed the plastic bag at the bottom of the closet, pulled out my phone and wallet, and headed to the door.

When I got home, I searched for Vivienne. My car was in the garage, but there was no sign of my Speaker. The last place I looked was in her bedroom. I called her name several times before I entered.

The room looked pretty much the same as it always had, but it smelled different. It smelled like Vivienne—fresh and with a faint hint of spice. I took a deep breath and turned a full circle. Her e-reader was on the desk next to a tattered duffel bag. I knew I shouldn't snoop, but I couldn't help myself.

Her screen came to life on her table of contents. Based on her attitude and appearance, what I saw was not at all what I expected. The books on her reader were classics and historical fiction; the newest selections were nonfiction books about learning disorders.

A door slammed downstairs. I turned the device off and put it back exactly as I had found it.

I slid out the door and into my bedroom before heavy footsteps sounded on the stairs.

I fought the urge to go peek. I was certain it was Vivienne's combat-type boots clomping up the stairs, but another set joined her footsteps. A clicking sound. The boots kept on tromping past my door, but the clicking footsteps stopped outside.

A faint knocking came from my door.

"Come in," I called.

"She's fine," Cinda said, twirling a rental car key chain and keys on her finger. "It all went smoothly."

I tried to not act as confused as I was. "That's good." I ran a hand through my shower-wet hair, hoping she'd give me a clue what had happened.

"Charles was very surprised when Vivienne made her request. He thought she would give it at least a week, but she was absolutely firm."

A horrible rush of nausea overcame me, and I covered my mouth as it dawned on me what had happened today. I held my breath for a moment and the urge to throw up passed. Vivienne had rejected me. I would go this cycle without a Speaker.

"She's packing now," Cinda said. "Are you okay? You look pale."

I took another deep breath, lowered my hand, and tried to smile. "Yes, I'm fine. I didn't get much sleep last night." I'd been too worried about protecting Vivienne from getting busted for breaking IC rules, only to discover she'd been messing around in the ward doing who knew what and then requesting a formal Council meeting to reject me. *Perfect.*

I could feel Vivienne's anxiety before she even got to my doorway. "Hey," she said.

She hadn't even given us a week! It took everything in me to not shout at her. Instead, I simply stared at her in silence.

She shuffled foot to foot, her transmissions of discomfort increasing until they bordered on dread.

"Ready to go?" Cinda asked.

Vivienne stared at me a moment longer. "Yeah, I guess so." She stayed planted, just staring.

The burning on the back of my neck flared. "Well, what are you waiting for? If you're going to leave, *leave*."

Cinda brushed past her and then, with one last look and a strong burst of regret, she followed.

I buried my face in my hands and tried to breathe. The back of my neck felt as though it were on fire.

The front door opened and closed, and it wasn't until I heard a car start in front of the house that I could move.

Gone.

She'd made up her mind in less than twenty-four hours.

My phone rang. "Race" lit the screen. Just what I needed—salt in the wound.

"Hello."

"Well, were you surprised?"

Surprised was not the right word somehow. I straightened the papers on my desk so that they aligned perfectly with the edge. "What do you want, Race? I'm not in the mood for hazing. Get it over with."

There was a long silence on the other end of the line.

"You don't know."

"Yes, I know!" I rubbed the back of my burning neck. It was almost as if I could feel Vivienne's emotions from wherever Cinda had taken her. But it couldn't be. What I felt from an outside source was sorrow. Surely, what she felt was relief. She was rid of me. "How could I not know?"

"Yeah, that's what I was thinking."

"Do you need something? Because if not, I've got stuff to do." Like try not to break down.

"Sure. Just wanted to say congrats."

I hung up without saying good-bye. "Thanks," I muttered. I thought back on what he'd said about how she'd ditch me if I was lucky. He probably genuinely thought congratulations were in order.

I opened the file on my desk and turned my computer on. I had to complete the report for yesterday's disastrous resolution. My vision blurred as I typed her name. Vivienne Thibideaux. I said the name out loud, and the back of my neck burned again. The horrible ache I'd felt earlier that I was picking up from outside myself flared again. *Great.* Just what I needed. Someone else's sorrow to compound my own. For the first time, being a Protector sucked. Truly sucked.

As I typed up the report, I realized the resolution hadn't been the loss I'd imagined it. She had resolved a Malevolent on her first attempt. No easy feat. Usually, a new Speaker was initiated with an easy assignment.

What would happen to me now? I sent the report electronically and filed the paper in my drawer. Would I end up in a desk job like Race's Speaker, or would I be a floating third used for odd jobs and exorcisms like Race?

The front door opened and closed again.

Cinda's delicate clicking footsteps rose up the stairs. This time, she didn't pause outside my room, she just burst on in.

"I didn't expect that from you." She shook her finger at me. "Sure, she's a bit unconventional, but you didn't have to be mean."

I almost turned around to be sure she wasn't scolding someone behind me. "Mean? How was I mean? I think I was pretty civil under the circumstances."

She was irrationally pissed. Shaking, even. Since she was a new Speaker, brand-new, I could barely feel her transmissions, but the sorrow from the other source kept a steady beat in my soul. "You didn't even say good-bye," Cinda said.

"*I* wasn't the one leaving."

Her jaw dropped. "You could have at least hugged her or shaken hands or something. She's a wreck."

"Yes, she is." And I was probably much better off for her decision, but still, my chest ached, and I felt like the total loser Vivienne believed me to be. And I felt lost. And hurt. And deep down, for some unexplainable reason, I missed her. I slammed my fist on my desk. Hell, I barely knew her. The whole situation was ridiculous.

"We'd only known each other a short while," I said. "I have no clue who she is—nor do I care." Which was an absolute lie. It was taking everything in me to not ask where Cinda had dropped her off.

"She cried the whole way home," Cinda shouted.

So it *was* Vivienne's emotions I was feeling from outside. She was sad. Why? The back of my neck felt like it was on fire. Maybe some Benadryl or cream for bug bites or poison ivy would make it stop. "I need to go to my car," I said, waiting for Cinda to get out of my doorway.

Her eyes narrowed. "I hope it's because you're going to go apologize."

I couldn't believe it. I was being bombarded with Vivienne's emotions from wherever she was, dealing with the ultimate rejection, my neck felt like it was infested with fire ants, and I was being hassled by this pushy girl blocking my doorway.

"Me, apologize? For what? I didn't leave. She did."

Cinda threw her arms up in the air dramatically and then huffed out. Fortunately, she went to her room and not downstairs. I wasn't up for more theatrics or guilt. Things sucked enough on their own without enhancement.

I pulled my medical kit out of my trunk and trudged to the kitchen. I could hear my phone chime upstairs, which meant I had received a text, but I blew it off.

I smoothed some Benadryl cream on the back of my neck, but that only made it worse.

I closed the kit and sat on a stool, resting my cheek on the cool counter. I could still feel Vivienne's soul transmitting, and it added to my own misery.

My text alert chimed from upstairs again. It could be Charles, and after last night, I needed to be on my best behavior.

With great effort, I made one foot go forward and then the other until I'd made it up the stairs and to my room.

I slumped into my desk chair and stared at my screen.

We need to talk—V.

What was she playing at? "No!" I shouted. The end was the end. Being around her would torture me.

I shuffled over to my bed and flopped down, exhausted. Too exhausted to reason this out effectively. I stared at the ceiling, seeing nothing. How had she wriggled under my skin in so short a period of time? She was obnoxious, abrasive, intentionally argumentative . . . and brilliant, beautiful, fascinating, and I had no idea how I could go without seeing her again. The burn on my neck flared.

"Damn!" I stomped to my bathroom, wet a hand towel with cool water, and wrapped it behind my neck. I was a master at pushing negativity and bad experiences into an inaccessible box in my mind never to be visited again, and that is where Vivienne Thibideaux would be relegated, just as soon as I could bring myself to do it.

ELEVEN

21st-Century Cycle, Journal Entry 4:

No events of significance to record.

Paul Blackwell—Protector 993

It was all I could do to keep my eyes open. I hadn't slept at all last night because of the situation with Vivienne, and the temptation to put my head down on my desk and sleep was almost too much to resist. I just knew that with my luck in this class, Ms. Mueller would call on me, and I'd do something stupid—like drool—and embarrass myself.

I stretched and yawned. Class was only half-over. This would be a test of my willpower to stay conscious.

Lenzi and Alden were not at school because they were on assignment somewhere with Race acting as the spare Protector. I looked around the room and realized how isolated a life

I really lived. I'd only been in school here a few weeks, but still, I didn't know anyone. It was probably better that way. Having to keep my real life secret would be more of a burden if I got close to someone outside the IC.

Ms. Mueller glared at me from her podium, cutting a perfectly good stretch short. "Am I boring you, Mr. Blackwell?"

Yes, you're boring me to tears. "No, ma'am." I ran a hand through my hair. "I'm sorry."

Once Ms. Mueller returned to her monotone lecture, the blond girl to my right smiled over at me and whispered, "Ms. Mule Face finds one person to pick on each year. Looks like you're it now. It used to be that Lenzi girl who sits in front of you."

I nodded and wondered what it was about me that had caught Ms. Mueller's attention, I did nothing to stick out . . . like dye my hair pink. I was the exact opposite of Vivienne, in fact. I tried my best to blend in, follow the rules, and conform. Perhaps Ms. Mueller had singled me out simply because I was the new student.

"My name is Clarice," she whispered.

"Miss Barton!" The girl shuddered at Ms. Mueller's shout. "Is there something you would like to share with the rest of the class?"

Clarice shook her head and stared at the notebook on her desk.

"Please confine your flirting to before and after school. My classroom is no place for it."

There were very few people in the world I didn't like. At

that moment, Ms. Mueller was one of them. I sat back in my chair, arms crossed over my chest, and studied her. "Size up your opponent," the IC rule book stated. "Study him to discover both his strengths and weaknesses."

Starting at the top of her head, I began my observations of Ms. Mueller, who, satisfied with Clarice's reaction, was droning on again about the Battle of Whateverberg. By the time I got to the bulbous turkey pin she wore in honor of the upcoming Thanksgiving holiday, I gave up my mission. The monstrosity had real tail feathers and was so heavy it made her blouse pucker, causing me to decide that she wasn't really an opponent after all, merely an inconvenience.

A burst of anxiety slammed into me, then a knock on the door interrupted the lecture.

"Open the door, please, Miss Sanders," Ms. Mueller directed.

A lanky brunette with a severe case of acne shuffled to the door and swung it open. I almost fainted.

Ms. Mueller gave an exasperated sigh. "What do you want?"

Vivienne stood in the doorway wearing her classic expression of hostility. "I'm a new student. The counselor sent me up here."

Ms. Mueller shuffled the papers in front of her. "My class is closed. The counselor must have made a mistake."

Vivienne waved a half sheet of paper and laid it on Ms. Mueller's podium. "Room 134, Margaret Mueller."

"Well, I . . ." Ms. Mueller's face pinched up into a scowl as she studied Vivienne with blatant distaste. "Just have a seat until we get it straightened out."

Vivienne looked directly at me the entire time she walked down the aisle to sit in Lenzi's vacant desk. Her transmissions were jumbled, but clearly she was nervous. I kept my expression neutral, but my insides were flipping over. One part of me was furious that I'd be forced to deal with her on a day-to-day basis—well, unless Mueller got her way and transferred Vivienne out. The other part of me was ecstatic. Perhaps it was because, as a Protector, I was naturally drawn to her because she was a Speaker. Or maybe it was because it was *her* . . .

She slid into Lenzi's desk, faced the front, and I could finally breathe. Clarice leaned closer. "Looks like you might be off Mule Face's radar for a while. Freak girl will be much more fun to pick on."

Vivienne twisted in her chair and glared directly at Clarice.

"Oops," Clarice said under her breath.

Yeah, oops. I'd seen that look before, directed at me, and it wasn't good. I looked around and noticed everyone was staring at Vivienne, including Ms. Mueller.

Instead of her usual Goth garb, Vivienne was dressed in the uniform worn by all girls at this private school: a white Izod, blue blazer, and a tan pleated skirt, but even dressed identically to every other girl, Vivienne stuck out. Her pale skin and hot pink hair were certainly eye-catching, but her demeanor was what made her truly unique. And she didn't seem to care a bit that she had caught everyone's attention. She stared back at them with calm indifference. I knew better. I felt her anxiety. This was terrible for her, and it made me want to intervene . . . but it wasn't my problem. She had rejected me. I owed her nothing.

Ms. Mueller cleared her throat and turned the page in her lecture notes. "So, who can tell me about the military order issued by President Lincoln on January 1, 1863?"

As usual, the class members exchanged clueless glances. Normally, Alden would chime in at this point and fill in all the details Ms. Mueller sought, but since he wasn't here, she was met with silence and shuffling of feet and papers.

Vivienne half raised her hand, wiggling her black-tipped fingernails. Ms. Mueller's eyebrows shot up. "Do you have a question, Miss . . ." She scanned the paper Vivienne had handed her. "Um . . . Miss . . ."

"Thibideaux," Vivienne supplied. "And no. I don't have a question. I have the answer."

Ms. Mueller smirked, and I felt Vivienne's anger surge, then that emotion was replaced by something else—something bordering on gloating.

"By all means, please answer," Ms. Mueller said.

And Vivienne did. In a manner Alden would have applauded, she described in detail the contents of the Emancipation Proclamation, including its positive effects and legal shortcomings as well as the social impact on the Southern states.

My classmates stared at her in absolute astonishment.

Ms. Mueller leaned forward. "You must have had a very fine history teacher at your previous school."

Vivienne shrugged. "Nah. My school sucked. I just read about it somewhere."

Well, she was consistently unpredictable—that I knew for sure. And I'd just discovered one of the things she was hiding behind her toxic plant disguise: She was supersmart. Smart and well educated—or at least well read. I thought back to the list on her reader and more clicked into place. She read classics, historical fiction, and books on learning disabilities. Why the last genre? I wondered.

My classmates eventually stopped gawking and turned back to the front, and Ms. Mueller resumed her lecture.

I leaned forward so that my face was close to Vivienne, sitting directly in front of me. So close I could smell her now-familiar scent that reminded me of the candle store. I whispered, "What are you doing here?"

"The same thing you're doing here," she whispered back. A twinge of irritation emanated from her.

Ms. Mueller kept on babbling, eyes only on her lecture notes.

"But I thought . . ." The burning on my neck flared when she swiveled in her chair and stared at me.

"Hi. Nice to see you too." She spun back around and crossed her arms over her chest, anger and sadness rolling from her.

Crap. I'd hurt her feelings. I rubbed my hand over the burning skin on my neck. "I'm sorry," I said a little louder. "I'm confused."

"No kidding."

Clarice leaned across the aisle. "You know her?" she whispered so quietly I had to read her lips. Her eyes went wide when I nodded.

For a very long time, I simply stared at the back of Vivienne's head. It made no sense that she was here, since she had rejected me. Maybe Charles was so desperate to have another pair protecting Lenzi, he had her here until he could replace . . . a wave of nausea rolled through me . . . until he could replace *me*. I would be the one to go. The Speaker had control, and she had chosen. It only made sense he'd plant her in the school Lenzi's mother had chosen for her. Alden was here to protect her, and so was I. Vivienne and I were to guard her as a pair.

Not now.

I took a deep breath and caught Clarice staring again. She immediately blushed and looked away. I wondered why I had never noticed her before. Probably because I was so focused on my job and only watched my mentoring pair. She was the total opposite of Vivienne. Her tanned skin and golden hair gave her the healthy look common to the girls at this school. I glanced over again, and she smiled at me before looking away.

In an unexpected burst, fear surged from Vivienne. She sat bolt upright and trembled. With the exception of Clarice, we were the only students at the back of the room, so no one else noticed. Not yet, anyway. The timing was terrible. There were still fifteen minutes of class left.

Vivienne turned and stared at me with huge, terrified green eyes.

I touched her shoulder and concentrated on silently sending her calming energy, but it didn't work. She made a squeaking sound in her throat and clutched her pen so tightly, her knuckles went white.

"We can't let the class know what's going on," I said. She nodded.

A quick glance at Clarice confirmed she was watching and was about to blow the whistle on us.

"She's okay," I told her. "It happens sometimes and will stop soon. It's kind of like a seizure. Just stay quiet, okay?"

Clarice nodded.

Vivienne twisted around in her chair to face me and grabbed my wrist so hard it hurt. The pen she was holding snapped with a crack. Gasping, she closed her eyes and shuddered. She moved her arm, smearing blood across the surface of my desk. She was under attack from a Malevolent.

"Keep it out of your body," I whispered, grabbing my jacket from under my chair. I only had two choices at this point: I could soul-share and keep the demon out, which would keep Vivienne safe but put my body in a terrible position and alarm the whole class, or I could haul her from the room and protect her in private, causing a scene but not revealing the IC. Detention was better than discontinuance; my choice was obvious.

I wrapped my jacket around her forearm to absorb the blood and cover the wound, then stood, keeping my hand on the jacket so it would remain in place. The metallic scraping of my chair on the floor seemed overly loud. I pulled Vivienne to her feet. Ms. Mueller said something, but I didn't even hear her over the fear and panic streaming from Vivienne.

Leaving our backpacks behind, I pulled Vivienne to the door. "She's sick," I said, not sure if my voice was audible. "I'll come back for our things."

Once outside the classroom door, I picked Vivienne up, ran to a storage closet near the end of the hallway, and flung it open. After shoving some mops and brooms out of the way, I shut the door. The only light was from under the gap at the bottom of the door that let light in from the hallway. We stood speechless for a while, catching our breaths. The musty, sour air made my nose burn.

"Do we need to soul-share?" I asked.

"No," Vivienne answered, still out of breath. "It's gone."

"Are you sure?"

I could feel her fear subsiding, and she felt more like herself emotionally. "Positive."

After a short while, my eyes adjusted to the darkness, and I could almost make out her face. "Are you okay?"

"What the hell was that?" she said. "That was nothing like Ethan."

I flipped the light switch. "I know." I unwrapped my jacket and examined her arm in the dim light provided by the bare lightbulb that hung just above our heads by a wire. The bulb was swinging, probably from being knocked by one of the brooms I'd shoved aside, which made it feel like the room was swaying. "The cuts are deep," I remarked, pushing down my nausea. The Malevolent had carved letters in her flesh, just like the attack on Lenzi. I yanked some stiff brown paper towels off a roll sitting on top of a box and wrapped them around her arm. The blood soaked through almost immediately. "We've got to get to my car for my medical kit. Are you ready?"

"Yeah."

I wrapped her arm with another round of towels. "Let's go. We've got to stop the bleeding." I opened the door and peeked out, then jerked back and closed the door immediately.

"What's wrong, Paul?"

"Stay here. I'll come get you when the coast is clear."

Her fear spiked again. "What is it?"

"Ms. Mueller. She's waiting in the hallway for us. Just stay here." I slipped out the door, leaving Vivienne alone in the dimly lit, foul-smelling janitor's closet.

"I hope you can explain yourself, Mr. Blackwell," Ms. Mueller said, her arms across her chest.

I hoped so too. "Vivienne and I know each other. She sometimes has spells like seizures. They're rare, but they embarrass her. I got her out of the room before she lost control."

She lifted an eyebrow. She wasn't buying it. "What about the blood all over the desk?"

"Nosebleed. They sometimes accompany the seizures." Pulling on all my training, I stood perfectly still, maintaining eye contact.

Her eyes narrowed. "We need to take her to the nurse's office to be examined. The school has a responsibility for her welfare."

God. That would totally blow our cover. The nurse would get one look at the words carved in her skin, and all hell would break loose. "Please, Ms. Mueller. She's really shy about it. Let me just get her home, and she'll be okay."

She rolled her eyes. "That girl isn't shy about anything."

"You don't know much about her, ma'am." Neither did I, really. "Appearances are deceiving." I could tell from her hand-wringing and the fact she was biting her lip that she was considering my words. Maybe she would let it go. "Please. I know what I'm talking about." The bell rang and students flooded into the hallway. "School is out for the day. Just let me take her straight home."

Clarice strode up to Ms. Mueller. "I brought their things, like you asked."

Ms. Mueller didn't break eye contact with me, and I held my breath for her decision. Wordlessly, she turned and lumbered back toward her classroom. I let out the breath I'd been holding and fought the urge to whoop and pump my fist in the air. She was letting us go.

I grinned at Clarice, who blushed. "Thanks for bringing our stuff." I took our backpacks and Vivienne's jacket from her. "See you tomorrow." She stood there as if she wanted to say something, but smiled and nodded instead.

I tapped lightly on the door before opening it so I didn't startle Vivienne.

"What happened to you?" she asked. "This closet smells like barf, and my arm hurts. I want to get out of this place."

"Me too." I slung both of our backpacks over my shoulder and scanned the hall. Ms. Mueller was nowhere in sight. I slid Vivienne's jacket sleeve over the paper towels wrapped around her hurt arm, and she put it on the rest of the way. Then I grabbed mine from the closet floor, where I'd dropped it.

"Sorry about your jacket," she said.

"It'll wash. Sorry about your arm."

"It'll heal." A twinge of sorrow washed from her to me, and she studied my face for a moment with those clear emerald eyes.

"We need to get you out of here and make sure you're okay." I took her good hand. She started to pull away, but I held fast. "We need to stay together. The hallway is crowded. If you're attacked again, I need to be able to protect you. At least for today." *Until a new Protector is chosen to replace me.* Again, a wave of Vivienne's sorrow washed through me, this time tinged with anger. *Speaker before self,* I chanted internally, relying on the words from the IC manual to keep me from breaking down and doing something stupid—like begging her to reconsider.

TWELVE

We pushed our way through the sea of students until they finally thinned out on the sidewalk to the parking lot. Vivienne pulled her hand from mine and stopped short.

I felt no fear from her, but didn't understand why she stopped. Wordlessly, I waited in case she was hearing a Hindered or Malevolent. She simply stood there, staring at me.

"What is it?" I asked. "Do you hear something?"

"What? No. I . . ." A group of laughing girls broke apart to pass us on both sides. Some of them turned around to stare at Vivienne. I'd become accustomed to her appearance, but she was new to the students here. She took a big breath. "I have a ride home. Thanks for helping me."

"No. You need stitches."

"Yeah, I know. I've got this. Sorry for the trouble." She stepped off the sidewalk and crossed the street to the parking lot.

Sorry for the trouble! Like a fish out of water, I stood opening and closing my mouth, fighting for breath. Once I collected my wits, I sprinted after her and caught up just in time to see her climbing into Race's truck. Her emotions were a tangled up mess, just like mine. She didn't look up, but as Race pulled out, he spotted me. He didn't wave or even give me his typical smirk. He just met my eyes with a somber look, then drove away with the girl who should have been my Speaker. At least I knew her injuries would be treated, and he'd do a better job than I would, for sure. *This is for the best,* I told myself. She didn't want me anyway. Prolonging the inevitable would only mess me up.

I rubbed my stinging neck and trudged to my car, still lugging both backpacks and my bloodstained jacket. The rain started right as I closed my car door. It came down in sheets, cocooning me in a safe, private, gray world that smelled like leather and familiarity. I tilted my seat back and closed my eyes, keys still in my lap, and decided to allow sleep to take me away from reality for just a moment.

I was awakened by banging. The rain had stopped, and it was dark outside. I was still in my car in the school parking lot, and Charles's Bentley was parked in the next spot. Cinda knocked again, and I sat up, shaking my head to clear it. I glanced at my watch. I'd been here for hours. *Crap.* Charles had been out looking for me. I buried my face in my hands, and Cinda knocked again. I pushed on the window button, but nothing happened. I reached into my lap to put the keys in the ignition so I could lower it, but they had slid off and were nowhere to be found. I unlocked the door manually and opened it.

"You okay?" she asked, pulling the door open the whole way.

"Yeah, I . . ." I leaned over to look for the keys on the floor-board. "I fell asleep, I guess." When I straightened, I smacked the side of my head on the steering wheel.

"Charles isn't happy. Where's your phone?"

Still groggy, I stepped out of my car and grabbed the keys from my seat, where they had evidently slid off of my leg. "My phone is in my backpack." Which was sitting on the seat under Vivienne's. My chest pinched.

She put her hands on her hips. "You didn't answer it. Charles has been trying to reach you forever."

I stepped over to Charles's car, and he lowered the window, phone to his ear. "Yes, we found him. He appears to be fine. Thank you, Horace." He set his phone on his dash and stared at me.

I placed my hand on the passenger door and spoke to him through the open window. "I'm sorry, sir."

"You've said that a lot recently."

I deserved that. "Yes, sir, I have. I fell asleep. My ringer was still off from class. I forgot to turn it on."

"You were distracted," he said. "That's not like you."

I stared at the lights on his dash, unable to come up with a suitable response.

"Distraction will get you killed in this business, Paul." I straightened and stepped back when he raised the window partway. "So will jumping to conclusions. Protectors are supposed to apply logic to discover effective strategies and truths. It is the IC's job to guide and support you, not provide you with the answers." Without looking at me again, he closed the window and drove away.

I'd prided myself on order and reliability. Alden and Race had teased me for being a walking rule book. Now it seemed like I was always in trouble, and I couldn't get my footing. My ordered, rule-oriented life had fallen into chaos. No, my life hadn't fallen anywhere. Vivienne had entered it.

I rubbed the back of my neck again. "Dammit!" I shouted.

Cinda cleared her throat.

I had been so wrapped up in my self-pity, I'd forgotten about her. "Sorry."

She was leaning against the trunk. "You okay to drive?"

"Sure." I walked around and opened the passenger door for her. I took my phone out of my backpack, slid it into my pocket, then pitched my jacket and both packs into the backseat. She paused a moment before getting in. "You make no sense at all." She slid into the seat.

"What are you talking about?" I propped my elbow on the roof of the car and waited for her answer.

"For example, you just opened the door for me." She snapped her belt. "You're all manners and professionalism with me and Charles, but such a jerk to Vivienne."

"I am not a jerk to Vivienne."

She reached over and grabbed the door handle. I jumped out of the way before she slammed it on me.

This was ridiculous. Cinda had been mad about my treatment of Vivienne yesterday too. I'd done nothing wrong. Nothing at all. I stomped around the back of the car and jerked my door open. "What did she tell you I did?"

"Nothing."

I got in the car and put on my seat belt. "Nothing. How does that make me a jerk?"

She turned in the seat to face me. "You were rude to her. You told her to leave and made her cry."

"She was already leaving! Ouch." I put my palm over the back of my neck.

"What's wrong with you?"

I flipped my visor down and opened the lighted mirror, craning my neck in an effort to see what was stinging my neck so badly. "I think I got into some poison ivy or something at that farmhouse when we were hiding in the bushes. Maybe it's a spider bite."

Her jaw dropped. Literally, her mouth hung open like she'd been stupefied.

"What?" I asked, snapping the mirror shut and putting the visor up.

And then she laughed. Really laughed until I became uncomfortable.

"What's so funny?"

She grabbed her stomach. "You!"

I put the key in the ignition but didn't start the car. "My pain is amusing?"

That set her off into another round of giggles. "Yes!"

I shook my head and started the car. Clearly she was unreasonable—or nuts—or both. Taking a deep breath, I put the car in gear.

"No, wait," she said, touching my arm. She calmed and composed herself. "I'm sorry, but it's kinda funny."

"Obviously." I shifted back into park and stared straight ahead at my new school.

"You are totally clueless, aren't you?"

I didn't answer. Obviously, I was, because I found nothing humorous about being bitten by a bug or stung by a poisonous plant. I turned the car off and waited for her to elaborate on my cluelessness.

"Vivienne didn't leave that night to get away from you. Her grandmother had gotten into town, and she went to her new home to be with her. The timing was bad, but it couldn't be helped."

Still not looking at her, I relaxed my grip on the steering wheel. "Staying wouldn't have mattered after . . ."

"After what?"

I dropped my hands from the wheel and looked over at her. "After what she did in Galveston."

Her gaze was intense. "Yes. It didn't matter where she was after that."

"So how does that make me the bad guy? She ended it. She's the one who quit trying, not me. *She's* the jerk." I started the car again before I got emotional. Driving was rule oriented. I could focus on that.

"Wait just a minute. What do you think Vivienne did in Galveston?"

"She severed our partnership. She rejected me as her Protector."

Cinda gasped, and I took my hand off the gearshift.

She shook her head, stunned. I could feel her shock, even though she was so new and it was hard to read her emotions.

"No," she said in almost a whisper. "That's not what happened at all." Then a big grin spread across her face. "Wow. No wonder Charles was pissed at you."

I drew in air though my teeth with a hiss as my neck felt like it had erupted in flames.

"She must be upset too for it to hurt that much. It'll stop hurting when you stop fighting it," Cinda said.

She was making no sense at all. "What are you talking about?"

Cinda punched me on the shoulder. Hard. "Her neck burns too." She gave a half laugh. "She didn't reject you that day in

Galveston, Paul. She accepted you. She got her soul brand. Your neck burns because your brand is coming to the surface."

It was a good thing I wasn't driving, or I'd have wrecked the car. The burning was my soul brand activating. I'd gotten it when I was ten and was unconscious when it happened. I had never even known where it was.

"She tied her soul to yours for lifetimes and then you told her to leave. She thought you were mad at her and unhappy to be bound to her."

I covered my face, horrified. I was so certain she had rejected me, I saw no other possibilities. I had jumped to conclusions—the wrong conclusions. Instead of the ultimate rejection, she had given me the ultimate acceptance, which must have been terrifying for her. Then, after she had jumped in with both feet, I cut her off at the knees and told her to leave. "Oh, God. I'm such a jerk."

THIRTEEN

21st-Century Cycle, Journal Entry 5:

Things are progressing normally.

Paul Blackwell—Protector 993

I texted Vivienne for the sixth time. She'd ignored my voice mails too—not that I blamed her. I pitched my phone on my bed and flopped down next to it. The girl had bound her soul to mine for who knew how many lifetimes, and I'd thanked her by basically telling her to get lost.

No wonder I'd been blasted with her sorrow.

I didn't have Cinda's cell number and she'd taken off before I'd thought to ask her for Vivienne's address.

"Now what?" I said out loud to no one. After staring at the ceiling for what felt like forever, it hit me. "Race!" He knew where she lived. He'd taken her there several times. Plus, I could check up on her injuries. I rolled over and grabbed my phone. I hit #2 on my favorites list and listened to it ring, and ring, and ring. Finally, it rolled to voice mail and I hung up, sending him a text instead.

After several hours of waiting, I figured out he was ignoring me too. I'd just have to wait until I saw Vivienne at school tomorrow to apologize in person.

But she wasn't at school the next day. I searched for her all over the campus. I even prowled the lunchroom looking for her bright pink hair, but had no luck. I waited outside Mueller's class, and when she hadn't shown up by the time the tardy bell rang, I panicked.

I ran out the front doors of the school and got in my car. A detention for ditching school was the least of my worries. Five lifetimes from now, a detention would be irrelevant, but screwing this up with Vivienne would be significant. I had only one resource left. I took a deep breath and dialed Charles. He answered on the first ring.

"Um . . ." Uncharacteristically scattered, I pulled my thoughts together. "I need to find Vivienne," I blurted out.

There was a long pause on the other end of the line. "Is she lost?"

"No, sir." But *I* was. "She's not at school, and I'm worried."

"Ah. Yes. She stayed home today to help her grandmother unpack and to make herself more . . . school approved."

School approved. "May I please have her address?"

"Why on earth would you need her address?"

I fiddled with the keys on my key chain dangling from the ignition. "So I can go talk to her."

He laughed. "I thought you had memorized the IC manual."

I had. Well, most of it. "I don't understand, sir."

"Think, Paul, or rather, feel." And he hung up.

Crap. Now what? I opened my console and then slammed it shut when I remembered I'd given my copy of the manual to Vivienne. I closed my eyes and visualized the book. "Think, Paul, or rather, feel," I repeated out loud. I could see the passages from the manual in my head. *A Protector can feel his Speaker's emotions . . .* No. That wasn't it. *He can transmit chosen emotions to aid in calming the Speaker . . .* No. I turned the imaginary page in my head. *At the beginning of each cycle, a Protector will feel his Speaker emerge to readiness through the soul brand. The soul brand enables the Protector to find the Speaker like a tracking device.* Yes! I'd had the answer all along. For a moment, I felt a twinge of jealousy for Alden's and Race's past-life memories. They already knew this stuff. I smiled. In a few lifetimes, I'd be proficient as well, with much less effort than it took right now. I had to get Vivienne back first, not that I'd ever really had her in the first place.

I closed my eyes and listened. It wasn't like regular listening. I listened with my soul. It was sort of like receiving a radio signal in the form of emotions. I pictured Vivienne and allowed my mind to focus only on her, relaxing my entire body. If I could locate her signal, she should be easy to find. I hoped Vivienne was close, since I had no experience with this and her soul brand was new. I couldn't believe how stupid I had been to not have thought of this.

I shifted in my car seat. "Come on, Vivienne. Where are you?" I took a deep breath and felt for her again. The back of my neck tingled slightly. It wasn't a burn at all this time. *There.* I put my car in reverse and pulled out of the parking spot. It wasn't like a hot/cold thing that let me know which way to go by stronger signals if I went the right way or weak ones if I took a wrong turn. Something in me just *knew* where she was. If I hadn't been so worried about what she'd do when I showed up uninvited, I might have laughed. It was an amazing skill, and it made me feel like a superhero with special powers.

Finding her was much easier than expected. I pulled up and parked in front of a tiny, white, wood-framed house that sat right on the edge of a residential area near downtown. It wasn't the safest place around, and certainly not convenient as far as working together would go. The house next door appeared to double as a dog grooming shop, with a hand-painted sign that said BAD TO THE BONE. The house on the other side had boarded-up windows and looked vacant. Farther down the street, a woman was hanging sheets on a clothesline, but other than that, the area seemed deserted.

After grabbing Vivienne's backpack, I got out of the car and locked it behind me.

The house had a new coat of paint and bright flowers in planters on the porch. A neon sign leaned against the railing. FORTUNES AND TAROT READINGS was scrawled over the shape of a palm. I could feel Vivienne's soul's transmissions as if her emotions were my own now. She was slightly frustrated, not upset or sad at all.

After slinging the backpack over my shoulder, I raised my hand to knock on the green door, but it opened, and I nearly knocked on the tiny woman's gray head instead.

"Hi," I said. "I'm Paul Bla—"

"I knew you were coming," she interrupted. A strange look came over her face. "I felt it. I saaaaaaaaw it." She dragged the last words out so that it almost sounded like an ominous song. "Please, come in, and I will commune with the spirits of your fuuuuuuture."

"Actually, I'm just here to—"

"Cut it out, Grandma!" Vivienne's voice called from the back of the house. "He's not buying it. He's here to see me, not you."

The woman shrugged and spoke in a perfectly normal voice. "Well, in that case, come on in and make yourself at home. Would you like some sweet tea?"

"No. Thank you." I stepped into the living area, which looked like something off a Hollywood movie lot. Persian rugs littered the floor and bright scarves were draped over lamps, casting pools of color on the walls and ceiling. All it needed was a crystal ball.

Incense burned by the door, and from the thickness of it, probably in every corner of the tiny house.

I was so overwhelmed by my surroundings, I didn't realize for a while that Vivienne's grandmother was staring at me. Studying me, really. The pupil of one of her eyes was cloudy, as if she were blind in it, which was unnerving. I clasped my hands in front of me to keep from fidgeting and focused on Vivienne's emotional transmissions while her grandmother focused on me. Vivienne felt . . . excited? Irritated too.

"You have had a life of luck," the old woman said. "Privilege."

Yeah, yeah. The old judge-someone-by-their-clothes-and-car routine. I said nothing. I certainly had been lucky, but I didn't come from privilege. I stared down at a black cat rubbing against my legs.

"I'll be out in a second," Vivienne called.

"No rush," I answered, meeting her grandmother's hard stare and stepping away from the cat.

"You're one of *them*," she said.

I remained quiet because the way she said it sounded like whoever *they* were was not a good thing.

"You're with the Intercessor Council."

"Yes, ma'am."

"Why are you here?"

"I . . ." Her tone was so changed, I wasn't sure how to proceed. "I'm here to see Vivienne."

Her face pinched up. "She knows. She knows what you did to her mother and her aunt. I'm only here because I had no other options. She can listen to the dead, but she will not belong to it like my baby did. She will not *die* for it like both of my daughters!"

I took a huge breath and said nothing for a moment. "I'm sorry for your loss. I'll protect her with my very life. She won't be harmed."

If looks could kill, I'd have been dead on the spot.

"Hey," Vivienne said. She was wearing a silk robe with Chinese dragons on it, and her hair was covered by a blue towel bound around her head.

"Hi. I, um . . ." I slid her backpack off my shoulder and held it out. "I brought this to you."

One side of her mouth quirked up. "Thanks." She relieved me of it and pitched it on a cushion on the floor.

"Sorry to just drop in like this. I tried to call and text, but you didn't answer."

Her amusement surged, and she smiled at me as if I were a little kid. "My phone was in my backpack, which was with you."

Well, that explained it. I never even thought to search her stuff. "How's your arm?" I asked.

She rolled up her sleeve and held it out for me to see. The whiskers of navy blue stitches stuck out from the letters carved into her that had evidently been the deepest.

I shuddered. "Looks like Race did a good job."

She turned her arm to examine it. "He did, but if he had called me sugar one more time, he would have needed stitches too."

I smiled, and the cat rubbed figure eights around my ankles. The silence stretched on forever.

"Is that all?" Vivienne finally asked.

I'd never felt so awkward. I needed to clear my throat, but that would have made it worse. "No. I also need to apologize."

Her grandmother made a harrumph sound.

"I do," I said, shifting my weight from foot to foot, causing the cat to slink away. "I had no idea you had . . . well, I had no idea you had gone to Galveston for that purpose."

Her brow furrowed. "What did you think I'd done?"

"Pulled the plug," I said, unable to meet her eyes. "Rejected me as your Protector."

For the longest time, she didn't answer. "Well, that makes a lot of stuff make sense."

"He's one of them. Don't trust him," her grandmother said. Despite the negative words, her voice had lost its hard edge from earlier.

"Come with me." Vivienne headed back the way she had come in, and I followed.

"No boys in your room," her grandmother called.

"Yeah, right," Vivienne muttered under her breath. "She's just showing off."

Vivienne's room was as unique as the rest of the house. Her walls were a deep purple, and her bed was more of a cushion on the floor than anything else, covered in crimson bedding. Brightly colored beads served as a curtain on the window, and dozens of paper Chinese lanterns hung from the ceiling. Boxes were strewn about, some open and some still sealed with packing tape bearing a professional moving company's logo.

She flipped the flap of a box open and pulled out a green shirt. "The stuff arrived three days ago, along with my grandma. She'll have this place whipped into shape in no time. She has way too much energy."

"She doesn't like me."

She shrugged and shut her door. "She doesn't like the IC."

I crossed to the side of her room farthest from the door. "Neither do you. Why did you agree to do it—become a Speaker?"

Her eyes didn't leave my face. "Do you really want to know? You're not going to like it."

I *had* to know. "Truth is rarely pleasant," I said.

She wrung the shirt in her hands. "Turn around."

I did. Rustling sounds came from her side of the room, and I realized she was changing clothes. I could feel the blood creeping up my neck. Her proximity was making me insane. I'd never felt like this before. It had to have been the

Speaker-Protector bond that made my body hyperaware of her. I knew I was going to need to get over it, because we would be working very closely, and it was sometimes necessary to change in tight quarters and even for the Protector to stitch wounds and provide medical aid regardless of the location of the injury. Race had often amused us all with the stories from the furthest imaginable end of the spectrum. He'd seen it all.

I hadn't. I was just beginning . . . with this girl who drove me crazy and made my heart beat too fast. A girl I knew nothing about, including why she had agreed to join the ranks of the IC even though her grandmother blamed it for the deaths of both of her children. "Why?"

I hadn't intended to think out loud, and my voice startled me a bit.

The rustling from her side of the room stopped. It took everything in me not to turn around.

"What did that ghoul carve into my arm?"

I shoved my hands in my pockets. "A word."

More sounds of her getting dressed. "What word?"

"Revenge," I whispered.

"The ghoul and I have a lot in common."

My heart sank. One word. One simple little word that changed everything. *Revenge* had a unique meaning among the IC community. It was the common factor that motivated almost all malevolent spirits. It was a toxic motivation. *Toxic*— the same word I'd used to describe her at the restaurant.

She turned me by the shoulder. "I warned you that you wouldn't like it."

She was wearing the green shirt with black pants and a different pair of boots. These zipped up, rather than laced. A thick belt with triangle-shaped studs hung low on her hips. She still had her hair wrapped up in a towel.

"You bonded yourself to me for multiple lifetimes for revenge? On whom?"

She flopped down on her bed or cushion or whatever it was. "I joined the IC for revenge. It's not why I asked to be tattooed or marked or whatever awful term they use."

"Soul branded."

"God. That's worse than what I came up with. Yeah. That. I didn't get soul branded for revenge. I could have gotten my revenge without that." She lay back and stared at the ceiling.

I took a step closer. "The two are intrinsically related. There is no one without the other."

She held her towel in place over her hair and sat upright. "Sure there is. I want to be a Speaker to get revenge on the bastard who killed my aunt."

"Revenge is a byproduct of something else. It's not what you really want."

"You're wrong. But that's not why I"—she shifted uncomfortably and placed her hand on the back of her neck—"did this."

Her grandmother opened the door.

"Just talking," Vivienne said. "Nothing to see here. Move along."

"Sassy!" Her grandmother chuckled and closed the door.

The room was small and intimate, and with the smell of this girl filling my head and her emotions flowing into me, I was a breath away from losing my mind. I needed to get out before I said or did something stupid and blew it again. "Are you hungry?" I asked. "I know a place that has great 911 enchiladas."

She grinned. "Starving. Can we bring something back for Grandma? She hasn't made it to the grocery store yet."

I offered a hand to help her up. "Would she like to come with us?"

"No."

"Yes!" her grandma's voice called from the hallway.

"No," Vivienne said more emphatically, taking my hand. Her eyes widened, and a jolt of excitement from her soul slammed into me when we touched. She felt it too, whatever this attraction was between us. She didn't pull her hand away, but just stood and stared.

"You need a chaperone," her grandma called. At this moment, I tended to agree with her.

"And you need to get a life! Preferably one that's not mine," Vivienne said, still holding my hand.

Her grandmother whooped and belly laughed from the hallway. "You get more like your mama every day." She laughed again and then her laughter faded as she went to the other part of the house.

Vivienne released my hand finally, and my heart started again.

"I like her," I said, taking a step back, grateful I could speak at all.

"I love her," Vivienne replied. "There's no one in the world like her." She grinned. "And she's totally nuts. Oh, I know what we should do. Let's go to the fried chicken drive-through place a few blocks away, and we can drop some off for her and then go hang out somewhere else. That'll make her happy and get her off my case for a while."

I was finding it hard to not watch her lips as she talked. I *had* to get out of there. "Sounds like a great plan. Ready to go?"

A funny look came over her face. "Not quite yet." She unwrapped the towel, and jet-black hair tumbled in a wet mass past her shoulders.

My twinge of disappointment came as a surprise. The pink hair that was so unnatural and shocking at first had grown on me.

She pulled a hairbrush out of a box by the door and ran it through her hair. "The school said that I had to have hair that was a natural color, or I couldn't go there." She grinned. "They said I was distracting." She pitched the brush back in the box. "Now I'll just have to find other ways to be distracting. Game on!"

I laughed. "No doubt you'll find a way."

"I always do." She snapped on a thick leather wristband with a serpent on it and looped silver serpent earrings through her earlobes.

As we left, her grandma was friendly to me, which was a huge relief. I had no chance of winning Vivienne over without Grandma's approval—no matter how slight. Grandma might hate the Intercessor Council, but I'd make sure she didn't hate me. In Vivienne's words, game on.

FOURTEEN

We dropped drumsticks and mashed potatoes off at the house for Vivienne's grandmother, and since it was a nice day, we drove to a park with a duck pond nearby.

Even in November, the temperatures in Houston could reach the sixties, like on this day.

Sitting on a park bench with a bucket of chicken between us, anyone looking on would think we were just normal people out enjoying a beautiful afternoon and an early dinner. But we were far from normal.

"Stop it," Vivienne said under her breath. For a moment I thought she might be talking to me, but then she closed her eyes and whispered, "Not now. Go away."

No fear flowed from her, only mild agitation, so I took another bite of chicken, glad she was at least communicating with Hindered rather than simply ignoring them.

The tiny park was empty with the exception of a couple on

the other side of the pond sitting on top of a picnic table with their backs to us.

Vivienne shook her head. "You thought I'd rejected you. No wonder you told me to leave the house that night. I can't believe Race or Cinda didn't fill you in on what went on down in Galveston."

"I can't believe you didn't tell me yourself."

She took a sip of her drink. "I wanted to surprise you."

"You succeeded." I wiped my hands on a napkin and put the remains of my meal in the trash can next to the bench.

Her hair had dried, and strands blew across her face in the evening breeze. The ink black was just as striking as the pink had been and made her skin appear even paler. She broke off a bit of biscuit and pitched it toward several ducks eyeing us from the water. "I should have told you."

"I should have trusted you."

She stared up at me. "You don't know me, and I'd given you nothing to trust."

That was true. I sat down and leaned back against the wooden slats on the bench. The ducks waddled from the water and waited patiently for Vivienne to share more biscuit. "What made you decide so quickly to bond your soul to mine?"

She pitched some more crumbs to the ducks, who had become emboldened and were only a foot or so away. "Are you unhappy I did it?"

"No. God, no." On impulse, I reached over to touch her,

maybe out of a need to express my sincerity, but stopped myself, dropping my hand in my lap instead. "I just didn't expect it, especially after having such a rough time with the farmhouse resolution." A duck with a green head nipped the cuff on my school khakis. "You didn't answer my question."

"Ah. Yeah, you want to know why I did it." She broke off another bit of biscuit, and the ducks made muffled quacking sounds, flipping their tails as they shuffled awkwardly on the grass, begging for food like puppies. "It was because of Race."

I groaned inwardly to know I'd now be indebted to Race for helping me out, even if he didn't mean to—which I was sure he didn't.

The white duck closest to her made a screeching sound, and she dropped a piece of biscuit right in front of it. "He explained the risk you'd taken by accepting the blame for my screw-ups. Well, more like he chewed me out for being a selfish bitch while you put your life on the line, risking execution to keep me safe."

I stared at the ducks squabbling over the bread at her feet. "I was certain it wouldn't come to that."

"But it could have."

"Theoretically."

"And you covered up for me, knowing you could be discontinued for it."

I kept my eyes on the ducks, unable to look at her. The intense emotion flowing from her made my body feel warm all over. I was afraid of being overwhelmed and saying something stupid.

She threw the remainder of the biscuit into the pond, and the ducks waddled away after it. "I told you the truth back at the house: I agreed to join the IC for revenge—revenge on the demon who killed my aunt and on the Speaker who stood my mother up. I had it all planned out. With the help of a temporary Protector—hopefully, a really experienced one—I'd dispatch the demon to hell, where he belongs, then I'd hunt down the identity of the Speaker who hurt my mom, and quit the IC once I had spoken with him. No fuss. No mess. No strings attached. Grandma would get a house out of it, and I'd be free to do whatever I wanted after that."

Still unable to read her intense emotions accurately or meet her eyes, I stared straight ahead at the couple all tangled up together on the table across the pond. "Sounds like you had it all planned out."

"I did. But I hadn't counted on you." She paused for a long time while I stared straight ahead. "Look at me," she whispered. Once I met her eyes, she continued. "No one other than family has ever done anything like that for me before. I've always been the one set up to get caught or take the hit. I've always been the target." Tears filled her eyes but didn't breach the rims. "You've asked me to trust you over and over. I do. It's why I changed my mind and got the soul brand. I need you to trust *me* now."

I stared out across the pond again, processing her words and her raw emotions blasting through me. Another layer of her toxic defense had peeled away. Underneath the harsh façade, I'd just discovered she was fiercely loyal. Loyal enough to take a huge, life-altering risk. Multiple lives, actually.

"Dang. They need to go get a room," she said. I glanced over, and she was watching the couple across the pond.

"Did it hurt?"

"What, the brand? I have no idea. I was out cold. Did yours hurt?"

"I was ten years old. It was done during a Protector induction ceremony. I was asleep under some kind of anesthesia." I rubbed my neck. "I didn't even know where it was until it started feeling like a beesting yesterday." Looking back, I should have known what it was. Charles had been right. I was distracted.

"Yeah. It evidently only hurts in this initial cycle when the souls are joined for the first time. Cinda says when we come back in the next lifetime, it'll start out like a big mole or birthmark, then it will darken and get sharp edges like it has now when we come into our powers or whatever."

"May I see it?"

She laughed. "You are acting so nervous. It's not like you're asking me to lift my shirt for Mardi Gras beads."

The image made my breath catch.

She laughed again. "Sure. It's in the same place as yours. At least that's what Cinda said." She leaned forward on the bench and lifted her hair. Just under the hairline, there was something that looked like a striking birthmark, or maybe a henna tattoo. It was in the shape of what appeared to be a bird in flight. It was fragile and beautiful . . . like Vivienne.

No. I shook my head to clear it. It had to be the soul branding bond making me into a sappy mess like this. *Focus,* I told myself.

"It's cool, huh? And it stung like crazy when I dyed my hair."

That explained the irritation I'd felt when I drove up. "It's very cool." Cool for so many reasons, most of which I couldn't even articulate.

"My turn."

Her excitement made my brain a little fuzzy, so it took me a moment to figure out what she meant. "Oh." I turned my back to her, still seated on the bench.

Her cool fingertips brushed my neck and I held my breath. I hoped the sensitivity to her would end soon so I could function normally again. "Yours is lower on the neck than mine. I guess that's so it's covered by a collar or something." She moved closer and her breath on my neck gave me chills. "Yeah. That's cool looking." Her fingertips skimmed over my skin again. "I love it. Very sexy."

My exhalation became a choking sound.

She chuckled and moved away. I caught my breath as she gathered up her trash from the bench.

A surge of irritation pulsed from her. She made a growling

sound. "Dang it, ghoul. Leave me alone." She stood, crushed her empty cup and threw her garbage in the can next to me. "This is driving me nuts. I can't even have a conversation without some dead guy barging in and interrupting. This one's been doing it since we got here."

"Why don't you resolve it? It just wants your attention so you'll help it out."

"Do we have time for something like that?"

I almost laughed. "It's what we do."

"Can we do it here?"

The couple across the pond were so caught up in each other, they wouldn't notice us at all. "It depends on what it needs, but probably. Give it a try. Ask what it wants."

She turned toward me slightly. "Just ask it what it wants? As simple as that?"

"As simple as that."

After looking around to see if the coast was clear, she cleared her voice. "So, um, ghouly. What is it you need from us . . . me? What do you want?"

She studied her lap and listened. No fear came from her, just nervous excitement, which made my heart beat even faster. This was how it was supposed to work. It was what we were made to do, and I soared at the thought.

"No way, you've gotta be kidding me." She rolled her eyes and shook her head. "Too stupid. Not gonna do it."

Well, maybe this was *not* how it was supposed to work. "What does it want?" I asked.

"He wants me to give some girl her yo-yo back." She raked her fingers through her hair, making it look even wilder.

"Why is this a problem for you?"

"Because it's silly and a waste of time."

I took her warm, soft hand in mine, and she met my eyes. "Nothing they need is silly. It's what's holding their souls here after death. We may not understand why, but it's very important to them."

She rolled her eyes but didn't pull her hand away. "What happens if I think it's too silly, and I refuse?"

I could feel her irritation growing, so I sent some calm her way through our linked hands. "If you refuse, it could become a Malevolent and hurt someone. Two things give them power: lingering a very long time and strong desire. That's why Malevolents are so powerful. They want something very badly. Badly enough to take your body and shove you out, ending your soul's hold on life."

She stared at our hands. "I like the buzzing thing you do when you touch me. Is that a Protector thing?"

"Yes."

"Keep doing it."

"Okay."

She slid her other hand in mine. "You think a yo-yo is keeping that dead kid stuck here?"

"Yes. It's a kid?"

She nodded.

"Excellent." Children were notoriously the easiest Hindered to resolve, because their problems were usually simple.

She pulled her hands away, then slid them right back into mine. "That's really cool. It calms me down."

I focused on keeping the current flowing to her. "That's the objective. Why don't you ask the Hindered?"

Again, no fear. She amazed me. In her place, I'd be terrified. Most new Speakers had a hard time getting used to it. Perhaps the fact she'd heard the voices of the dead since she was a little girl helped. She was also inquisitive and bold. She was going to be a brilliant Speaker.

"Okay, ghouly kid. What's with the yo-yo?"

She stared at a point just over her right shoulder and then met my eyes, brow furrowed. "Dang. He's hard to understand. He's talking fast and has a lisp or something. I don't understand him at all." She closed her eyes. "Slow down, kiddo."

She was quiet for a while, and I kept the calming energy running from me through her. Her hands were so small in mine. She didn't have the big, creepy rings on today.

"It's not working," she said, pulling her hands away. "He's too hard to understand. He keeps saying 'Let me, let me.' And I've no clue what he wants." She fiddled with the metal shapes on her belt.

"He wants to use your body to solve his problem."

She groaned. "My aunt's partner used to do that all the time—let the dead guys use his body to do weird stuff. It scared me to watch it."

I placed my hand over hers at her waist. "It's by far the most effective way to resolve their problems. Much more direct. I can kick it out of your body anytime you want."

She stood and took a step away from me. I could feel her anxiety, but still no fear. "I don't want to lose control like that." She walked to the edge of the pond.

I joined her at the water's edge, purposely keeping my voice level and calm. We were so close to performing our job as prescribed by the IC. We needed to do this resolution. "You won't lose control. It's not like a possession. You only allow it the power you want it to have." I touched her shoulder briefly, and she turned toward me. "You'll be there the whole time, and you can talk to me when you want to. I'll help and ask questions and take it where it needs to go." I could tell from the lessening of her anxiety she was considering it. "You can end the soul-share any time you feel you are in danger or compromised. Hindered aren't evil or out to hurt you. They just want to move on."

She was still nervous, but not afraid. I felt her decision before she voiced it.

Purposefully, she strode to the bench and sat, ready for work. "Okay, ghost kid. Hop on in and do what you need to do." Despite her casual words, she sat as rigid as a board.

"Just relax," I said, lowering next to her on the bench, "and give him control of your body."

"Come on, kid. Do it." She took in a sharp breath through

her teeth and shuddered. "Crap, that hurts," she muttered. Almost immediately, her posture changed. She scooted to the edge of the bench and looked over at me. "Who are you?" a boy's voice said from her mouth.

"I'm Paul. What's your name?"

"Jathon. Jathon Lynch. Hey! Leth go chath the duckth!"

At that, Vivienne jumped up and raced to the edge of the pond flailing her arms, causing the ducks to freak out and scatter in all directions, squawking madly. I couldn't help but laugh at Vivienne, in her badass Goth clothes, acting like a little kid chasing ducks along the edge of the water. The couple on the picnic table across the pond had come up for air to watch the bizarre scene. The girl got to her feet, straightened her shirt, and grabbed her purse. The guy stood too, and they headed to the parking area. Good. They were leaving.

Vivienne darted toward the white duck, giggling maniacally, and I laughed out loud. She stopped abruptly and put her hands on her hips. "You'd better not be laughing at me," she said in her own voice.

I grinned. "Me? Never. Laughing *with*. Always with."

"Run, duck, run!" the boy's voice yelled from her mouth and Vivienne took off around the edge of the pond again.

"Hey, Jason! Come here a second, okay?"

"'Kay!" Vivienne ran up, breathing heavily, and plopped down in the grass right in front of me.

I leaned forward, hands clasped in my lap. "I'm glad you're having fun, Jason, but Vivienne needs her body back soon, so you're going to have to tell me what you need to do."

Using Vivienne, he plucked a blade of grass and studied it. "I need to give Thamantha her yo-yo back. Ith her favorite."

"Where is it?"

Jason put the blade of grass between Vivienne's thumbs and blew, making a harsh screeching sound. The ducks squawked and flew in a rush of flaps and splashes to the other side of the pond. "In a hole in a tree."

"Can you show me where?"

"Uh-huh!" Vivienne ran to a huge oak tree in the corner of the park and tried to climb it. "The low limbth are gone. Gimme a bootht."

The hole was about a foot out of reach. "Okay." I placed my back against the tree and laced my fingers together, then stooped so that my hands were a foot off the ground. "Step into my hands."

"Okay!" Jason placed Vivienne's palms on my shoulders and her foot in my hands.

"Ready?"

"Yep!"

I stood up, lifting Vivienne, her hands still on my shoulders for balance. Her body pressed against me with her waist at my face level. She smelled so good it made me dizzy. Like spiced candles and incense and . . . Vivienne. *Focus.* "Can you reach it?" I called.

"Hold on. I feel it. Ith all covered in thtuff."

The bottom of Vivienne's boot dug painfully into my palms. "Hurry up."

"Got it!"

I lowered her down, and Jason backed her away, studying the yo-yo. It was one of the big butterfly kinds popular a long time ago that looked sort of like a stubby hourglass. It was covered in black debris that looked like mildew maybe. It had been in that tree a long time.

Manipulating Vivienne's body, Jason pulled on the string, and it broke free from the yo-yo. "The thtring ith rotten."

A sickening feeling gurgled in the pit of my stomach. "Jason. What happened to you?"

"I died."

"Yeah, I know. How?"

"Thumbody wrecked into our car."

I took Vivienne's shoulders in my hands. "Do you know when this happened?" My fear was that is was so long ago, we might never find the yo-yo's owner.

"Thurthday. I know that becauth I wath on the way to a thcout meeting in the thtathion wagon. It wath raining. I don't like rain now." He picked up a stick from the ground and jumped back. "Hey! Wanna play army?" Vivienne ducked behind the bench, then popped up, aiming the stick

165

at me and making machine-gun noises. I couldn't help but smile.

Nobody had station wagons anymore. They had minivans and SUVs. He'd been dead awhile. "So what do you need me to do with that yo-yo?"

"Give it to Thamantha Briggth. I took it and hid it. It wath her favorite. I feel bad I took it."

"May I see it?"

Jason—well, Vivienne—plopped it in my hand. "Uh-huh. Then can we play army?"

"Maybe. How old are you, Jason?"

"Theven."

I wiped some of the grime off the side of the yo-yo and discovered writing. More rubbing revealed exactly what we needed. The name, Samantha Briggs, and an address and phone number.

"Are you okay in there, Vivienne?"

"Yeah. Feeling kind of cramped, though. Is it almost over?" she answered in her own voice.

"It is." I put my hand on her shoulder. "Hey, Jason?"

"Uh-huh?"

I had to convince him to leave before Vivienne became too uncomfortable. I'd been told it was like extreme claustrophobia when a spirit had been sharing the Vessel for too long. "It's time for you to leave Vivienne's body. We have Samantha's name and address now, see?" I turned the yo-yo so the writing was visible. "I promise you that Vivienne and I will return it to her as soon as you get out of Vivienne's body, okay?" I was hopeful that the promise alone would resolve him, and he wouldn't require witnessing the actual hand-off in case it proved difficult because the little girl had grown up and moved away. The chances were good he'd be satisfied with the promise, since he was so amiable.

"It's getting kind of uncomfortable now. How do I get him out?" Vivienne's voice asked.

Hindered almost always did this. They resisted leaving once they were in a body. It was the only dangerous part of Hindered resolutions. Malevolents were another story entirely. "I'll come in and push him out. It's easy. The weakest soul, which always the one ready to move on, is forced out."

"Okay," she said, sitting on the bench, arms folded over her chest in a protective position. "He's trying to push his way back up to control my body again, but I want him out."

"Hey, Jason? I'm going to help you out now. We're going to do what you want and return the yo-yo, okay?"

"He says okay," she said.

I sat on the bench. "Vivienne. Touch me."

She placed her hand in mine, and for the first time since the resolution began, she transmitted fear. She scanned the park. "What about your body being all empty again? That didn't go so well last time."

"Not a problem. You'll be here with it, and I'll get right back in again. It's not like last time. Ready?"

She trembled, but her fear subsided, and she gave a slight smile. "Yeah, do it."

"Out," I commanded my soul. Immediately the ripping sensation began in my extremities and continued until I hovered over us on the bench with no physical sensation whatsoever. "In," I said, and my soul obeyed, shooting into Vivienne's body, causing her to curse between gritted teeth. It didn't take long to push Jason out. He was ready.

Through Vivienne's eyes, I watched Jason materialize in the blue hologram-like form. He had on a Scout uniform and a big grin. He waved like crazy, then dissipated in a white flash.

"Okay. That was a lot cooler than Ethan," Vivienne said, pushing to her feet.

It certainly was. I need to get back in my body now. Please touch it. Through her eyes, I saw my empty body sitting on the bench, my vacant eyes staring straight ahead.

"You look like a zombie," she said. "Well, a zombie before the flesh falls off and stuff. It's pretty weird."

Touch me before somebody sees me like that.

She placed her hand over mine. She gave a squeak as I exited the Vessel, then poured my soul back into my own body, reanimating with a gasp. I looked up into her eyes.

She smiled. "Do you always come back like that?"

"Like what?"

Her hand still covered mine. "Like you were startled out of a bad dream or somebody just nailed you with defibrillator paddles?"

"I suppose so."

She released my hand and stared at me a long time. "That one was kind of fun, huh?"

I nodded. "You were fantastic. Well done."

She laughed. "I just stayed out of the way. You did the hard part."

"We make a good team."

"Yeah, we do. Let's go deliver that yo-yo."

FIFTEEN

A woman in her sixties opened the door. Her expression was puzzled, but then I supposed that was justified, considering a Goth-looking girl and a guy in a preppy school uniform were standing on her doorstep holding a filthy yo-yo with her address on it.

I held the yo-yo out for her to see clearly. "We found this in a knothole in a tree at the park around the corner. It has Samantha's name and address on it. Is she here?"

The woman held out her hand, and I placed the yo-yo in it. A wistful look crossed her face. "Well, I never thought I'd see this again." She smiled at us. "No. Samantha isn't here. She moved out ten years ago and has a family of her own now." She shook her head and studied the yo-yo. "She lost this a long time ago. It's been more than twenty years. She was in second grade." She turned the yo-yo over in her hand and stared into the distance. "I'll never forget it. She was so upset. I bought her a new one just like it, but it just wasn't the same for her. We always thought that little Jason Lynch boy stole it just to be mean, God rest his soul."

His soul *was* at rest finally. Vivienne reached over and entwined her fingers in mine.

The woman pulled herself out of her reverie. "Thank you for bringing it by. I'm sure Samantha will get a laugh out of knowing it made it home at long last."

When she closed the door, we stood on the porch for a moment, smiling at each other. Happiness flowed from Vivienne, and it made me feel fantastic. I wanted to shout *yes!* at the top of my lungs and give her a huge hug, but instead I walked to my car and opened the door for her.

"Let's go to the grocery store on our way back to your house," I said, pulling out of Samantha's neighborhood. "I noticed you don't have a garage, and there isn't a car parked out front. You have no way to easily get groceries."

Her happiness dimmed. "We're fine."

"But we're already out, and it's on the way. Let's get some stuff to hold you over for a bit."

"I don't have any cash on me," Vivienne said, her mood shifting entirely. She felt almost hostile.

"I do."

She smirked. "Of course you do."

I turned into a grocery store around the corner from her house, baffled by her behavior, the high from the resolution completely gone. "What is that supposed to mean?"

She laughed and waved her hand toward me. "Look at you. You have everything. You live in the perfect house, drive the perfect car. I bet you make perfect grades too."

I gritted my teeth.

"You do, don't you? What are your grades? I bet you've never made a B."

I pulled into a parking place. Clearly, I had hit on some sore spot accidentally. "What's your point?"

"The point is, I don't need charity from the rich kid who has no clue what it's like to not get everything he wants."

I put the car in park, but left it running. "Charity is the furthest thing from my mind." I could barely control my outrage. Closing my eyes, I took a breath, counting down from ten until I had my temper under lock and key again. Rarely could I be roused to anger. Something about this girl stirred me up. "You know absolutely nothing about me." And I was determined that she never would. My past was irrelevant. It would be completely different in the next lifetime and had no bearing on my future. Past was past. "I was simply trying to make it easier for you by stopping in here. If you don't want to, that's fine. I was being polite . . . kind . . . courteous." I turned to face her at last. "Try it sometime."

After a few moments, in which she said nothing but felt plenty, I put the car in gear and drove her home, bearing up to the onslaught of anger and regret flowing from her.

I pulled up in front of her house and cut the engine. It was dark already, and the streetlight closest to her house was out. I didn't get out to open her door in the hopes she would explain what the hell was going on with her.

"I'm sorry, Paul." Her voice was so quiet, I could barely hear her. "I'm not used to people being nice to me. I guess I come with a lot of baggage."

I nodded, which was the best I could do in the way of accepting her apology.

"I hate the IC so much, and I guess I took it out on you, which was wrong." She stared down at her hands folded in her lap.

Now we were getting somewhere. This was an issue we needed to work through—this and the revenge thing. "Why do you hate the IC so much? I know your aunt was a Protector and died in the line of duty, but that's part of the job."

"Part of the job," she repeated. "She spent years protecting her Speaker, Phillip, but who protected her? Nobody. She got run down in the middle of the road by a demon named Smith. He only killed her because he wanted to get the IC's attention and bring some Speaker named Rose out of hiding." A tear rolled down her cheek. "Her death was random and pointless. She died because a dead guy was mad at someone else who was hiding from him."

Lenzi went by the name Rose in her past cycles. Most likely, it was Lenzi's attention Smith was trying to get when he killed Vivienne's aunt, but explaining that right now didn't seem like it would help. Vivienne was too upset. I wanted to touch her, but kept my hands on the steering wheel. "I'm sorry. I know this isn't much consolation for you, but she'll come back in the next cycle."

"That doesn't help me right now."

"No, it doesn't."

She ran her hands through her hair. "And it doesn't make up for what the IC did to my mom."

I put my hands in my lap but remained quiet, knowing she would tell me what happened if the time was right for her.

She stared out the windshield, wearing a blank expression that belied the intense sorrow pouring from her. "She died a long time before the cancer killed her. She died of a broken heart." She met my eyes, unblinking. "Did you know that could happen?"

"No."

She turned back to face the windshield, and I prayed she wouldn't leave it at that. I needed to hear this girl's story, no matter how painful it was for her to tell. To my relief, she continued. "My dad was a Speaker. He met Mom through my aunt. He wooed her, won her over, got her pregnant, promised to marry her, then disappeared. Just took off, never to be heard from again. Grandma said my mother was never the same. She died when I was eight. His name was the last thing she ever said." Tears flowed freely, but she didn't sob. "I'd never heard his name before that last breath."

She said nothing for a while, the tears coming down her face, while she remained still. No sobs or sniffles. And wave after wave of painful sadness that made my insides churn and ache. She took a deep breath. "I told you I come with a lot of baggage."

I wiped a tear away with my thumb. "I can help you carry that baggage. You don't have to shoulder this alone anymore. We're partners now."

She caught my hand at her cheek as I wiped away another tear. "Race was right."

I tried to smile. "I doubt it. He's full of hot air. What was he right about?"

Lowering our hands, she held mine captive with my palm against her neck. She was so warm. "He said I was lucky that you were assigned as my Protector. He said you're the best."

"I stand by the hot air statement I just made. He's totally full of it."

"I'm really sorry about being rude to you."

Finally, she released my hand, and I withdrew it slowly, my palm feeling so cold away from her. "Soul-sharing with a Hindered is draining physically and emotionally. That's why only one resolution a day is recommended. I should have just brought you right home."

She wagged her finger at me. "Oh, no. You took the hit on losing your body, but you're not taking the blame for me being rude to you. You were just trying to help. And it bugged me that you were so observant about the cars and us needing supplies." Her emotions were returning to a level state again. "Grandma has a cab coming in the morning to take her to the store. It's how we did it in New Orleans, and we'll manage here." She looked out the passenger window at the little white house with multicolored lights shining from inside. "We just need to get the sign up so that she can get some business. The IC has been pretty cool so far and is covering all of our initial expenses. They wanted to buy her a nicer place, but she insisted on having her business in her home. The choices were limited, since most neighborhoods don't allow you to run a business out of your house. Still, it's a lot nicer than where we lived in New Orleans."

I was relieved she hadn't gotten out of the car angry. We'd made huge progress today, and I wanted to be sure it continued. Every lifetime was a foundation for the next in our business. Race was the perfect example of how one lifetime could derail the relationship in the future. I was determined to make a solid go of it this first cycle. "How are you going to get to school?"

"Well, we only have one more day of classes before Thanksgiving break, and Cinda is picking me up in the morning. I guess I'll come up with some options over the break."

"Please consider me an option. I'd love to drive you to and from school."

She gave a bittersweet smile. "You're a really nice guy, Paul."

Under all her aggression, she was nice too, but I knew she didn't want to hear that. So instead of returning the compliment, I just smiled.

She unbuckled, and I did the same, rushing around to open her door for her.

"Always a gentleman," she said, stepping onto the curb. "Your parents certainly raised you right."

If only. Again, I just smiled. "I'll type up the report for today's resolution for you to sign." She was staring at me in the strangest way as pulses of energy transmitted from her soul that I couldn't interpret. I closed her door but stayed in place next to the car. She stepped to the edge of the curb, which brought her body within inches of mine. Being on the curb put her at almost eye level. I cleared my throat. "Um. I guess I'll see you in class tomorrow."

She tilted her head, the peculiar expression still on her face. "I wonder . . ."

"You wonder what?"

I held my breath for the longest time until she finally answered. "I wonder what your lips feel like."

Oh, God. My heart pounded so hard I could feel it in my throat. I'd kissed girls before, but this was different. Perhaps it was the fact our souls were bonded and that I could feel her emotions and give her mine in return, but I suspected this kiss was unique because it was with Vivienne, who was unlike anyone I'd ever met.

SIXTEEN

21st-Century Cycle, Journal Entry 6:

*The resolution of a child Hindered was
executed without incident, resulting in a
positive conclusion. The Speaker is assuming
her role effectively. The working relationship
between Speaker and Protector is satisfactory.*

Paul Blackwell—Protector 993

Thanksgiving was usually a terrible time for me.
Loved ones traveling all over the country to
spend time with their families and give thanks
for their blessings . . . Yeah, not something I
could relate to.

This year was different, though. Standing in front of the
school, I shared some of the buzz and adrenaline experi-

enced by my classmates who were preparing to go on trips or have huge feasts with family. There was a great deal of excitement about having a five-day weekend too. That certainly appealed to me. Vivienne was staying in town and had asked me to have dinner at her house.

My stomach churned as I waited for her to arrive, wondering how she'd act when she saw me today. I'd been up most of the night replaying her kiss over and over in my mind.

I grinned as she got out of Cinda's rental car and approached the front doors of the school. She smiled back, and a wash of excitement from her flooded through me. Good. No regrets.

She looked great in her uniform. She had her jet-black hair pulled back in a braid, but layers of bangs framed her face, giving her a bit of a Goth edge, even with the uniform. I noticed she had on no jewelry and much less makeup than usual. Her fingernails were natural instead of black. Her skirt seemed a little short, which might get her busted by the administration, but was totally okay by me. I almost laughed out loud when I noticed the bandage on her arm was held in place by black Band-Aids with pink skulls on them. Where in the world would someone buy something like that?

"Hey," she said, stopping several feet away.

"Hey, yourself," I answered.

She shifted her backpack to her other shoulder. "Did you sleep well last night?"

"Not a wink."

She laughed. "Good." She turned in a circle. "Do you like my new look?"

"I kind of miss the old one," I answered honestly. "But rules are rules."

She took a step closer. Too close. "And you like rules, don't you, Paul?"

"Some of them." Her nearness and smell were driving me crazy, as was the memory of the heated kiss up against my car last night. "I don't like the detention-if-we're-late-to-class rule, for sure."

The bell rang and saved me from breaking another rule: the no-public-displays-of-affection-on-campus rule.

Vivienne was in all my classes, as were Lenzi and Alden. The day was a total blow-off. None of the teachers were in the mood to really do any meaningful work the last day before a holiday, which was a good thing because the students were too rowdy to settle down enough to listen. We watched movies in two classes while my mind wandered to last evening. We had free reading in English, but we all just chatted instead while our teacher gossiped with the teacher across the hall. Everyone was ready for a long break. Everyone except Ms. Mueller, that is. She held class as usual.

"Pull out your notes. Today is no different in this classroom from any other."

No words had ever been less true.

Everything went along fine—well, fine if monotonous lecturing on the post Civil War reconstruction is fine.

Except for Alden, no one in the class was listening to a word Ms. Mueller was blabbing. He always listened, because history was his thing. Maybe it would be my thing too when my soul was centuries old. For now, history was history and not my own past.

Lenzi gasped. Alden immediately spun to face her. I felt Lenzi's fear spike, but Vivienne's trumped it.

"What the hell is that?" Vivienne whispered. "Ugh. It stinks." She covered her nose and mouth with her hand.

Alden stood right as Ms. Mueller grabbed the sides of her podium, slumped over, and groaned. A bizarre, glazed look crossed over her face and then she straightened back up. It was obvious what had happened the moment she grinned.

"Shit. She's been possessed," Alden whispered. "We need to do something before the demon hurts a student."

I looked around and was relieved that, as usual, no one was paying attention.

"I've got this," Vivienne said before bolting out the door.

Ms. Mueller's face contorted several times as if she were putting up a fight to regain her body from possession.

Then the fire alarm went off. Vivienne had found the perfect way to clear the building.

Desks and chairs scraped the floor as students emptied

their desks and left the room in record time. The three of us, however, remained perfectly still, eyes fixed on Ms. Mueller. I'm not sure I'd ever given her my full attention before, but she sure had it now.

Vivienne returned, and once the room cleared completely, Alden took several steps toward Ms. Mueller, who stiffened and spoke in a horrible male voice. "Were we discussing the Civil War? We know a lot about the Civil War, don't we, Speaker 102?"

Undoubtedly, the Malevolent was Smith. I felt Lenzi's fear, but she didn't show it. "We do. Leave the human's body now."

Ms. Mueller threw her head back and laughed in the voice of a man.

Fire alarm still screaming from the hallway, Alden shut and locked the door, then pulled out his phone and furiously punched buttons.

Far faster than Ms. Mueller's usual waddle, the Malevolent bolted toward Alden, stopping just out of reach. "Calling backup? No need. This won't take long."

"Don't you dare hurt her," Lenzi shouted over the shrill clanging of the fire alarm.

Its evil laugh filled the air. "What, like this?" Ms. Mueller picked up a pair of long scissors from the podium, splayed her fingers over the top, and stabbed the blades through her hand, pinning it to the podium. Her face contorted into a grimace of pain, then the grin returned. "Mmm. The sweet pain of having a body again."

The fire alarm fell silent.

"What do you want?" Vivienne asked, striding toward the podium. Alden grabbed her by the elbow and pulled her back. She shook him off. "Cut it out! I'm not scared of a ghoul that has to stuff himself in the body of a middle-aged history teacher because he's too weak to take me on."

Alden and Lenzi looked horrified, and Lenzi transmitted complete alarm. I wasn't sure if Vivienne was bluffing, or if she knew more than I did about the powers of Malevolents and possession in general. She certainly appeared confident, and her emotions flickered among excitement, anger, and occasionally, fear.

"Why didn't you take one of the students? You could have done some damage in one of those football players' bodies." Vivienne paced in front of the podium. "Because they were too strong and you couldn't get in. You knew that."

The demon growled and yanked on the scissors that were plunged deep into the wood of the podium.

"Ha! You're too weak to even free yourself from your own stunt." Vivienne did a little pirouette and laughed. "Caught ya! If I were you, I'd worry about that poor woman's body bleeding out with you in it. Wouldn't that end it for you? Don't you have to skedaddle before the heart stops beating?"

Ms. Mueller's eyes opened wide, then narrowed into a menacing glare.

"Stay ready, Paul," Alden said.

Vivienne strolled closer to the podium. "If the big bad ghouly here were able to invade a Speaker, he'd have tried that first." She put her hands on either side of the podium facing Ms. Mueller. "Isn't that right, loser?" The demon growled and made a swipe at her with its free hand, and Vivienne ducked.

After she was out of reach, she laughed again. "I bet that used a ton of energy. Are you done yet?"

"Nicaragua Smith will never be done," he howled from Ms. Mueller's mouth.

Rage rolled through her. "You're Smith? No way. You're telling me that Smith is just a weak demon wearing a polyester pantsuit?" She shook her head. "You're not at all what I expected."

The demon leaned forward. "Who are you?"

Vivienne's grin gave me chills. It was as terrifying as the demon's had been. "I'm your worst nightmare. I'm the person who's going to dispatch you to hell, where you belong."

Ms. Mueller's body became very still. Her head tilted as Smith studied Vivienne through her eyes. "I've wronged you somehow, haven't I?"

"Yeah. And it was a big mistake on your part."

He stretched the lips in an unnatural smile. "You seek revenge. Revenge for something so insignificant, I don't even remember it."

Vivienne's calm cracked just a bit. He was trying to weaken

her—perhaps to make the jump into her body. "*I* remember it." Her voice trembled slightly.

Crap. I had to do something, but had no idea what.

"Well, you'll have to wait," Smith said from Ms. Mueller's body. "I'm here for something else."

"Now, Alden," Lenzi said. Alden sat and went still as his soul entered Lenzi's body.

At least Lenzi was safe. I gave Vivienne a pleading look. Even though her in-your-face approach seemed to be working, I didn't think she was up to taking Smith on from the inside. "Now?"

"Don't you dare, Paul," she said, eyes on Mueller.

There wasn't as much blood from the wound through Ms. Mueller's hand as I'd have thought there would be, but she looked awful. Her skin was pasty and slick with sweat.

"Ah, predictable as always, Speaker 102," Smith said to Lenzi, then he turned Mueller's gaze to Vivienne. "You, however, are not. You are far more entertaining."

"Oh, really? Well, you're boring me, Smith. Even Mule Face Mueller is more interesting than you, and that says a lot."

Smith growled in rage, baring Ms. Mueller's teeth. Vivienne laughed. "Hey, you've got something right"—she pointed at the space between her front teeth—"there."

Smith made an effort to remove the scissors again, but only caused the wound to bleed more.

Never taking her eyes off of Smith, Lenzi moved closer

to me. "Alden says we need to simply hold steady and wait for backup."

"I don't want to wait for backup," Vivienne said.

Lenzi shook her head. "No."

Ms. Mueller's eyes looked unfocused. Her body was about to pass out.

Vivienne pulled her eyes away from Smith and faced Lenzi. There was no anger coming from her at all, which was a relief. "I don't know you, Lenzi. I don't know anything about you, but there is no way you want that demon gone as much as I do. I'm going to get rid of him for good, and I think I can do it right now."

Ms. Mueller had put her head down on the podium, but her eyes were open.

"No," Lenzi said. "Both Alden and I say no."

"Yes," I said back. I trusted Vivienne and was going to back her up no matter what. "I think we need to trust Vivienne's intuition on this one," I said. "So far, so good."

My phone buzzed. "Hey, Junior. I'm outside the door. Let me in quick."

I strode to the door and let Race in, locking it behind him. Race took a look around and figured out the state of things quickly. Lenzi was protected, and Mueller was possessed and immobilized by the scissors, blood slowly falling one drop at a time from the corner of the podium to the floor.

"Do you want me to cover or soul-share?" he asked.

"Leave me open," Vivienne said. "Come on, Smith. What are you waiting for? Come on in and talk to me."

The body slumped over the podium and didn't move.

"Well, crap," Vivienne grumbled. "The chicken took off."

I didn't know whether to be relieved or disappointed for her. At least she was safe.

Race nudged Ms. Mueller's shoulder, and she didn't react.

Lenzi sat in the desk next to Alden. "I think you're right. I think he's gone, which is the best possible outcome."

"No, it's not." Vivienne's anger surged. "The best possible outcome is dispatching him. He got away."

Race put his fingers on Ms. Mueller's neck and studied his watch. "She's okay." He checked out the scissors and made a face. "That's nasty. And it's going to bleed like crazy when the scissors are pulled out. The pressure is keeping it from gushing." He shuddered. "Poor woman."

Vivienne joined him where Ms. Mueller lay slumped across the podium. "Yuck. Her notes are under her hand." She stepped closer. "I hope this means we get to move on to a different subject."

"Out, Alden," Lenzi said, placing her hand on his shoulder. His body gasped to life, and he took his phone from her.

Race walked over to the door and peeked out the narrow window at the side. "Wonder when the medical team will be here."

"According to their texts, any minute," Alden said, looking up from his phone. "Charles is coming too. This one is a mess, because it's a teacher. They're going to have to do a lot of fancy footwork to keep it secret."

Race leaned back against the door. "I guess it all revolves on how cooperative the teacher is."

"And how much money the IC has donated to the school," Lenzi added.

"The IC is its biggest benefactor. I imagine they hold some clout," Alden said.

Vivienne leaned closer to Ms. Mueller, peering at the notes. "I don't think she deviates from these during class. I bet if we copied them, we could ace her tests." She fingered the edge of a page.

Quicker than I imagined possible, Ms. Mueller's free hand shot out and grabbed Vivienne by the throat. "Stupid little girl. Your hate makes you strong, but you can't even begin to fathom hate like mine," Smith said from Ms. Mueller's body. "You asked what I wanted. I want revenge."

"Now, Alden," Lenzi whispered. I didn't need to look back to know they had soul-shared again. Lenzi was safe, but Vivienne wasn't and couldn't even give the command to soul-share because she was being choked.

I had to do something. I charged the podium and knocked the entire thing over, Mueller and all, which caused Smith to turn loose of Vivienne's neck. "Race! Protect Vivienne!" I shouted, grabbing Mueller's free arm. "Vivienne, let him in."

"Okay, Vivienne?" I heard Race say.

"Yes," Vivienne responded. Then she cried out as Race poured his soul in her body.

Smith struggled underneath me, but wasn't strong enough in Mueller's weakened body to fight me off. It had all been an act, and he had probably planned to possess Lenzi or Vivienne after he finished his diatribe. He was certainly pissed I'd tackled him. In pushing the podium over, I'd dislodged the hand that had been stabbed to the wood, and blood was everywhere. The blades were still through the hand, fingers wrapped around them.

"Give it up, Smith," I said, getting a better hold.

"Never," he growled from Ms. Mueller's body. A searing pain shot out from my left shoulder blade. Smith laughed, and I punched him in the face; well, actually, I punched Ms. Mueller in the face, knocking her out cold. Fear spiked from both Lenzi and Vivienne.

"There he goes," Lenzi said, pointing to the far side of the room. "His voice was over there before it faded away. You got him out, Paul."

Yeah. But he hadn't been weak. Ms. Mueller could never have fought that hard. It was as if he was scoping us out. Playing with us.

"Oh, no!" Vivienne ran over to me. "The scissors."

"Yeah, I know," I groaned. "Pull them out, will you?"

She leaned over me. "They're stuck through her hand into you, just like the podium." It must have looked pretty gross, because her fear spiked. She stood up. "No, I can't . . . Shut up, Race."

It was bizarre hearing her argue with Race while they soul-shared, and I would have been amused were it not for the pain in my shoulder.

"Okay, fine. Race is telling me what to do, so if I screw this up, it's his fault," Vivienne said, kneeling beside where I was sprawled over Ms. Mueller's body. "He says he won't leave my body yet because Smith might come back, which is total BS. He just wants me to be the one to yank this out."

"Just do it, Vivienne." I felt her fear and concern. She was frightened and compensating for it with belligerence, like she'd done before. "I'll be fine. You can do this."

I used words I didn't even know I knew, but before long, the scissors were out. Vivienne had me stay still, lying on top of Ms. Mueller, while she put pressure on my wound.

Race's body reanimated with a gasp, and he strolled over. "Oh, man. I wish it weren't against code to photograph this, Paul, because I'd have blackmail material forever," he said.

In less than a minute, backup arrived, and a dozen or so people charged into the room. Four wore lab coats, some wore what looked like special ops gear, a couple had on suits, and then there was Charles, whose concern blasted me for a moment as he knelt down. "How bad is it?"

"I have no idea," I answered.

"I wasn't talking to you. I was talking to Vivienne."

"The shoulder bone deflected the blade," Race said. "The wound is shallow."

From my embarrassing facedown position on top of Ms. Mueller, I couldn't see Charles's face, but I could swear there was a smile in his voice. "While I appreciate your expertise, Horace, I wasn't addressing you either."

Vivienne shifted a bit, but kept the pressure on my wound. "I don't have a clue about this kind of stuff."

Charles stood. "You'll need to get a clue. It appears Paul here has an adventurous streak no one anticipated." I lifted my head to look at him, and he winked. He motioned to the guys in lab coats.

"Lift your hand, please," one requested of Vivienne. The injury pulsed with pain when she took her hand away. I almost asked her to come back as she moved to sit in a desk on the front row. I wanted her to touch me. Needed it. Instead, I took a deep breath as the guys poked at the wound.

Before long, they had me move to Ms. Mueller's desk chair, leaning forward with my elbows on the tops of my thighs. One guy attended me, while the other three hovered over Ms. Mueller. A couple of the guys in suits spoke on their phones, and the guys that looked decked out for warfare each stood in a corner.

"Please take your shirt off," the guy in the lab coat treating my wound said.

Panic made my mouth dry as cotton, and I wasn't sure I could speak. "No." My response had been so quiet, he hadn't heard.

"Please remove your shirt."

"I can't." Still only a whisper.

He crouched beside me. "You can't because it hurts somewhere else, or is it too painful from the wound on your shoulder blade?"

A pulse that felt like a twinge of regret came from Charles. The transmission was so unusual, I sat up and turned to look at him. He looked away—something I'd never seen him do. I wondered if it was because he'd let some emotions slip out or because he knew why I couldn't take my shirt off.

"I have to look at the wound. I can just cut this shirt off, okay?" The guy moved to a large, metal medical supply kit a few feet away. Thoughts of bolting from the room ran through my mind. I plotted out several strategies to escape before they could stop me, but Vivienne killed my scheme by taking my hand.

"Hey. You okay?"

I nodded and focused on her slim, tiny hand holding mine. I closed my eyes and took a deep breath, intentionally letting my memories drift back to the incredible kiss outside her house last night.

She sat on the floor in front of my chair and gave my fingers a squeeze. "You look a little panicked. Does it hurt a lot?"

I shook my head. The wound from the scissors didn't hurt that much. It was the least of my worries.

The guy in the lab coat pulled a chair up beside me and

reached for the hem of my shirt, holding scissors in his other hand. I flinched.

Vivienne took my other hand. "It's okay."

No. It wasn't.

The sound of the blades cutting through the fabric on my back seemed amplified as if it were being broadcast through speakers. The guy stopped midtask. He made no sound, but that bizarre regret emotion pulsed from Charles again. And then I placed that emotion; it was pity. Pity was my enemy.

I took a shaky breath. I couldn't stop this from happening. But I wouldn't allow it to beat me now, not after all these years of successfully dominating my past to create a real future.

I stared into Vivienne's eyes as the guy made the last few cuts in the shirt, then pulled it away from the wound. At least only my back was exposed, and right now, Vivienne was directly in front of me. "You still okay?" she asked. Her sweet concern and tender emotion almost made me weep. Were it to turn to pity, I didn't think I could remain in that chair.

The guy at the door opened it to admit a man rolling a gurney. I was relieved when they put Ms. Mueller, who was still out cold, on it. She had a black eye from where I'd punched her.

"You need stitches," the guy at my back said. "We should

do it off-site." He pulled out a bandage. "We'll do a temp solution until then."

Still shaking, I nodded.

Vivienne squeezed my hand. She thought I was nervous over stitches.

Then she stood, and my worst fears surfaced. I clung tighter to her hands, willing her to stay in place, but even from where she stood, she could see. She pulled her hands away and peered over for a better view of my back. A pulse of surprise. Then horror. Then, yeah, there it was: pity.

I groaned and dropped my head to my hands as she moved to get a closer look.

The guy placed a bandage over the wound, but all I felt was Vivienne looking at my back.

"God, Paul. What happened?" she whispered.

That, of course, prompted Alden, Lenzi, and Race to come view the freak show. I remained silent. What could I say?

Then she touched me, and it felt like fire. She ran her fingers over my skin in some kind of macabre connect-the-dots from one scar to another. I shut my soul from receiving any emotional transmissions at all. Something I was not allowed to do by IC rules, but at that moment, I wasn't a Protector. I was a five-year-old boy being examined by strangers. I had shut out their emotions, but I couldn't stop mine—or my shaking.

She laid her palm flat on my spine while the guy still worked. "Was it measles or chicken pox or something like that?"

The guy had finally finished and pulled off his gloves.

"Yeah, something like that," I said, still trembling.

The guys in suits spoke with Charles, who was nodding but still watching me. Ms. Mueller was strapped down on the gurney, and the medical team seemed packed and ready to go.

Alden, Lenzi, Race, and Vivienne said nothing, but I could feel them behind me, staring. Emotional block still in place, I replayed the memories from outside Vivienne's house last night.

"We'll take care of the Protector," Charles said. "The teacher needs to be transported to a real hospital. The principal understands that the official story is that she somehow lost her balance while holding scissors and fell, impaling her hand and hitting her face on the corner of a desk and whatnot. He is aware of our presence and will stick to that story to keep it under cover. He will contact her family."

The men in the room spoke in quiet voices as they wrapped up. "You're good to go," the guy who bandaged me said, helping me to my feet. I didn't turn around to see the others. I knew I wouldn't be able to bear the looks on their faces.

Charles slid off his suit jacket as he walked over to stand in front of me. "Let's go home," he said. "Race will stitch you up there."

I nodded.

Charles helped me into his jacket, and I almost sighed with relief. It was like a suit of armor protecting me from the arrows of pity. Pity was stifling. It kept people distant. I'd learned that when people felt sorry for you, it was impossible for them to divorce that feeling from any other emotion, like respect . . . or love. And unlike respect or love, once in place, pity was permanent.

I pulled the jacket closed and, without looking back, walked out the door.

SEVENTEEN

"Hey, wait up," Vivienne called, running down the hallway after me. I couldn't even bring myself to slow down. What I wanted to do was take off running.

She caught up as I reached the front doors. "Stop. Just for a second," she said. "Please."

I stopped and waited. Not turning because I dreaded seeing that look—the one people wore when they knew. And I'd made certain that very few knew. I supposed I should have expected this to happen; I just hadn't thought that far ahead with regard to this.

"Can I ride with you? Alden and Lenzi are going by her house for something, I don't want to be stuck with the old man, and I'd much rather be with you than Race." She put her hand on my chest, over my heart. "I'd rather be with you than anyone."

I closed my eyes and hesitantly lowered my emotion block

just enough to get a reading off of her. No pity. None at all. Concern . . . and something else. Something different and intense. The same thing I felt from her outside her house, but it was different. Richer.

I pulled her against me in a hug, and after a moment, she wrapped her arms around my waist. I held my breath as she ran her hands up my back over the jacket. I remembered her touch on my bare skin and shuddered, partly from fear and partly from something stronger than the mortification of her discovering my private past. I had come to like this girl and trust her—probably more than I should.

"Are you sure you're okay?" she asked, head against my shoulder.

She smelled so good. I took a deep inhale. "Yeah. I am now."

We were silent on the way to the mansion, except for an occasional comment about the possession. Vivienne tactfully avoided any mention of what had come after.

I pulled into the garage and killed the motor. My shoulder blade ached, and so did my head. Vivienne grabbed my arm as I unbuckled.

"Thanks for standing up for me," she said.

I held my breath as she leaned across the console until her face was inches from mine. I knew the wise thing to do would be to stop her, but being wise didn't seem possible when she was this near. She stared into my eyes for a moment before our lips met. And then I was lost. Hopelessly lost in this amazing girl who was smart and brave and kissed like she was on fire.

She pulled away. "Wow," she said.

"Yeah, wow." I ran a hand through my hair and shook my head to clear it.

She laughed and got out of the car, leaving me alone with my pounding heart and scattered thoughts. Soon, I mustered enough strength to follow her into the house, where Race was waiting for me in a modified clinic he and Cinda had created in the kitchen. Vivienne was leaning against the refrigerator.

"Hop up on the operating table, Junior, and let's get this done," Race said. "My lovely assistant, Cinda, will act as nurse." Cinda blushed and stared at the floor.

"No." I caught myself and chose my next words carefully. "I mean, okay, but I'd like it to be just you and me. I don't want an audience while I'm being stitched up."

Race's eyebrows shot up. "You scared you'll blubber like a baby?"

"Yeah. That's it. You got me, Race."

He shrugged. "Okay. You heard the man. Clear out, ladies."

Vivienne shot me a puzzled look as she left, but no strong emotions transmitted from her.

"I was going to let your hot little Speaker distract you, Junior. You missed a great opportunity there."

I slid Charles's jacket off and laid it over a stool. "Hopefully, it won't be my last opportunity to be distracted by her. I just prefer it not be in front of an audience."

"Don't knock it till you've tried it." He chuckled and put on a pair of surgical gloves while I pulled off my shirt. He was going to see my entire back up close under bright lighting, so wearing the blood-soaked, ripped-up shirt made no sense. I wadded it up and dropped it into the trash can.

He paused in putting on the second glove and stared at my chest. I braced myself for the worst. Instead, he turned his attention back to his preparation.

"You can either lie down on the island counter or sit on a stool for this." He picked up a syringe, and I slid onto a stool. I folded my arms on the counter and laid my head down, feeling no fear over the stitches at all. Still, my stomach churned at my exposure.

I closed my eyes and waited through several sharp stings, each one less intense than the one before. Race pulled a stool around to the other side of the bar and sat down to wait until the anesthesia took effect. "You want a Coke or something?" he asked.

"No. I'm good."

He pulled off the gloves, then went to the fridge and grabbed a grape soda, Charles's favorite. "I always wondered why you wore shirts when we swam laps at the academy." He popped the top on the soda. "You also ran sprints in a shirt and showered at odd times when nobody was around." He took a swig of soda. "Now I know why."

I closed my eyes. "Now you know."

He said nothing for a long time. "I thought you had a hang-up or something."

"I do."

"Is it just your chest and back?"

I opened my eyes and met his. "Yes."

He nodded and looked at his watch. "Almost time." He took another swallow of soda.

I heard the kitchen door open, and my whole body tensed. "Whoa, Junior. It's just Charles," Race said, patting my elbow. I took a deep breath and let it out slowly.

"How's it going in here?"

"The anesthesia has another minute or so before I test it," Race said, finishing off his soda.

Charles nodded and pulled a grape soda from the refrigerator. "How are you holding up, Paul?"

"Fine, sir," I answered. Race got up and moved the tray of medical supplies. Charles retrieved a glass from a cabinet and sat on the stool Race had just vacated.

"Do you have any questions or concerns, Paul?" His question surprised me. He used to ask that at the end of every day when he was training me. I hadn't heard it in a while.

"Yes, sir." It was the first time I'd ever answered affirmatively.

He popped the top on his soda and poured it into the glass. "I thought you might."

"Do you feel that?" Race asked. I knew he was testing with a needle to see if I was numb from the anesthesia.

"No. Go ahead."

Charles took a sip of his soda as he waited for me to return my attention to him.

"Vivienne told me something in confidence, sir. Perhaps this conversation should wait." I looked over my shoulder at Race, who appeared completely focused on his task.

"Nonsense. Horace is sworn to secrecy. He knows a multitude of confidential things. I trust him." Charles put his glass down and emptied the rest of the soda into it.

Race said nothing, but continued sewing, causing strange, painless, tugging sensations where he worked.

If Charles trusted him, then so should I. "Vivienne said her father was a Protector. She said he abandoned her mother."

Charles turned his glass a half turn, then met my eyes. "Why does this trouble you?"

"Because it troubles *her*. She blames the IC for it. It ripped her mother up. She plans to find him and engage in some kind of confrontation."

"That sounds like her personal business and not that of the IC, which means you, as a Protector, must honor her privacy."

"It affects her ability to perform as a Speaker."

He lifted an eyebrow. "The magic words—'it affects her ability to perform as a Speaker.'"

"Done," Race said. I could hear him snipping off the ends of the stitches.

Charles took a swallow of soda. "Vivienne's father did not abandon her. He was killed the day before his wedding. It was a controversial resolution, and the IC had to cover it up. For practical purposes, he just disappeared. We didn't tell anyone, including his fiancée, that he had died." He picked up his glass to take a sip.

"You should have. You were wrong."

He froze before the glass reached his lips. He put it back down on the counter and paused before answering. "In retrospect, you're right. We had no idea she was pregnant. I didn't know about Vivienne until her aunt told me about her existence and her extraordinary abilities. I made arrangements for her the minute I found out."

"And what if she hadn't had abilities?" I regretted asking it the second it came out of my mouth. I had let my anger get the best of me.

"If she hadn't had abilities, she'd be living a life of extreme poverty in New Orleans with her grandmother, none the wiser. Like you, her talents have given her the opportunity for a better life than she would have had otherwise." He leaned forward. "What we do is bigger than any one individual. Sometimes sacrifices are made. Her mother's situation was unfortunate." His pointed look told me that not only had I gone too far, but that the conversation was over. His eyes strayed from my face to my chest, and his look softened. "I'm glad you're okay." He stood and left the room.

For a long while, I played Charles's words over in my head while Race silently packed up the medical supplies.

When I looked over at him, he shook his head and gave a low whistle. "Dude. You like walking on a razor's edge, huh? No wonder they paired you up with the wild girl. Both of you are danger junkies."

I stood. "That's ridiculous. I was never in any danger."

He snapped his kit shut. "I wouldn't dare challenge Charles. I'd be struck by lightning or something."

"I didn't challenge Charles. I questioned the IC."

"Same thing. Be careful, Junior."

Someone knocked on the door. I still didn't have on a shirt. "Don't," I said, not intending to sound as panicked as it came out.

Race nodded. "We're almost done," he called toward the door. "What's up?"

"You need to get out here, Race," Lenzi called from the other side. "We have a surprise for you."

"We'll be out in a sec," he called. He scanned me, pausing on my chest. "You need a shirt, don't you?"

I nodded.

He cracked the door. "Hey, Cinda!" He continued to peek out the door for a moment. "Hi, sugar. Could you please go grab a shirt out of Paul's room and bring it back here?" She didn't say anything, but he stuck his head farther out and made a *mmmm* sound in his throat. Surely, they weren't kissing. Yep, they were, I discovered when he pulled his head back in with a self-satisfied smirk and lipstick smeared across his mouth.

I threw him a towel. "You look like a drag queen."

He laughed and wiped the lipstick off. "She's pretty fine, huh?"

"You say that about every girl you meet." I stood and stretched my sore shoulder.

"Yeah, but she's different." He took a few steps closer. "Can you keep a secret?"

"No."

"Sure you can. Beatrice has severed our official bond at Charles's request, and he's assigned Cinda as my new Speaker. She'll be given a soul brand tomorrow or the next day that matches mine!"

My head reeled. She barely transmitted emotion, which meant she didn't hear the Hindered completely yet. "She's not ready."

"For what?" He wagged his eyebrows, and I stifled a groan.

"To be a Speaker. Her powers aren't fully in place yet, are they?"

"No. Charles wants her to just hang out with me and learn the ropes until they are. He thinks we're a good pair. He wants her to get used to me and the job and then he'll put her in the field when she's ready."

I sat back on the stool. "Well, you do take some getting used to."

A gentle knock came from the door, and Race opened it, returning to me with a black T-shirt from a concert I'd gone to last year. I slipped it on over my head and looked down. The pleated, navy blue school uniform pants with the black 30 Seconds to Mars T-shirt looked ridiculous.

Race gave me a thumbs-up. "You're stylin', man."

I rolled my eyes and followed him out the door, fully intending to dash up the stairs and throw on some blue jeans before anyone saw me like this, but squealing and laughter broke out in the media room before I made it to the stairs. My curiosity got the best of me, and I peeked into the room. Race was in a bear hug, being showered with kisses by a girl with short blond hair and a powerful build, decked out in western wear. Cinda looked as pale as a ghost in the corner.

Race finally broke free long enough to catch his breath. "Hey, Maddi! Glad to see you too. How was Venice?"

"It was great," she said. "Helena and I resolved a zillion Hindered, and I can say some words in Italian now. Wanna hear?"

He noticed Cinda in the corner and gave her a smile. "Not now, Maddi. I want to introduce you to my new Speaker . . . well, she will be tomorrow or the next day." He gestured for Cinda to join him, and she blushed as she crossed the room. "This is Cinda. Cinda, this is Maddi, one of my very best friends."

The expression on Maddi's face indicated they were more than friends. Alden and Lenzi looked uncomfortable too. Vivienne cast me a puzzled glance, and I shrugged.

Maddi held out her hand. "Hi, Cinda. Great to meet you. It's about time he had a real Speaker. I'm getting kind of sick of babysitting him, you know." Maddi was a Protector, obviously, since she had been involved in resolutions, but I felt no emotions coming off of her. Her eyes gave her away, though. She was shaken by this news. "Yeah. Race and I hang . . . hung out together every cycle until my Speaker showed up, since his old one had ditched him and he didn't have anything better to do." She shrugged in a jerky, awkward movement. "I guess he has something better to do now."

Lenzi bit her lip, and Alden studied the carpet. Everyone was uncomfortable except Race, who seemed totally relaxed. He put his hands on either side of Maddi's face. "We knew this would happen. We talked about it, right?" She nodded. "I am always happy for you when your Speaker emerges. I need the same from you."

"I am," she said. "I just wish you had called me and told me privately or something instead of this."

"I only just now found out myself. Be happy with me." He put his arm around Cinda. "Please, Maddi."

"So, I guess this means they'll be pulling you off of Smith's case?" Maddi asked. "A new Speaker wouldn't stand a chance."

Vivienne's anger pulsed into me. Her eyes were glued to Maddi. "Why couldn't a new Speaker do it?" she asked.

I stepped into the room a few feet.

"Well, come on. Smith has been around forever. He's killed Rose over and over." She gestured to Lenzi. "And if she can't off him, a beginner sure can't."

"Rose," Vivienne said under her breath. My hackles stood up when her emotions rolled through me. So many conflicting feelings, the dominant one was sorrow, followed by anger. She stared at Lenzi. "You're Rose?"

Lenzi took a step back and nodded once. "That was my name in past cycles. I prefer Lenzi."

"You're the one Smith was looking for when he killed my aunt." Vivienne's eyes met mine. "You knew. You knew she was Rose when I told you why I accepted this job in the first place, and you didn't tell me."

"Yes, I knew that she used to be Rose. She wasn't even a Speaker in this lifetime when your aunt died. I didn't know it was relevant."

"Everything is relevant." She took a deep breath. "I would have handled Smith much differently had I known. You should have told me. I trusted you, Paul." She shook her head. She looked over at the doorway to where Charles stood. I had no idea how long he had been there. "I trusted *all* of you."

Charles held out his arms, offering a hug, and she shook

her head. "No. Not again. I'm not falling for the IC's lies and promises again. We're done here," she said. "I need a ride home."

I took a step forward. "Not from you, Paul," she said, holding her palm up.

My insides churned as she turned her eyes to Maddi. "You're the only one here who hasn't lied to me. Can you take me home, please?"

Maddi's eyes darted from one person to the next, ending up on Charles, who nodded. "Um. Sure."

Vivienne stomped out of the room, not looking at any of us. Her emotions were as stormy as her expression.

"Come back when you're done, Maddi," Race said. "We really want to hear all about Venice."

"You do?"

He smiled. "Of course we do."

"Yeah, we missed you," Lenzi said, wrapped in Alden's arms.

Cinda smiled. "I'd love to hear some dirt on Race."

Maddi laughed. "I'm gonna like this girl." She winked at Cinda. "I could make your ears catch fire with stories about him. See y'all soon."

Race caught my arm as I shot for the door. "No, buddy. Let her go. She's way too pissed to listen to you, and trust me, I know all about pissed females." He loosened his grip but didn't let go. "You felt her emotions just like I did. She feels betrayed and hurt, which is different from just being mad."

"I know Smith and Vivienne have some kind of history, but what does it have to do with me?" Lenzi asked.

I slumped down onto the leather ottoman. "Smith possessed a truck driver and ran her aunt down because he couldn't find you and wanted to get the IC's attention so you'd surface. It happened last year, I think."

"Oh." Lenzi turned to Alden. "I bet that was Phillip's Protector."

"Who is Phillip?" Alden asked.

"He's the guy we met on the sea wall in Galveston last month."

"That's right! He said he had a desk job for the rest of the cycle because his Protector was run down by Smith."

"Poor Vivienne," Lenzi said.

Then they all seemed to look at me at once. I knew what they were thinking before they said or felt it. I slammed up my emotional block before I had to feel it as well. Pity. They all felt sorry for me because I was paired with Vivienne.

I had planned to go to my room for a while, but Charles caught me on my way out of the media room. "May I have a word with you, Paul?"

"Sure." I didn't have a choice. He was my boss and my benefactor. Race was right; I should be careful. Without the IC, I'd have nothing. I followed him into his office and sat across from his desk. Instead of sitting at his desk, he chose the chair next to me.

"How are you holding up?" he asked, leaning back and crossing his legs.

"I'm fine, sir." I stared at the glass paperweight on his desk. Tiny bubbles inside the heavy glass had been frozen midflight to the top when the glass had cooled and hardened.

He steepled his fingers in front of his chest. "You wouldn't tell me if you weren't fine, would you?"

"No."

He picked up a piece of paper from his desk and folded it in half. "You are not fine, Paul."

I said nothing, but stared at the bubbles that were stuck halfway through their journey. Just like me.

In my peripheral vision, I could see his fingers working with the paper. He'd done this as long as I'd known him. Lenzi did it in class sometimes too. He made another fold, but said nothing. I shifted to lean back, careful not to touch the side with the stitches. He turned the paper over and made two more folds. "The first time I saw you, you were sitting on the sidewalk talking to a bird." He glanced over at me, but I said nothing. I had no recollection of the event. "It was a tiny bird of some kind, and you sat very still and offered it a bit of a sandwich you had found somewhere. I was impressed with your patience and stillness. Most small children fidget, but not you."

I lifted my shoulder slightly to relieve the ache. The paper in his lap looked like a lopsided triangle with a tail now. He turned it over and kept working.

"After a very long time, the bird eventually felt comfortable enough to come closer. Finally, the bird trusted you enough to hop onto your arm and eat out of your hand."

Through the window behind the desk, I could see that the sky had grown dark and stars twinkled between clouds. When I glanced back at his lap, the paper had been transformed into a bird. I raised my eyes to meet his for the first time since entering the room, and he smiled.

"It was amazing to watch a half-starved boy sit still for hours on end to gain the trust of a tiny, frightened animal so that he could share some food he desperately needed himself." He held the paper bird out to me, and I took it, balancing it in my palm.

"Why are you telling me this?"

He shifted to face me. "I want you to know that you stood out to me long before I knew about your talents. You are not just another Protector I have brought into the ranks of the Intercessor Council."

A wave of emotion that felt like warm water flooding through me took my breath away. He had lowered his guard. This was what he was feeling.

He leaned a little closer. "Were I lucky enough to have a son, I would want him to be like you. I am certain that I would have intervened on your behalf, regardless of whether you had the gift and even if you had not come over to talk to me that day—but I'm glad you did."

"So am I." Tears pricked behind my eyes. I never cried. Never. Not even as a child.

He stood and walked behind the desk to stare out the window. "Vivienne is like that bird. The slightest disruption causes her to fly, but she'll come back because she wants what you offer. She wants friendship and trust. You just need to be still and patient." He walked to the door but paused in the doorway. "I'm proud of you." His emotions stopped instantly as he blocked them, and I could breathe again.

EIGHTEEN

After changing into some jeans, I drove to Vivienne's house. I knew she wasn't home before I pulled up, but I needed to stop here first before I sought her out. Her grandmother opened the door before I knocked—an unnerving habit.

"She's not here," the tiny woman said.

"I know."

She cocked her head. "Then why are you here?"

"To speak with you."

Her face pinched up. "I've got nothing to say to you."

She started to close the door, but I stopped it with my palm. "But I have something to say to you."

After a stare-down with her one good eye, she sighed. "Come on in, then. I'm not going to be gabbing with you through an open door, letting every bug in the county fly in." She gestured to a red velvet chair. "Sit."

I did.

"What do you want?" she asked, sitting on a matching chair, crossing her arms over her chest.

"I don't want anything." That wasn't entirely true. I wanted a lot of things—too many things. "I'm here to give *you* something." The black cat jumped up in my lap and rubbed against my chest.

"Well, what is it?" She sounded disinterested, but her body language gave her away. She uncrossed her arms and leaned forward.

"I have information about Vivienne's father."

She sat back and gave a disgusted snort.

"He's dead."

She stilled.

"He was killed the day before the wedding. The IC covered it up. They should have told your daughter, Mrs. Thibideaux. He didn't abandon your daughter and Vivienne."

The cat startled and jumped off my lap when she shot to her feet. She walked out of the room, leaving me baffled. As I stood to search for her, she returned with two glasses of iced tea and handed me one.

"Call me Tibby." She sat back down, and so did I. "She always said he'd never desert her. She knew something had happened or he'd have come back. She believed it until the day she died."

I took a sip of tea. It was so sweet, I was amazed it was liquid rather than granulated. The cat jumped back up in my lap, giving me an excuse to put the glass on the table next to me rather than try to drink it. I placed it carefully on a coaster near a deck of cards. The cat purred and settled down in my lap.

"That creature doesn't like anyone but Vivienne. Not even me," she said. "You must have a good spirit."

The cat's purr rumbled against my legs. "I'd like to think so."

"Vivienne has a good spirit too."

I rubbed the cat's head. "I know."

She put her empty glass next to my full one and picked up the deck of cards. "These tarot cards belonged to my mother. They're very powerful. Do you want me to read for you?"

"No, thank you."

She patted the deck in her hand. "You don't believe."

"No."

She smiled and leaned back. "But you believe in Vivienne." She placed the deck back on the table. "She's in the ward right now."

"Why?" I placed the cat on the floor and stood.

"I have no idea. She goes almost every night. I don't like her in that part of town by herself." She pointed at my glass. "Are you done?"

I nodded, then looked at the door. "Thank you, Tibby. I'm gonna . . ."

She picked up my glass, took a big sip, then held it up as if to toast and grinned. "Yeah, you go get her, tiger."

Once in my car, I closed my eyes and felt for Vivienne's soul. It took a while, but I finally pinpointed it. Nausea churned my stomach and pinpricks traveled over my skin as I drove down the familiar street, past the park, and pulled up in front of the house where Vivienne's soul pulsed feelings of happiness.

Happiness? My immediate thought was that she had scored drugs of some kind, but I knew that wasn't right. She had never been high since I met her. Why was she here? I closed my eyes and beat back the long-abandoned feelings associated with this place. I was here for one reason only—to protect Vivienne. Past was past.

Going up to the door would be the wrong strategy. My best bet would be to wait it out and talk to her after she left. I'd know if she got into trouble because I'd feel her soul. I drove down the street several houses and turned around so that I wasn't parked right in front. I wanted to see who came out with her, so staying out of direct view seemed wise.

My phone rang. "Hey, Race."

"Where are you?" he asked.

A woman with a little girl left the house and walked across the street to go into another house. "I'm waiting to talk to Vivienne."

"Bad idea, Junior. Trust me. It's too soon. She was really upset."

I didn't respond. I turned the radio off and stretched my sore shoulder.

"If she hasn't seen you yet, you should come back to the house. You need to be patient."

Patient. That was the same word Charles had used. Vivienne stepped out onto the doorstep of the dilapidated house, followed by a dark-haired woman.

"I've gotta go." I unbuckled and ended the call even though he was talking.

As I got out of my car, she gave the woman a hug, then descended the stairs and headed down the sidewalk in the direction of my car. Surely she hadn't planned to walk all the way home from here. She wore tight black jeans and a shirt that was painted to look like blood was running from a wound at the collar. As she got closer, I realized it was a souvenir T-shirt from a production of *Macbeth*. What a fitting combination for her—shocking and smart. She looked over her shoulder and told a Hindered to leave her alone. Then she gasped and stopped several yards away when she spotted me. "What are you doing here, Paul?"

"I assume that's rhetorical."

She rolled her eyes and took off again, passing me on the sidewalk. I followed. "Let me drive you home, please."

She didn't slow her pace. "No way."

"This is a dangerous part of town at night."

She spun to face me. "I'm surrounded by pushy dead guys who won't shut up. Live people are not a big concern. . . . and at least the ghosts don't lie."

"I didn't lie."

"If I had known Smith's primary target was in the room, I would have used that. I could have resolved him. Instead, he got away."

A sidewalk at night in this neighborhood was not the place to have this conversation. "I'm just offering you a ride home. I won't say a word to you, I promise."

She sighed and put her hands on her hips. "It *is* a long walk." She adjusted the bag on her shoulder. "And I'm pissed off, not stupid." She looked behind her. "Take a hike, ghoul. I'm not helping anyone but myself tonight." Then she turned her attention back to me. "I'll take you up on your offer."

I unlocked and opened her door, but she didn't get in. "You were spying on me," she said.

"No. I was protecting you."

"That's crap, and you know it." She got in the car and crossed her arms over her chest. I closed her door and got in on the driver's side. She glared at me. "You were spying like a creepy stalker."

I started the car. This girl was nothing like a frightened bird. More like a bird of prey. "I don't have to spy. I can tell where you are at any given time, and I can feel your reactions to being there."

"And just what do you think I was doing?"

"You know, that's a really good question, Vivienne. What *were* you doing?"

"It's none of your business."

"It's totally my business, because it puts you in jeopardy. It's my duty to protect you."

She stuck out her chin and stared straight ahead.

Clearly, we weren't going anywhere until we got this solved. I couldn't drive and have this conversation. I turned off the car. "I need to know why you're in a heavy crime area at night on a regular basis."

"A resolution."

"What? On your own? That's forbidden. You read the manual."

She waved a hand. "I know, I know. But I hadn't read it when the ghost came to me. I hadn't even met you yet. We were looking at the house to see if it would work for Grandma and then this dead woman asked me to do it just once, so I did it to make her go away. And she did. Well, I liked it so much, I just kept going back."

Dread trickled down my spine like tiny needles. Surely she wasn't messed up in drugs. I'd never heard of a Hindered requesting it of a Speaker. Ever. And she wasn't high at all. I'd feel it if she were.

She turned in her seat and looked at me. "You have a really weird look on your face."

"What did you just keep going back to do?"

"Oh, my God!' Her anger flared. I'd offended her. "What do you think I'm doing?"

Based on her transmissions, she knew exactly what I thought, and she didn't like it. "Honestly, I have no idea. You sneak out at night. You worry your grandma. You worry me. You even had to leave me at the hospital to do it. It looks like you're doing something shady, Vivienne."

"Shady?" She laughed, but anger still pulsed from her. "First of all, that's the lamest word ever. Second, you're way off base."

"Then tell me what you were doing."

"God. Working with you is going to be like working with a probation officer or something." She grabbed her bag from the floor. "You wanna go through my stuff? See if I've got any stash?"

Her emotions were almost out of control. She was furious. I remained very still and waited for her to calm. "No, I insist." She pulled out a children's picture book with a puppy on the front. "Here." She placed it in my lap. "It's as addictive as crack." She pulled out several more. "And these. Oh, man. Be careful of these. One read, and you're hooked for life." She slammed the books back into the bag and shoved it onto the floor.

I ran my fingers over the book in my lap, then handed it to her. She yanked it away and pushed it into the bag with the others. I tried to soften my voice as if she were the bird Charles mentioned. "Are you babysitting?"

Her anger subsided a bit, but was now tinged with what felt

like embarrassment. "No. I'm tutoring. I'm teaching little kids to read because their school sucks, and their parents were never taught and don't speak English, and if they never learn to read, they'll never get out of there. And you're going to tell me not to do it because it's in a scary part of town."

"It *is* a scary part of town." But I would never tell her not to do it. I felt horrible that I had even considered she was doing something . . . shady.

I turned on the car and looked over at her. She was furious. Perhaps because she resented my interference. Or my discovering she broke the IC rules. Or maybe she was so caught up in maintaining her uncaring, badass image she didn't want people to know she was a tender person donating her time to help little kids. I stared at her a moment longer. With the minimal light coming in through the windshield, she looked almost unearthly with her unnaturally black hair and pale skin.

"Now that you've stalked me and spied on me, are you going to drive me home, or should I go ahead with plan A and walk?"

I put the car in gear and pulled away from the curb. "I wasn't spying. I was worried about you being here."

Her laughter made my hackles stand on end. "That makes sense. Little rich boy is frightened of the poor side of town. It figures. Unfamiliar things are scary. Well, it doesn't scare me, because I'm used to poverty and hardship. Something you can't even comprehend in your Mercedes and your mansion."

I pulled up to the curb at the park and turned the car off.

Her emotions were conflicted. Behind her harsh words, she felt doubt and regret—probably because meanness wasn't her real nature. It was an affectation from the hardship she mentioned. I took a deep breath and got out of the car. She needed to know about my past, or we'd have a lifetime of this. Many of them, maybe.

"I thought you were taking me home."

I walked around the front of the car and opened her door. "I am. Get out, please. I want to show you something first."

After a brief hesitation, she stepped out of the car and followed me into the pitiful little park, which was no more than a metal slide, two teeter-totters, and a swing set with one operable swing. Graffiti decorated the wooden benches set in concrete throughout the park. Litter from the trash cans overflowed onto the pavement, and all but two of the streetlights were out.

She shuddered. "Why did you bring me here?"

"This is where I met Charles for the first time." I pointed to the bench closest to the slide. "Right there, in fact."

"What were you doing in a place like this?"

I walked to the bench where I had first met Charles and sat down. "Looking for food."

"Here?"

I pointed to the trash can over by the teeter-totters. "There, actually."

Her horror and confusion blasted me as she sat next to me on the bench.

I gestured to the apartments across the street. Many of the windows were boarded up. "I lived there."

She said nothing, but stared at me openmouthed.

"After my mom died of an overdose, her boyfriend would send me out to beg money off of people. A four- or five-year-old starving boy drew a lot of pity and could score pretty good cash. Since he took all the money from me and rarely bought food with it, I would come here to find stuff in the trash cans. That's how I met Charles. He was here with a Speaker he was training. She was trying to resolve a ghost that haunted the playground. I didn't know all of that, of course. I knew he had come here with her a few times. I noticed them because they obviously weren't from around here."

Vivienne remained silent, but her emotions were a jumble of shock and pain. No pity still.

"I felt the woman's fear and came over to where they were." I patted the bench. "Exactly where you are sitting now, and I asked her if she was okay. I told her I knew she was scared, but that she'd be okay. Charles figured out right away that I was a born Protector, and he hunted down where I lived and had me moved to a foster home. From there, I went for IC training at Wilkingham Academy, then to the house I'm in now."

She remained seated as I got up and walked toward the car. When I turned to see if she was following, her eyes met mine, and I immediately blocked her transmissions. I couldn't bear to feel her pity. It's why I had never told anyone about my childhood.

"Let's go, Vivienne. I promised you a ride home." I lowered my block as I neared the car.

She stopped short on the sidewalk, and her fear flared. She spun around and looked behind her.

"What is it?" I asked.

She hurried to the car, and I opened her door. She glanced at the park again. "Nothing. I just felt something." She shivered and snapped her seat belt. "I'm fine. It was just my imagination. Let's get out of here."

She was silent on the ride home, but I knew she was thinking about what I'd told her at the park. Flickers of sorrow and guilt pulsed from her occasionally, and whenever I glanced over, she was looking at me. When I pulled up to her curb, she turned to me. "Why a foster home?"

I put the car in park. "Because Charles already had an intern and I was too young to train yet."

"No, I mean, why did he take you out of your real home?"

It was a question I hadn't seen coming. I'd intended to tell her what was safe and leave it at that. I took a deep breath and put up a block. "Because my living conditions were less than ideal."

I was glad I had blocked her emotions because her face said it all. She had put the pieces together. "Oh, my God. The scars on your body . . ." Tears filled her eyes, and I closed mine. "Are cigarette burns."

The air stirred, and I looked over to find her reaching for me. She moved slowly, just like one would with a frightened animal, until she touched my face. Her fingers were so warm and gentle. Then, without another word, she opened the car door and walked up into her house.

NINETEEN

I t was a party in full swing when I returned home. I would
have been angry that they were making so much noise
and mess in the house without my permission, but then
I remembered Cinda lived there too now, and she was
having a great time.

Maddi, arm in arm with Cinda, told inappropriate stories
about Race, who objected and tried to tell his side with no success. Alden and Lenzi lounged on the rug in front of the TV,
laughing at Maddi's tales. Like a family.

I relaxed in a chair while Maddi revealed how Race hit on
Rose every lifetime and how she and Alden placed bets on how
long it would be before she told him to shove off.

"Hey, Junior," he said. "How's wild girl?"

"She's fine."

He rubbed a hand over his spiky red hair. "Dang, you're
tight-lipped. What happened?"

I shifted to where my shoulder didn't touch the back of the
chair. "We talked."

"Why didn't you bring her back with you?" he asked.

"I said she was fine, not over it."

Lenzi propped up on an elbow. "She seems to be over it. She called Race, asked to be put on speakerphone, and apologized to me. Said she'd overreacted."

"Did she say anything else?" I asked, praying she hadn't told them anything about our trip to the park.

They shook their heads and exchanged glances, but no pity came from them. She had kept my secret.

"Go get her and bring her here," Cinda said.

It was better to give her space right now. Better for me too. I knew she'd ask more questions about my childhood, and though letting some of it go felt good, I didn't want to talk about it anymore. I needed to get myself together first.

I stood. "Nah. I'm going to go to sleep. It's been a long day. I'll see you guys around."

Even though I knew there was no way I'd be able to sleep, I went through the bedtime routine: showering, brushing my teeth, and slipping into warm-up pants and a T-shirt. It had always calmed me to do things in a particular sequence. Routine usually made order of the chaos, especially the chaos in my mind. But not tonight.

For the first time ever, I had revealed my secret to someone else. It wasn't inferred or discovered as it had been when I was removed from my home or when Race had stitched me up. I had given it freely, and it felt good. It was as if a heavy backpack

I'd been carrying around had been lightened just a bit. Still, it made me uneasy. And while hiding it from others for the rest of this cycle would be a burden, the inconvenience was not as bad as pity.

I pulled a book off of my nightstand, but the words just garbled together. The restlessness was killing me. I closed my eyes and searched for Vivienne's transmissions. She was happy and a little nervous. I smiled knowing she wasn't upset. I wondered if she was lying on her round cushion of a bed unable to sleep, like me. Then the yearning started. I needed to be with her, I *had* to be with her. I rolled over and tried to get comfortable, but I couldn't quit thinking about how she looked, how she smelled, how she sounded when she laughed, how her lips felt and tasted. It had to be the soul brand. It wasn't natural to feel so bonded to someone so quickly. I needed to put the brakes on. I didn't want to end up like Race, with no Speaker for cycles because I let my emotions get carried away. I groaned and buried my face in my hands.

A light tapping sent me to my feet. I knew who it was before I ever opened the door. I felt her soul as if it were my own.

Vivienne slipped inside my room wordlessly, and I shut the door. Without any prelude, she grabbed me and wrapped her arms around my body. "Well, hello to you too." My voice came out in an embarrassing, breathy whisper.

She stepped away and ran her hands through her hair. "Sorry. I just needed to . . . I felt like I had to—"

"How did you get here?" I remained by the door, gathering the shreds of my self-control.

"Race."

That figured.

She wrung her hands. "Sorry."

My heart had calmed to a reasonable rate again. "You don't need to apologize." I stepped closer and took her hands. "You took me by surprise, though. Are you okay?"

She was so nervous. Her emotions ran through me like a live electric current. "I'm sorry. I'm sorry for the mean things I've said about you being spoiled. I'm sorry I was rude to everyone."

"I know you are." I laced my fingers through hers. "And I want you to know that I'm sorry I didn't disclose that Lenzi was Rose. You made a good point. You need all the information possible to do your job. I'll keep that in mind and be totally open from now on."

"Smith is right. Hate is powerful. It makes me stupid. I overreacted. I just want to get rid of him so bad."

"Nothing about you is stupid," I said.

She shifted from foot to foot, fingers still laced with mine. "And Grandma told me what you found out about my dad. It sucks, but it's also a huge relief that he wasn't a complete jerk. My mom always knew something had happened. The IC should have told her."

"They should have."

She looked at the floor for a while before meeting my eyes. "Anyway, I'm sorry, and thanks."

I pulled her against me, transmitting calm through my hands.

She took a deep breath, and I felt her emotions tone down slightly. "I like it when you do that."

I smiled against her hair.

She pulled back to look at my face. "Can you transmit things other than calm?"

I lifted an eyebrow.

"We could have a lot of fun with that, you know."

I pulled up one of her hands. "Your nails are black again."

"Yep. School code says clear polish only. No school for a few days, so I'm back to being me again." Her brow furrowed. "Do you not like the black?"

"I like *you*. Your nail color is irrelevant, but I like the black,"

She grinned, then took a deep breath and her smile faded. "I need to be the one to dispatch Smith, you know."

I sat on the edge of my bed. "I know."

"I mean, I'd be happy however he goes, but it would mean a lot to me to do it myself. Did you know he has killed Lenzi every cycle since the Civil War?" She strolled over to my desk and stared at it. "You are ridiculously organized."

"So I've been told."

"Are you going to bring your OCD into the next lifetime?" She ran her fingers over my perfectly lined-up files that were exactly square with the edges of the desk.

"I have no idea."

She stood directly in front of where I sat on the bed. "Alden says you keep a journal so that you can track the 'trends of the Speaker' from lifetime to lifetime. That indicates we take baggage with us."

She sat next to me, touching from shoulder to knee. "You have a lot of baggage, Paul." She reached over and took my hand. "To me, emotional baggage is like a horrible rotten piece of something . . . maybe like an old piece of steak. You can keep it bottled in, sort of like putting it in a jar with a lid and leaving it in the sun to fester and rot. It sits in that jar, breaking down, getting more and more disgusting." She moved her hand to my neck and played with my shirt collar. "But if you take the lid off, clean air gets into that jar and the moisture evaporates out of that rotten thing. Maybe ants get in and carry parts of it away and there's less of it. Maybe it just dries and shrivels up until it's just a little hard clump. After a while, it breaks down to dust. Yeah, it's still there, but it's not a slimy chunk of garbage stinking the whole jar up. You need to take the lid off, Paul. Let some of it out. And let someone in."

I stared in her eyes for the longest time. I'd never seen eyes as green or as deep. "You."

She ran her hand across my back, avoiding the stitches, and I thought she was going to kiss me, then to my horror, she reached under my shirt. I went rigid as a board.

I held my breath as her fingers glided over the skin of my back, pausing at each scar.

"Breathe, Paul." She continued her exploration. "So many. Did it hurt?"

The panic rose to where I thought I would scream. Instead, I whispered, "I don't remember it. I was very young."

"Was it your mom's boyfriend?"

"Yes." I leaned forward and covered my face.

She got on her knees facing me, fingers still exploring my past. "When it was going on, why didn't you tell anyone?"

"I thought it was normal. I'd never known anything else. I thought all kids lived like me. Honestly, I don't remember much of it, and what I do remember is foggy. I was a little kid."

She pushed me to my back and ran her hands over the skin of my chest. I knew she could feel the scars there as well. "He was careful to keep it where it wouldn't show." She shook her head, but no pity came from her. Just that warm feeling like when we had kissed outside her house mixed with sadness.

A tear welled in the corner of my eye and rolled down my temple as I stared at the ceiling, trying to keep a lid on my feelings. Then there was a sob. It sounded like it came from someone else, but it had come from me. I had never, to my recollection, actually cried like this before, and it was a painful, horrifying sensation. I rolled away from her, covering my face.

She climbed behind me and wrapped her arms around my body, and I suddenly felt calm. I'd hidden my past for so long, and talking about it with Vivienne had been a relief. Empowering, even.

I took a deep breath and focused on her touch, rather than the scars she was touching. She knew the worst of it and didn't look down on me or feel sorry for me. That was all that mattered. This girl at this moment was more important than any wrong done in my past.

I rolled over to face her. "I'm really okay. I just got overwhelmed. I've kept it to myself for so long. It was the hiding it that was the burden, not what happened."

She traced my lips with her thumb. "Do you hate him?"

"I don't even remember him, really, only that I feared him. I was too young. Besides, hate isn't worth the energy."

"Then why do you hide it? Why do you freak out when I touch your back?"

I took a deep breath, trying to find a way to articulate it. "You don't like it when people ask you if you need help."

Her brow furrowed. "No. I don't like it when people think I'm incompetent."

"Well, I don't like to be pitied. I want people to admire me or respect me . . . heck, they can even hate me, but I don't want anyone to feel sorry for me."

"You don't think someone can respect you and still feel sorry that something bad happened to you?"

"I think the pity trumps everything else and diminishes the view of the person."

"I think you're wrong."

I smiled. "I often am."

She ran her fingertips down the side of my face. "You're solid, you know? Even after what you went through, you're so well adjusted and together. I'm glad you let me in. You can always talk to me, you know." She snuggled closer. "Which is a good thing, since we're stuck together for a really long time."

I propped up on an elbow and smiled. "So you'll be my private psychotherapist?"

"You bet." She ran her hand down my side to my waist and slid her fingers back under my shirt. "I'll be your private physical therapist too."

I stopped her before her lips touched mine. Her nearness felt so right, but I knew taking this to the next level could end in disaster. "We should address what we're doing here."

Her fingers paused for only a moment and then continued their maddening trail across my skin. "I'm pretty sure we both know what we're doing here."

It was almost impossible to talk with her touching me. "I don't want to jeopardize our working relationship. I'm thinking we should step back and—"

She covered my mouth with her hand. "Nuh-uh. Don't overthink this or apply one of your silly rules. Pretending I'm not attracted to you or that you don't feel the same way would be a lie. Lies are what will hurt our working relationship."

The smell of candles and incense filled my head, and my chest felt tight. I pulled her hand away from my lips. "Yes. I agree, but I don't want to screw this up. It's too impor—"

She jerked upright and her terror shot through me. For endless moments, she held her breath and trembled.

A crash loud enough to wake the whole neighborhood came from downstairs. It was followed by shouting and a scream.

"He's here," she whispered.

TWENTY

Vivienne threw her legs over the side of my bed. "Smith is here. Oh, God, he's . . ." Her panic was so high, I couldn't breathe. Another huge crash from downstairs brought Vivienne to her feet. Our footsteps sounded like thunder as we bounded down the stairs and sprinted across the marble foyer, coming to an abrupt stop in the media room entry.

There was blood everywhere.

I placed my hand on her shoulder. "Don't do anything until we assess the situation."

Alden's limp form slumped in a chair across from Maddi's equally empty body. Cinda cowered in a corner behind a claw-footed table.

Race sat on top of Lenzi's chest in the middle of the floor, glaring at Cinda. He was so pale, his freckles stood out in stark contrast. "Call it in now, Cinda!" he shouted. "Medics, backup, Charles. We need help!"

"Can't," she muttered. "N-no phone."

Lenzi's body jerked hard enough to almost dislodge Race. "God almighty, Cinda. Come get my phone from my back pocket and call for help," Race commanded. "Or she will die." He repositioned himself on top of Lenzi again. "Maddi, make her do it."

Cinda covered her ears and chanted, "No," over and over again. Maddi was obviously soul-sharing with her, which meant Alden's soul was in Lenzi's body.

Vivienne charged to the middle of the room and grabbed Race's phone from his jeans pocket. As she pulled it out, Lenzi's body levitated, lifting Race with it, then shot to vertical, dumping Race on the floor. Right as he hit the ground, Lenzi screamed and her body went limp and dropped to the wood floor with a thud. The blood all over the room appeared to be coming from a wound on the side of Lenzi's head and a gash on her palm. As Race dove to throw himself over her, Lenzi's body launched a good six feet into the air, catapulting across the room as if she had been thrown like a football. Her back slammed into the bookcase before dropping to the floor in a cascade of books.

"Protect the Vessel, Paul," Race shouted. "Now!"

Vivienne nodded, and I sat on the floor, then ripped my soul out of my body and poured it into hers. Smith's laughter filled Vivienne's head. *An audience. I'm so glad you joined us.*

Cinda whimpered from her corner.

"Hit number one on speed dial and tell Charles we're under attack and need medical backup," Race said, pulling books off of Lenzi and taking her into his arms. Vivienne called immediately and calmly relayed the information to Charles, who had answered on the first ring.

An invisible force jerked Lenzi from Race's arms and flung her across the room, where she crashed sidelong into a display case that held Asian figurines. Glass and porcelain rained down on Lenzi's body. She made no sound, and her eyes were closed. Her transmissions, though weak, were still present, so she was still alive. Another slam from Smith, and that might not be the case.

Vivienne dashed across the room, but Race held up a hand and stopped her from getting close to Lenzi. "Stay out of it so you don't get hurt." Race staggered to where Lenzi lay, arms outstretched as though he planned to catch her if she launched again. Her body convulsed in several distinct pulses, and she moaned. "Keep him out, Alden. Hang in there, Lenzi!" Race shouted.

"Give up, Speaker 102, and the pain will end." Smith's voice sounded like it was everywhere. *"Haven't you grown weary of this? I have. Leave by choice, and your Protector will be safe."*

If she leaves voluntarily, she won't recycle, I explained to Vivienne. *Her soul has to be in the body when it dies.*

"Fight, Lenzi!" Vivienne shouted.

As if invisible hands had grabbed Vivienne by the shoulders, her body slammed against the paneling behind her.

"It's not your turn yet, little Speaker. Be patient and enjoy," Smith said.

Vivienne's fear skyrocketed, but her body remained relaxed. "How much fun can it be to pick on a helpless, unconscious girl?" she said. "Why don't you leave her alone and talk to me?"

"You're right. She's tiresome. You, on the other hand, are not. I knew you couldn't resist a good show and would join us. Now for the finale."

The force that had pinned Vivienne to the wall released her. Then Race fell to his knees as if he'd been hit from behind just before Lenzi's body arced across the room and smashed headfirst into the enormous television with a sickening crack of bones. The television toppled from the stand and shattered into pieces around Lenzi's broken body when it hit the floor.

"No!" Race cried, crawling to her. He reached as though to pick her up, but let his arms fall limply to his sides.

Smith's laughter was as horrifying as the scene itself. *"I'll tell your fortune at the place where I died, little Speaker. Don't make me wait."* His voice faded to almost nothing on the last few words.

Vivienne held her breath, then let it out slowly. "He's gone," she said. "I don't feel him at all anymore." She ran to Race's side and fell to her knees next to Lenzi.

Race shook his head. "Don't touch her. If her back or neck is broken, moving her could paralyze or kill her."

Cinda howled in pain, and Maddi's body gasped to life across the room from the chair. "You're supposed to warn me so I can touch your body so it doesn't hurt like that!" Cinda shouted.

"Oh, gee. I totally forgot," Maddi said. "Maybe I would have remembered if you had done something other than hide in the corner while Smith threw Lenzi around like a toy."

A pulse of sorrow shot from Lenzi. *She's alive,* I told Vivienne from inside her body.

"There she is." Maddi said, feeling the transmission too. She grabbed Alden around the waist and dragged him toward Lenzi. Vivienne jumped up and helped. Maddi put Alden's hand on Lenzi's chest. "Come on out if you can, Alden," she whispered.

"Get Paul to his body, Vivienne," Race said. "We're going to need him."

Lenzi groaned, and Alden's body animated.

Headlights flickered through the front windows as cars pulled into the driveway. *Hurry!* I said.

Vivienne crouched in front of my lifeless body, which was leaning against the entry room wall, and placed her hands on my shoulders. The second my soul was in place, I bolted up the stairs, changed into jeans, and put on my shoes. By the time I made it back downstairs, the medics had put a neck brace on Lenzi and were sliding a backboard under her. She groaned in pain, teeth gritted. "Wait," she whispered. "Alden . . ."

Alden kneeled by her head.

"Find Smith." Lenzi's voice quavered with the obviously painful effort to speak. Her eyes found me. "Paul. You can do this. End this. You and Vivienne." The sorrow and regret pouring from her into me made me dizzy. "All of you. For me, okay?"

Alden covered his face and choked back a sob.

I nodded, feeling like I'd just been tasked with something way beyond my reach.

Race sent Cinda and Vivienne to get coats and supplies together. Maddi retreated to the corner of the room and pulled out her phone.

"Go with them, Alden," Lenzi murmured as the medics lifted her on the backboard.

"I'm staying with you."

She shook her head, then whimpered when the motion caused pain. "No. I need you to do this for me. Go for me. Get rid of Smith. If I don't make it, I'll see you in the next cycle—but get rid of him first." A tear mixed with the blood on the side of her face. "I love you forever, Alden."

Trembling, he reached for her, then dropped his hands helplessly by his sides as the medics moved toward the door. "No. Not now. Not when . . . We finally got it right. Not now." He ran along beside her as the medics hurried her out the front door into a black Suburban that was one of the IC's undercover ambulances. "What if he comes back for her?" He ran to Race.

"I can't just let her go like this. I need to be with her this time."

Race took him by the shoulders and shook him hard. "Pull it together. There's a Protector among the medics if Smith comes back. There always is. Go say what you need to say, and let's get rid of this demon once and for all. We can't do this without you. He needs to be dispatched whether Lenzi lives or dies, or this will never stop happening. You don't want to do this again in the next lifetime." He gave him another hard shake. "Go . . . go say good-bye."

Alden sprinted to the back of the Suburban and climbed in.

Maddi joined us on the sidewalk. "Charles is on his way from Dallas, but he's still a few hours out."

"Do you know where Smith took his last breath?" I asked Race and Maddi.

Race shook his head. "Alden will know. It'll be in Galveston, though. That's Smith's home turf, so that's where he died." He glanced over at the ambulance and looked at his watch.

"Any idea what the fortune thing means?" Maddi asked.

I had a horrible suspicion that I did, but I hoped I was wrong. "I might. I want to talk to Alden first."

Cinda and Vivienne joined us with several coats and blankets.

Race took the blankets from Cinda. "Is your medical kit stocked and in your car, Paul?"

"Yeah."

"I'll take Alden and Cinda," Race said. "You take Vivienne and Maddi. That way we've two Protectors for each Speaker."

"Cinda can't go," Maddi said.

"Why not?" Cinda asked, face flushing.

"Because you're a liability."

"I am not! Charles said—"

Maddi cut her off. "You totally choked in there. You're not ready. Your powers haven't developed fully yet. I can hardly feel your transmissions."

Cinda shook her head. "I know what to expect now. I'd never experienced a Malevolent before, and I was scared. I can help. I just know it. I'm coming with you."

"No way." Maddi folded her arms over her chest. "Being scared is part of the job, and you froze."

Cinda's eyes filled with tears, and her shoulders slumped.

Maddi's tone softened a bit. "Besides, you haven't been soul branded. If you die, you die. That's it. Kaput. No reincarnation, no Race, no nothing."

"You guys aren't my bosses. I'm supposed to stick with you."

"Maddi's right," Race said. "The lack of a soul brand is a kill-deal." He shook his head. "Sorry, sugar."

Cinda glared and then stomped toward the house, muttering under her breath.

The Suburban pulled away with Lenzi inside, leaving Alden behind in the driveway looking totally lost. I thought for a minute he was going to run after it.

When Alden joined us, it appeared that all the life had left him. He looked like he did when his soul was absent, only he was moving. He ran a hand through his blond hair and opened his mouth as if he were going to say something, then he just shook his head.

"Okay. So, we're all here. Let's load up," Race said. "Are you up to driving, Junior? Your car is biggest."

"Sure."

"I can't do this," Alden said. Then he strode off toward his car, and Maddi ran after him. She caught up and wrapped her arms around him. He buried his face in her short blond hair and clung to her as if his life depended on it.

"She'll convince him to come," Race said. "He just needs a little time to get it together."

"Is Lenzi going to die?" Vivienne asked.

Race shrugged. "It's hard to tell. I heard her skull crack. There's also certainly some internal abdominal damage and lots of broken bones—her neck even, maybe. If she lives, it'll be a miracle."

"Miracles happen," Vivienne said. "I've seen them myself. I'm holding out hope for a miracle. In the meantime, let's do what Lenzi asked us to do and get rid of Smith."

TWENTY-ONE

lden was no more than a shell sitting in the front passenger seat of my car. Maddi had helped him wash Lenzi's blood off, and I'd loaned him a new shirt, but his legs were too long to fit my pants, and we didn't have time to go by his house, so he still wore his bloodstained jeans.

I opened the garage door and started the motor. "Where did Smith die exactly?" I asked Alden.

"Galveston." Even his voice was hollow.

I put the car in reverse and backed down the driveway. "Where specifically in Galveston?"

"Old City Cemetery." His voice cracked.

Race reached up from the backseat and patted his shoulder. "Easy, buddy."

I turned onto the road leading to downtown.

"This isn't the way to Galveston," Maddi said from the backseat.

"I know." I turned into Vivienne's neighborhood. "I need to check out a hunch." A hunch I hoped was wrong.

In the rearview mirror, I saw Vivienne stiffen. I felt her anxiety spike as well. "Oh, God. You think Smith's remark about reading our fortune has to do with me or Grandma, don't you?"

I pulled onto her street. "I'm ruling it out."

"Grandma reads fortunes." She unbuckled her seat belt before I pulled up in front of her house. "He'd better not hurt her!" Before I came to a complete stop, Vivienne was out of the car and sprinting up the sidewalk.

Maddi, Race, and I didn't need to go in to confirm my hunch was correct. Vivienne's anguish from inside the house hit us like a shock wave.

Race cussed under his breath and pulled out his phone. "I'll call the IC to come get her."

"No, wait," I said. "Let's see exactly what we're dealing with. I don't think he killed her. Not yet. I imagine he'll use her to bait us. I bet she's alive and unharmed."

The inside of the house was littered with broken lamps, overturned chairs, and shattered glass strewn on the floor. I found Vivienne in the kitchen leaning over the table catching her breath, clutching the edges of the linoleum tabletop so hard her knuckles were white. The kitchen looked untouched except for an empty knife block turned on its side on the counter. There was an uneaten plate of food and a full glass of tea on the table in front of Vivienne. She reached out and pushed some brightly colored pills by the glass around with her finger.

"Not her," she whispered. "She's all I've got left."

"He's using her to bait us, Vivienne." I put my hand over hers. "Let's go get her back."

She met my eyes and nodded.

Maddi and Race were putting furniture to rights when we entered the living room. "She put up a good fight," Race remarked.

"Of course she did," Vivienne said. "Grandma Tibby is tough."

Maddi moved a chair and the cat hissed and scurried into the back of the house.

"We need to go now," I said. "I have no idea how he's getting to Galveston in Tibby's body, but none of the options are good."

Vivienne was pretty shaken, so I had Race drive so that I could sit next to her in the back. I sat in the middle between Maddi and Vivienne, who folded up against me in a ball. Maddi stared stoically out the window.

I knew that Smith was luring us to Galveston because Malevolents were strongest where they had died. It took way too much energy to fight us in Houston. Ordinarily, we would never take him on in his most advantageous venue, but he'd made sure we would by taking a hostage.

"He's really strong this time," Race remarked. "And he's different. Usually, he's sneaky."

"I thought he was as good as gone when he possessed Mueller," I said.

"It's all been an act." Vivienne sat up straight next to me. "He's playing us. He has been all along. I've felt him a couple of times. He's been watching us and waiting." A shudder ran through her. "He has Grandma." A tear slipped down her cheek, and she curled against me.

"We need another Speaker. She'll never pull it off," Maddi said as if Vivienne were not present.

"Stop it," Race said.

"You feel it too, Race. She's a mess."

"She's all we've got!" he snapped.

Vivienne sat up. "Who? Me?" Her anger surged. "I won't pull it off?" For a moment, I thought she was going to lunge for Maddi, but to my relief, she sat back and crossed her arms over her chest. "He's got my grandma. He's as good as gone."

Alden shuddered and then moaned as if his very soul had died. He crumpled over with his head in his hands.

"You okay, buddy?" Race asked.

For the longest time, he said nothing. He just rocked forward and back. Finally, just above a whisper he said, "She's gone." He took a long, shaky breath. "The soul bond just broke. I can't feel her anymore." He fisted his hair and continued to rock.

No one said anything. There was nothing to say that would help. My heart broke for him. I couldn't even imagine what he was going through or how much it hurt. And then it hit me.

Vivienne was right. Pity didn't diminish a person in someone else's eyes. I felt sorry for Alden. Horribly, fantastically sorry, but it didn't make me admire him any less.

We rode the rest of the way to Galveston in silence until we hit the causeway bridge to the island. The lights from the Texas City refineries reflected in the water across the dark bay.

"I need you to tell me what you guys know about this demon in order to beat him," Vivienne said.

Race reached over and rubbed Alden's shoulder. "Hey. We need you to help us out here."

Alden didn't move.

"Alden. Get it together, man. We're almost at the cemetery. We need you. Lenzi needs you to make good on this so she doesn't have to go through this again in the next cycle. Pull it together now."

Alden lifted his head and ran his hands through his hair.

"It's important," Race said. "Do it for all the times he killed Rose. Do it for Lenzi. Tell us everything you know about Smith."

Alden stared straight ahead and spoke in a monotone, as if numb. "He was a crook who went by the name Nicaragua Smith, but I know that wasn't his real name. In 1862, he set me up for a crime I didn't commit, so Rose seduced him and got the evidence that freed me and convicted him. He had fallen in love with her and took it very personally. Enough to kill her in every lifetime, as soon as he could find her."

He glanced over his shoulder at Vivienne, and when he spoke, he sounded like he'd pulled himself out of his trance. "That's why your aunt died. He was looking for Rose and trying to get her attention, but she hadn't emerged for the cycle yet."

"How did he die?" Vivienne asked.

He put his head down and took some deep breaths and rocked, then began again in the same flat tone, as if he were reading from a textbook or reciting a memorized passage. "In 1863, Nicaragua Smith was court-martialed by the Confederate Army stationed on Galveston Island. They loaded him on a wagon with his coffin and took him to the cemetery for his execution. He stood next to his grave and tapped his foot on his coffin, grinning like it was a party while he waited to be shot by a firing squad. He vowed revenge from the grave and refused a blindfold, saying he wanted to look at his killers' faces as he died. He demanded to be buried facedown, looking toward hell."

"Yeah, well, I'm all for sending him there," Vivienne said.

The cemetery was on our right, its monuments visible through the iron fence standing at odd angles in the moonlight.

"We need a strategy," I said.

"There are too many unknowns to formulate any plans. We're going to have to make it up as we go along." Race pulled onto the street in front of the cemetery entrance and parked at the curb. The iron gates that were closed at night had been smashed open by an old blue Ford Mustang that stood in the middle of the road that ran through the cemetery. "There's how your grandmother got here."

"She's never driven a car in her life," Vivienne said.

Maddi unsnapped her buckle. "Showtime, kiddies."

"Stop," Alden said. He shook his head as if to clear it. "Wait." He turned in his seat to face us. "Vivienne's new," he said directly to Maddi, who took her hand off the door handle. "There are some things we can do to help her. Basic things that Vivienne needs to know."

"I read the manual," Vivienne said. "I get how it works."

I took her hand and transferred calm to her. She yanked her hand away. "Cut it with the calming crap, Paul." She crossed her arms in front of her body. Her anger was palpable, and being Protectors, everyone else in the car felt it too. "I'm new at this, but I'm not stupid. And I'm not a wimp."

"No one ever said you were," Race said.

"I'm all you've got, remember!" she snapped.

"You are," Race said calmly. "So you'd better cool down. Anger weakens your soul, and you're going to need all the strength you've got."

She grabbed my hand. "Do it."

Immediately, I transferred calm to her, and her emotions dialed down significantly.

"Okay, I suggest we assess the injuries to the hostage or hostages first," Alden said. "It would make sense if he forced someone else to drive him here since Vivienne's grandmother doesn't know how."

"He'd better not have hurt her. She's diabetic, and her wounds don't heal easily. She'll probably die if he cuts her up."

"She's diabetic? Really? She drinks sweet tea like crazy," I said.

"Artificial sweetener. So we check out the hostage situation and then what?"

Maddi rolled her eyes. "Then you weaken him until you think you're stronger than him and are ready to let him into the Vessel so you can finally beat him down to where he leaves forever. They have to be too weak to stay behind or they have to choose to move on voluntarily."

I could feel Vivienne bristling at Maddi's condescension, so I spoke before it got worse. "Possessing a body uses a ton of his energy. He will also lose energy when he gets mad or remorseful."

"Forget the remorse," Alden said. "He doesn't have any."

Vivienne nodded. "Okay, so the plan is to keep him talking and piss him off in my grandmother's body without letting him hurt her, until he's weakened. Then I have him possess me and because my soul will be much stronger, I kick his butt to oblivion or hell or whatever."

"Yeah, while we put our souls wherever they're needed to protect vulnerable bodies. Even yours," Maddi added.

"Especially yours, Vivienne," Race said, glaring at Maddi.

"What? You're pissed at me? Really?" Maddi said. "This is a suicide mission. She doesn't stand a chance. We need Rose."

I held my breath as Alden turned in his car seat to stare directly at Maddi. "We don't have Rose, Maddi. Rose is dead." He glared at her a long time. "Again," he said quietly, as if to himself. He faced front, ran both hands through his hair, and then flung the door open. "Let's get this over with." He slammed his door and strode into the cemetery.

Race unbuckled. "Keep your eye on him, guys," he said. "He's likely to do something really reckless."

Maddi opened her door. "Yeah, like get himself killed."

After they had closed their doors, I remained in the car, holding Vivienne's hand for a few moments in the welcome silence.

"He has Grandma," she said. "What if they're right? What if I can't do it?"

I sent as much calm her way as I could conjure, but it was hard because my own emotions wanted to surface. I was terrified for her. I also understood her anger and fear. "You can do this. They don't know you. They've underestimated you."

"Everyone underestimates me. It's one of my weapons. Nobody sees it coming until it's too late."

I took her face in my hands. "I don't underestimate you. You're powerful and smart. Go in there and take charge. You're the Speaker. We're just Protectors at your command. Our only purpose is to facilitate your success." I kissed her. "Remember that." I kissed her again, and this time, she kissed me back so hard I thought the windows would fog up.

She pulled away and stared into my eyes a long time. "I have to be successful, because that is way too good to put off doing again until the next lifetime. Let's go get rid of this demon."

I opened my door, and she slid out after me. She took my hand as we entered the cemetery together. "Game on!" she said to the others, pumping her fist in the air.

TWENTY-TWO

"The motor was still running," Alden said from the driver's side of the Mustang, holding up a set of keys on a long smiley-face lanyard.

Vivienne leaned in through the passenger window. "Grandma's tarot deck is on the backseat." She opened the door and dug the cards out from among the fast-food wrappers and empty cigarette packs. She fanned through the deck. "Some of them are missing."

Maddi put her hands on her hips. "So, some game cards are missing. It's irrelevant."

Vivienne got right up in her face. "Tarot is not a game, and it's my grandmother he's got, so to me, nothing is irrelevant. If you want to cover up your grief over Lenzi, or your fear of Smith, or your jealousy of Cinda, or whatever baggage you've got by being a hostile bitch, do it to someone else. I've got a job to do."

With that, Vivienne tromped down the middle of the narrow road, deeper into the cemetery. For a moment, we all stared at each other in amazement, then Maddi chuckled. "You know, I think she really might pull this off."

"I know she will." I ran to catch up with Vivienne. She had slowed her pace by the time I fell in step beside her.

She stopped and turned a full circle, eyes closed.

"You won't be able to feel him if he's possessed someone," I reminded her.

"Well, that sucks," she said, opening her eyes.

Alden joined us, and not long thereafter, so did Race and Maddi.

I scanned the north side of the cemetery, looking for any signs of life among the broken, vandalized monuments. I had to squint against the relentless salty wind blowing off the beach that made the bushes and trees sway in the moonlight as if they were human. "There!" I said, pointing to a larger mausoleum in the back corner. Its black iron doors were thrown open wide with a light coming from inside.

"Oh, crap, I hate creepy stuff like this," Vivienne said, striking out toward the light. We followed in silence.

"It's probably a trap," Maddi said.

"It's certainly a trap," Alden answered. "But we're on his turf now. His rules. He plays dirty. Even when he was alive, he played dirty."

"So do I," Vivienne said.

Our feet crunched in the long, dry grass as we passed through several rows of unkempt and neglected graves—tragic testimonials to long-forgotten lives—and I suddenly felt very small and insignificant. Just one more person.

But I wasn't just one more person; I'd been given a chance to make a difference. It wasn't about being remembered, it was about being worthwhile.

A retaining wall no more than a foot high surrounded an elevated plot on our right. Four stark white headstones with lambs on top stood between two larger headstones adorned with stone urns. I studied them as we crept past. All four in the middle marked the graves of small children ranging in age from less than a year to seven years old. That could easily have been me, had it not been for Charles and the IC.

When we were within several yards of the mausoleum, Vivienne stopped, tilted her head, and listened.

Behind us, Race stepped on something that made a loud crack, and we all flinched.

Vivienne held up her hand, and we stilled, holding our breaths, but no sound came from within the mausoleum.

Vivienne shook her head, then moved forward.

"You kept me waiting," Smith's voice called from inside the small, pale stone structure shaped like a chapel. "I don't like to wait."

Race gestured to Maddi, who crept around behind the building.

Vivienne was the first to go inside. She had to stoop to get in the arched doorway. I followed.

Tibby sat on a stone bench at the back of the cramped space, holding a knife against the throat of a terrified girl with red hair who looked to be just out of high school. Her eyes darted to each of us as we entered, making a silent plea to save her. I kept my face emotionless and my eyes on Tibby, hoping to not agitate Smith to the point he killed the girl. He gestured for us to sit on the long concrete slabs, which had at one point held coffins.

Vivienne positioned herself at Smith's right side, closest to the girl. I sat next to her. Alden and Race occupied the slab on the opposite side of the space.

In the center in front of Tibby was a small, round table covered with one of the scarves from Vivienne's house. A candle flickered in a brass candlestick, illuminating the objects on the table: five kitchen knives and five tarot cards placed facedown in a straight line.

"Well, isn't this cozy?" Vivienne said. "I see you've taken up a new occupation, Smith, besides being a thief."

Tibby's head jerked toward her in an unnatural motion.

"That's what you were executed for, right? Being a petty thief?"

Well, she had certainly come out of her corner swinging. Smith's eyes narrowed, and hate seemed to ooze out of every one of his host body's pores. "I was executed because I was betrayed." He tightened his grip on the redheaded girl and she cried out.

Vivienne shrugged. "Spin it however you want."

Through Tibby's eyes, he looked at each one of us. "Two are missing. I want all of you, or I kill this girl."

The girl squeaked again and squeezed her eyes shut. The blade at her neck pressed a dent in her flesh. Any more pressure, and it would break the skin. I swallowed the lump in my throat. It was essential I stay calm in order to keep Vivienne safe.

"Come on in, Maddi," Race called. "The other one is back in Houston."

Smith grinned at him. "So you are in charge. Led by a buffoon, are we?"

"I'm in charge," Vivienne said.

Tibby's head tilted. "Ah. Much better choice. Your hate makes you a more interesting opponent."

Maddi ducked under the archway to the mausoleum, and after checking out the room, she sat to my right, eyes fixed on the knives on the table. Maddi was excellent at hand-to-hand combat. She had taken first place in the dagger competition at Wilkingham.

Smith chuckled through Tibby's tiny body. "Take one, Protector 454. You know you want one." Maddi remained still as stone. "No, really," Smith continued. "Every one of you take one now, or—" The girl cried out as he pushed the blade against her skin.

Each of us took a knife from the table in silence, returned

to our spots, and waited. The girl's ragged breathing and terrified whimpers were the only sounds.

I did a mental checklist of the environment. The structure was all stone, with the exception of the iron doors, and there were no windows or other openings. The floor was dirt. Nothing appeared flammable but the occupants. I eyed the candle. Not much risk of that. We were all armed except the redheaded girl, but having the weapon made me ill at ease.

"Now that we are all here," Smith said, settling back, "we can begin."

Vivienne's anxiety spiked slightly, and Maddi tightened her grip on the knife.

"I'm going to lower the knife now . . ." Tibby's body loosened its grip on the terrified girl a bit. "But you are not going to move, do you understand?" Smith tilted Tibby's head in that strange jerky fashion characteristic of possession victims. "I'm sorry. I've forgotten your name, dear."

The girl said something indecipherable, and Smith shook her. "I'm sorry, I didn't understand you."

"Rachel," the girl screeched in a voice bordering on hysteria.

"Rachel," Smith's voice repeated with an eerie calm, dragging each sound out as if it tasted good on his tongue. "That's a lovely name, and you are a lovely girl. I've not killed a girl named Rachel yet." He looked straight at Vivienne. "Need to keep it fresh, you know."

Vivienne crossed her legs and shot him a bored look. "No

doubt. Nothing worse than repetition. Good thing her name's not Rose. Been there, done that."

She was brilliant. Playing this just right. She was letting him go on in Tibby's body to wear him down. His objectives, though, were unclear, which bothered me.

"Did you call the others to come help?" he asked, lowering the knife from Rachel's throat. "The ones from the classroom?"

"Nope." Vivienne picked at her fingernails with the knife as if giving herself a manicure without a care in the world. "They can't come in until the possession is over and the open Vessels are secured."

Tibby's eyes narrowed as Smith glared at Vivienne. "If you are lying to me, I will kill you outright. All of you."

Vivienne met his eyes and smiled. "Promises, promises. I think you're just screwing with us."

A low growl came from Tibby's throat. "Why did you leave the other one behind? The female Speaker who can't feel me yet?"

Vivienne shrugged. "Who? Cinda? She had better things to do."

"Pity," he said. "I wanted to initiate her into her new job in a way she'd never forget."

Vivienne leaned closer to him. "Well, as the Rolling Stones say, you can't always get what you want." She sat back up. "What *do* you want, by the way? What do you *really* want?"

Rachel had inched away from him a short distance during the exchange. He reached over and yanked her flush against him by the hair, and she screamed.

"I want revenge," Smith said.

Vivienne waved the knife she was holding in a loose grip as if it were a conductor's baton. "For Rose ratting you out who knows how long ago for whatever may or may not have happened?"

"I *died* because of it."

"So did she. Over and over again." She placed the knife across her lap. "Time to move on now, dude. Give it a rest."

By his spastic movements, I could tell Smith was agitated. Beads of sweat broke out on Tibby's brow and glittered in the golden candlelight. "Never."

Vivienne rolled her eyes. "Ugh. Whatever. She's dead again now, so what do you do until she turns up again in . . . oh, say, sixty to ninety years?"

He chuckled. "I kill *you*."

She laughed and leaned back against the stone wall behind her. "Man, if it takes you sixty or more years to kill me, you're doing it wrong." She laughed again.

Smith evidently didn't like being laughed at. He shoved the girl away and stood, knife pointed at Vivienne, who didn't even flinch. A quick look around verified that every one of us was ready to intervene, poised on the edges of the coffin slabs.

Vivienne began cleaning under her nails again, not even looking at him as he stood, knife in hand, ready to kill her. "See, you can't kill me right now for two reasons."

Rachel scooted to the corner of the mausoleum, huddled on the dirt floor, trembling.

"First," Vivienne continued, "these fine folks would stop

you before you could get to me." She gestured to us with a flourish of the blade. "As you know, I'm the only Speaker here, and when you go for me, two of them, Alden and Maddi, will fill the open Vessels while the other two take you down, leaving you nowhere to go but out." She met his eyes. "And what fun would that be? You'd be right back where you started. No dead Speaker. No dead Protector. Nothing. Just you waiting again. And waiting sucks, doesn't it?"

Smith sat Tibby's body back down on the concrete bench and placed the knife on the table. "And second?"

I met Alden's eyes briefly. He understood that she had just given us directions as to how she wanted this handled when it went down. Alden flitted his eyes to the girl huddled on the floor, and from the corner of my eye, I saw Maddi nod almost imperceptibly once, letting him know she would soul-share with Rachel or Tibby, whoever was open at the time.

"Uh-uh," Smith said, wagging a finger at Alden and Maddi. "Everyone stays in their own body, or I kill the girl and Grandma. Are we clear?"

Vivienne got up and stretched. "Nope. You won't do that either. The Protector that gets into the girl's body will instruct her, and her body is a lot stronger than you are in Grandma's. To top that off, killing Grandma puts you back at floating around and waiting again."

She stood opposite him at the table. "Which brings me to my second point. You brought us all here for a reason. You already killed Lenzi, or Rose, or whoever she was to you . . ."

I looked over to find Alden balanced on the very edge of the coffin slab, knife clutched in his hand with his other in a fist. I hoped he knew her nonchalance was an act. He could feel her soul just as I could, so certainly the calm, uncaring outside was clarified by her controlled rage on the inside.

"And after killing her, you could have just disappeared again, but you didn't. You want something, and you've set up this elaborate scene to get it." She gestured to the table in front of her. "You've gone to a whole lot of unnecessary trouble, seeing as how you've already achieved your usual objective. You want something else, and I know what it is."

A twisted grin stretched across Tibby's face. "Do you, now?" Smith's voice rumbled. "A fortune-teller like your grandmother, are you?"

She smiled. "Yep. You bet. Do you want me to tell your fortune?"

"Let me guess," I said. "Smith dies."

I was worried she would be mad that I'd interrupted, but she grinned at me instead. "Nah. That's his past. I was going to read his future."

"No." His voice was loud and harsh. Then, it softened into the sickening cordial voice he used on us at first—the one that made every one of my nerve endings burn and tingle. "No, I believe I will tell you your fortunes first." He gestured for Vivienne to sit, and she did.

"Now, um . . ." He closed his eyes and snapped his fingers. "Ah, yes. Rachel. Sweet Rachel. Please come sit next to me again." He patted the bench with Tibby's hand. "I would like a cigarette, please." He held out his hand and waited while Rachel, shaking so hard it took her several tries, fished a pack of cigarettes out of her Windbreaker pocket. "Anyone mind if I smoke?" He looked right at me, and I almost vomited. "No? Excellent."

Rachel held the pack out to him, and he stilled her hand and took a cigarette. "Do you have a lighter, dear?" He asked, holding the cigarette between his thumb and forefinger.

Shaking so hard she dropped the pack of cigarettes on the floor, Rachel dug in her pocket again and pulled out a lighter. Smith nodded as a cue, but her hands trembled too hard to even light it. Over and over again, she tried to make the lighter ignite, until she crumpled to her knees sobbing.

"No matter," he said, snatching the lighter from her limp fingers.

"You," he said, looking directly at me. "You do it."

I kept my face placid and simply stared at him, focusing on not allowing my fear to show. My job was to protect the Speaker. Weakness would impede my ability to do my job.

His smile widened, and despite my best efforts to retain control, my terror welled. Images from my childhood filled my brain.

A jolt of concern and fear blasted from Vivienne. She knew what this was doing to me. At least she couldn't actually read my emotions like I could hers.

He grasped the knife and pointed it at Tibby's chest. "Come

light this, or I kill the body I'm in," he ordered. He raised an eyebrow. "What exactly are you afraid of, hmmm?"

He must have been spying on us all this time. He was using my past to weaken me, and for a moment it worked. For fleeting seconds I was that five-year-old boy Charles had found all those years ago. But I wasn't that boy anymore. I was Protector 993.

"Go to hell," I said.

Tibby's eyes widened. I'd surprised Smith. "Undoubtedly, I will. Now light this, or I will drive this knife right through her feeble heart!"

It took everything in me to not grab the lighter and do as he asked, but Vivienne believed he wouldn't hurt her grandmother, and so far, her instincts had been spot-on. "Kill her. I'm not lighting it."

He laughed and lowered the knife, then leaned over the table, lighting the cigarette in the candle. He took a long draw, then exhaled through Tibby's nose, making her look like a dragon . . . or my mom's boyfriend.

Illuminated in the flickering candlelight, a plume of smoke rose to the pointed apex of the tiny mausoleum, causing a haunting burn in my nose and eyes.

He sat back and grinned. "There are demons within, and there are demons without. It takes one to know one, as they say." He took a drag off the cigarette, still studying me, then exhaled slowly, the smoke swirling around the candle flame.

"Only *your* demon is much harder to exorcise. Long after I'm gone, yours will remain."

I knew what he was trying to do, and it wouldn't work. Past was past. I stood and walked within a few feet of him. "Dwelling on the wrongs of the past is unhealthy. Like smoking." I reached out and took the cigarette from Tibby's mouth and extinguished it under my foot. "You should stop both."

He raised Tibby's eyebrows in surprise. Then he clapped. "Bravo." He nodded his head toward Vivienne. "You might end up being worthy of her." He leaned back against the wall. "I must admit that I'm a little disappointed, though. A breakdown would have been so much fun."

"Sorry to disappoint," I said, returning to my place on the cold coffin slab. Vivienne's relief and approval wrapped around me like a blanket.

He gave a theatrical sigh. "Where was I? Ah, yes. Fortunes."

He'd been possessing Tibby a long time. Probably two hours or more, which had to be wearing him down. I glanced at my watch to check.

Smith used that nerve-frying cordial voice. "Am I boring you?"

"Stop grandstanding and get on with it, Smith, because you're boring *me*," Vivienne said.

He turned his attention to Alden, whose eyes narrowed immediately. I worried about Alden's self-control if pushed too hard. Though he was far more likely to hurt himself than Vivienne's grandmother. "I will tell your fortune first, Protector

438, since you and I have known each other the longest." He turned the center card over. "Ah. The Fool. So appropriate. Now that she's dead, will you kill yourself to join her sooner, or will you simper and mourn and wait it out like usual?"

Alden remained completely unchanged and still as if he were frozen.

Smith shot a look at Vivienne, and she rolled her eyes. His brow furrowed.

He moved on to Race, who met his eyes directly. "This one is for you and your girlfriend across from you." Maddi's hand tightened around the knife she was holding. He took the card to the right of center and held it up for both of them to see. "The Lovers. Isn't that sweet? Only you're not anymore. You've been replaced, haven't you, my dear?" he said, smiling at Maddi.

Anger and doubt weakened the soul. He was systematically trying to break us down to make his chances of success greater. Only, I wasn't so sure at that point what he would consider success. He hadn't made any move to possess Vivienne or destroy her, which was his usual MO.

Vivienne gave a long-suffering sigh, and Smith, through Tibby's body, scowled. It was as if he sought her approval. As if he *cared* what she thought. Then she yawned.

"You next," he said to Vivienne.

"Bring it, demon. Do your worst." She smiled.

He flipped over the card and held it up with a triumphant

grin. "Death," he said. Rachel squeaked from where she huddled on the floor.

Vivienne stood and snatched the card from his hand. "You're doing it wrong."

He appeared disappointed. Like a child who had not gotten the correct flavor of ice cream.

"Just like everything you do, it's all about show and not substance. A little research would have prevented this embarrassment."

I expected him to rage or growl, but he just watched her with a disappointed look on his face . . . well, Tibby's face.

Vivienne picked up Alden's card. "Here, let me tell you what these really mean." She got on her knees within a few feet of Smith so they could look at the card together.

"Don't get too close," Race warned, turning his knife in his palm.

"Nah. He doesn't want to kill me yet. He's got something else in mind first. Don't ya, demon?"

Tibby's face simply showed confusion. I wondered if he had been weakened or was truly baffled by Vivienne. She was certainly disarming, all calm and didactic when Smith expected her to quake with fear like Rachel.

"So, here we go. I'll start with Alden. You assigned him the Fool card. If the tarot cards are like numbers, Fool is zero. The Fool is where it all begins." She looked right at Alden, and I knew she was telling us something important. "He is the spark that sets everything into motion."

She moved to Race and Maddi's card next. Smith appeared completely engrossed, caught up in her lesson. Perhaps he hadn't communicated in so long, he was enjoying it. That or he was lulling us into complacency again. After his acting job in Mueller's classroom, I wouldn't put anything past him.

"The Lovers," Vivienne said, holding the card up for him to see. "You used it to make a dig at the fact Race just got a new Speaker, huh? Trying to pit him and Maddi against each other, which indicates you've got something in mind for us later where that animosity would be useful." Smith nodded, and Vivienne rewarded him with a smile. "It's actually a good card for them. The Lovers card is about more than just the relationship between two people. It also addresses the necessity of proper choice. The card can tell us to consider all consequences before acting. To be on your toes." She smiled at Maddi without acknowledging Race, and laid the card back on the table.

I was certain that ignoring Race meant she was addressing Maddi specifically. I assumed she wanted Alden to take the first open body and Maddi the second, but Maddi would have to choose something. Maybe when or even who.

Her emotions were still level, and I was in awe of how confident and calm she was, sitting so near the closest thing to the devil himself. The demon who had killed her aunt. And it hit me like a ton of bricks. If she could handle her fear and hate like this, so could I. I wouldn't hide my past. I'd faced my demon and turned it away. The timing for an epiphany was terrible. I almost laughed. Wouldn't it suck to finally realize I no longer had to hide my past just in time to die?

"Death," she said, showing Smith the card. "It's interesting you picked this one for me. You really might have been a decent tarot reader if you had learned how. But you could have been a lot of things if you had learned how, huh? Nobody ever really gave you a chance, did they?" She placed her hand over Tibby's. "Rose never gave you a chance."

Tibby's eyes widened, and Smith shook her head almost imperceptibly.

Vivienne removed her hand and flicked the card with her fingers. "You were trying to freak me out by insinuating I was going to die, right? Well, that's not what this card means at all." She leaned even closer to Smith as if she were telling an important secret. "Death is transformation to the next level of life. It means my perspective has changed. An old attitude is no longer useful to me." She dropped the card in his lap and moved to the center of the room. "Hate is no longer useful. I'm done with revenge, Smith." She walked directly toward the door to leave.

"Stop!" he shouted, grabbing Rachel by the hair and pulling her against him, knife back at her throat. His hand shook, but it might have just been his anger. "*I'm* not done with revenge."

Vivienne turned around and sighed. "Give it a rest." She appeared totally calm, but her anxiety spiked at the sight of the helpless girl with the knife at her throat.

He smiled that sickening inhuman grin through Tibby. "Let's make a deal."

She shook her head. "I don't deal with demons. You sneaky little devils never keep your end of the bargain."

A glance around the space showed me that Maddi, Race, and Alden were all ready for whatever Smith pulled.

"It's an offer you can't refuse." Smith folded Tibby's hands innocently in her lap. "I'll leave permanently and move on— 'Give up the ghost,' as they say—if you meet my demands."

Still in the center of the room, Vivienne put her hands on her hips. "Spill it, Smith."

Smith fanned Tibby's flushed face. She looked overheated, but it was chilly. "Everyone pick up your knives and stand, please."

"I'm already thinking your deal sucks. Forget it."

Rachel screamed and a thin trickle of blood dripped down her neck. "I'll kill her, and you know it. Pick up your knives." The voice wavered a little. Perhaps he was weakening.

Vivienne grabbed her knife from the coffin slab, and we stood in the center of the small space facing Smith in Tibby's body.

He stretched her face in a sick smile, pleased we had obeyed and given over control. "Here is my offer. One person dies. Only one."

My stomach dropped to my feet. The walls seemed to close in even tighter than they were in the confined space.

"One of you must kill someone else. I'll even throw in a

bonus. Grandma and Rachel are included." Rachel sobbed, and he shoved her away. She landed on her knees on the dirt floor. "Anybody is fair game except for him." He pointed at Alden. "He *wants* to die, so that would be no fun at all." He winked at Alden. "You may kill someone, though, if you wish."

The look Alden gave him made it more than clear who he wanted to kill if it were possible. Smith waved Tibby's arms. "Discuss, discuss."

We huddled in a circle while Rachel sobbed at Smith's feet. Vivienne and I had our backs to Smith, with Maddi facing him and Race and Alden flanking her.

"Who's it going to be?" Vivienne whispered just loud enough for Smith to hear over Rachel's wails.

"What the hell are you talking about?" Maddi said in a regular voice. "Have you lost your mind?"

Vivienne narrowed her eyes, but her emotion didn't flare at all as it would if she had really been challenged. "No. It sounds like a reasonable deal. We recycle. He's gone forever. Win-win."

"You've gotta be kidding me," Maddi said.

Vivienne paced the floor—as much as she could in such a small space. I knew she was checking out Smith. When I turned to watch Vivienne, I noticed Smith breathing heavily, and there was more sweat. Tibby's whole face was slick in the candlelight. Her eyes followed Vivienne's movement, but she didn't seem as alert. Vivienne paused in her pacing and winked at us. She began pacing again. "So, who's it going to be? I'm the only

Speaker, so I'm out. Alden's out. I won't let it be Paul, because I'm kind of partial to him, so that leaves Maddi and Race."

Race had figured it out. Something was wrong with the body Smith was in. If we stalled long enough, Tibby would pass out, and he'd be forced to move to Vivienne or Rachel, which would take even more of his energy. "Well, I shouldn't be sacrificed, because I've finally been assigned a Speaker so I won't be the odd man out all the time." He returned to his place on the coffin slab and crossed his arms. Alden sat next to him, glancing at Smith out of the corner of his eye.

Maddi had finally caught on too. "You'll be odd no matter what, caveman. You're not offing me. No way." She sat down, clearing the center of the room for Vivienne, who no doubt would want to resolve him by having him possess her rather than let him escape. If he took off with any power at all, he'd be back.

I wanted to remain standing, but knew if I soul-shared, my body would fare better seated. Every fiber of my being focused on Vivienne and her feelings, which were a mixture of fear and excitement. We'd almost done it. Hopefully, she was strong enough to take him. He'd possessed Tibby for a long time. Much longer than the average Malevolent could hold on to a body with another soul in it, especially after expending a huge amount of energy on what he'd done to Lenzi. And then a horrible thought crossed my mind. What if he had forced Tibby's soul out? He could use that body indefinitely.

Vivienne picked up a card from the table as Smith watched through droopy lids. She turned the Fool toward Alden, then flipped the card at him as if disgusted. Smith sat up straight in Tibby's body as Vivienne grabbed Rachel by the arm and pulled her to stand in front of Alden. "Kill her. We all have too much value. She's expendable."

"I knew I liked you," Smith said.

"No!" Rachel screamed. Vivienne tightened her grip around the girl's rib cage to keep her from collapsing. My heart went out to Rachel. She had no idea what was going on, only that it was way beyond normal. She was living a nightmare that with any luck would have a happy ending for her.

"Do it now," Vivienne said, shoving Rachel into Alden's lap. The minute contact was made, Alden's eyes glazed over and then Rachel screamed and kept screaming. "Get her to shut up," Vivienne said, never taking her eyes off of Smith. "Shut her up, Alden."

I jumped up and grabbed Rachel, moving her out of Smith's reach. I covered her mouth and sent calming current through her while Alden talked to her from inside her body. Hopefully, she'd calm down soon. It was too risky for one of us to leave to take her outside—Smith might go for Vivienne.

"You tricked me," Smith said, still seated. He didn't seem surprised. That or his body was too weak to show it.

Vivienne shrugged. "When in Rome . . ."

He placed Tibby's palm on her forehead. "What's wrong with this body?"

"Diabetes," Vivienne replied between Rachel's screams. "Rachel. Be quiet or I'm going to have Paul knock you out."

Her screams lessened to groans, and I turned my back to Smith. "I would never do that," I whispered in her ear. "But you need to be quiet so we can help you." She calmed a bit more, and I uncovered her mouth. She muttered something, probably in response to Alden talking to her from inside, and I turned back to face Smith.

"Diabetes," Smith repeated. It was probably a new term for him.

"Yeah. She didn't take her meds, and she hasn't eaten. She's going to pass out any minute, so it looks like I'm the only party in town. Ready to get in here so I can evict you to where you belong?"

"Is that what's taken so long?" he asked. "You actually believed I'd do it voluntarily. That I'd just give up." He laughed. "I could evict your weak soul right now if I wished it, little Speaker."

Vivienne walked closer and stood right across the tiny table from him. "You are so full of crap. You couldn't begin to overpower me. I'm smarter, I'm stronger, and I want you gone a whole lot more than you want to stay. So come on in and prove it."

And right when I thought he was going to go for it, just when he opened Tibby's mouth to speak, Cinda stuck her head into the mausoleum, and time moved in slow motion.

Maddi's body went still as her soul departed it, then Race's.

"Leave me open!" Vivienne shouted as Cinda screamed and Tibby fell sideways on the bench.

Rachel started up screaming again, just as Cinda stopped.

"Alden! Get Rachel out of here," Vivienne ordered.

Rachel staggered on shaking legs toward the door while I wondered what the hell had just happened.

I didn't have to wonder long, because Cinda blocked the doorway with her arms, keeping Rachel in, then threw her head back and laughed in Smith's voice.

TWENTY-THREE

Cinda's appearance had been totally unexpected, and it was unfortunate—for her especially. Smith made no move, though, and just leaned against the door frame, smiling in as if we were the greatest entertainment in the world.

"Surprise!" Smith's voice said from her body.

Rachel scooted away, grabbed a knife from the floor, and crouched on a bench. Alden, who was still soul-sharing with her, must have told her what to do.

Tibby sat up. "Oh, my. Well, if that don't beat all." Her speech was slurred, and she looked awful, but it was, without a doubt, Tibby. Smith had not shoved her out.

"Hang in there, Grandma," Vivienne said, eyes still on Cinda.

"Oh . . . oh!" Tibby's eyes flew wide. "There's another person in my head now. I'm mighty tired of this." She slumped back against the wall, shaking her head.

"So am I," Vivienne said, knife in hand.

Smith laughed. "Sick of me so soon?" He still had Cinda's body positioned in the doorway.

I did a quick check. Maddi was in Tibby, Alden in Rachel, Smith had Cinda—because Race couldn't get there in time—and Vivienne was open. Where was Race?

"We appear to be missing one," Smith said from Cinda's body. "Come out, come out, wherever you are."

I had no idea what Race was up to, but I hoped it wasn't some reckless stunt that would get one of us killed. He was probably checking out what was going on outside to be sure Cinda was alone. We needed him back in here to act as second in case I needed to soul-share with Vivienne. I doubted Smith had enough strength at this point to throw someone around noncorporeally like he had Lenzi, but I didn't want to bet on it.

To my relief, Race's body gasped to life. He assumed a casual pose, leaning back against the wall and crossing his legs. "Did I miss anything?"

"I'm an attractive brunette now," Smith said, gesturing to his new host's body.

I could tell Race was upset that the demon was possessing his new Speaker's body by the tightness around his mouth, but his body remained relaxed.

"This could be great fun. There are so many things I could do with this girl's body. Just like I did with Rose," Smith taunted.

Race placed the knife he was holding beside him on the bench.

"Yes. That is wise. You don't want to accidentally hurt her if you have to stop her from slamming her head into a hard surface, would you?" Smith turned his gaze to Vivienne. "And if I destroyed this body, that would leave just you, wouldn't it?"

Vivienne put her hands on either side of her face and gasped. "Oh, no. That would mean you'd have to stop screwing around and wasting time with all the theatrics and deal with me directly, and we both know how that will end. You'll be dispatched." She put her hands down and narrowed her eyes. "That or you'll have to just run away like a coward again."

In Cinda's petite body, he stormed to stand toe-to-toe with Vivienne, and I readied to intervene if he made a move to hurt her. Instead, he lunged at Alden's soulless body and slammed the knife into his thigh near the knee.

Vivienne's horror and anger washed over me in a staggering wave.

Smith straightened Cinda's body and smiled at Rachel, who was housing Alden's soul. "Ouch." He chuckled, and the hair on the back of my skull tingled. He gestured to the knife in Alden's leg. "Something to look forward to, Protector 438. That's going to hurt—that is, it will hurt if you decide to abandon your duty and return to your body before you bleed to death."

Alden would have to put his soul back into his body before it died in order to recycle in the next lifetime.

"Ugh," Vivienne groaned, sounding disgusted and bored. I

knew better; I felt her panic. She rolled her eyes. "That was such a cheap shot. I'd really hoped you were above childish stunts like that." Without pause, she strode to the doorway, stooped under it, and left. Smith looked confused, but I knew Vivienne was leading him away from the mausoleum to keep Alden's and Maddi's bodies safe. Rachel's and Tibby's too, for that matter.

Smith growled from Cinda's body, yanked the knife out of Rachel's hand, grabbed her by the hair, and bolted through the doorway after Vivienne, dragging Rachel with him. Race and I followed.

Vivienne, only a few yards away from the mausoleum, spun to face Smith, hands on hips, and scowled at the screaming girl struggling to free herself from his grasp.

We needed medical backup. It was policy to wait until the resolution was complete, but Tibby and especially Alden needed medical attention right away. I pulled my phone out of my pocket, hit the top name on my favorites list—Charles—and held it behind my back, knowing if he heard Rachel screaming, he'd send help.

"I've gotta go back in and check on Alden's body," Race said, voice low enough for only me to hear. "Slow the bleeding down somehow if it's bad." He eyed the phone behind my back. "Vivienne promised they wouldn't interfere. If they come now, they'll compromise the resolution."

If they didn't, Alden could die. But he was right. Alden was not the most valuable player. "Speaker first," I said out loud, quoting the IC manual. Phone still behind my back, I felt for the button on top and pressed it, canceling the call, then slid the phone back in my pocket. Race nodded and ducked inside the mausoleum.

"Let her go so she'll shut up," Vivienne said. "She's giving me a headache."

To my amazement, Smith obeyed and made Cinda's hand release Rachel's hair. Rachel scurried away a few feet, then bolted toward me, ducked behind my back, and grabbed my shirt.

"What are you doing?" I whispered over my shoulder.

"The guy in my head told me to come over here with you."

"Now what do we do?" Smith's voice said from Cinda's mouth.

Vivienne gave a choked laugh. "You're asking *me*? This is your circus, dude. Play it however you want."

He tilted Cinda's head in a jerky motion and studied Vivienne. "I'm not playing. This is not a game."

"Sure it is." Vivienne leaned against a granite obelisk and folded her arms over her chest. What sounded like hushed whispers hissed all around as a gust of wind rustled the olean- der bushes and dry grass, blowing strands of hair across Vivi- enne's face. She brushed the hair aside and pushed away from the monument, strolling toward the back of the cemetery.

"If you plan to run away from me, it's impossible," Smith said.

She smirked at him over her shoulder. "Do I strike you as someone who runs away?"

"No. No, you don't," he said.

"I'm not afraid of you. I don't think you really want to kill me." Vivienne dropped the knife she was holding into the tall grass and gestured for him to join her in her leisurely meander between the tombstones. "Come on, we'll just be a couple of girls talking."

He followed. "I'm not a girl."

She stopped, smiled, and looked him up and down. "You look like one."

"An unfortunate circumstance." He held up the knife clutched in Cinda's hand. "You would come with me even though you are unarmed?"

Vivienne pointed at her temples. "I have my rapier-sharp wit."

"That you do." Smith smiled. This time it wasn't the kind that made my skin crawl. He seemed genuinely amused. He placed his knife on top of a low, wide grave marker.

Race joined me.

Vivienne shrugged. "Besides, I would never hurt another Speaker, no matter what ghoul is animating her." She nodded to me and Race. "That's what they're for."

Smith gave us a hateful glare, then returned his attention to Vivienne.

"Come on, I want to check out that creepy-looking angel

thing over there." Vivienne pointed to a monument a short distance away.

"Maybe she's going to talk him to death," Race said.

Vivienne looked over her shoulder and held her hand up, indicating she wanted us to stay back. No way was I letting her stay alone with a Malevolent, even if he was unarmed and in Cinda's tiny body.

"Alden should be fine," Race whispered. Like me, Race kept his eyes riveted on Smith and Vivienne. "No major blood vessel damage. Still, it might be wise for him to return just in case."

That would leave Rachel open. A civilian casualty would be awful and was to be avoided at all costs.

I glanced over my shoulder at the frightened girl hanging on to me. "Rachel. I need you to take Alden back to his body."

She clutched my shirt tighter. "No. No, please don't make me go back in there. Please."

Vivienne and Smith weren't going anywhere fast, but I didn't want them to get too far away in case he tried to hurt her physically. I untangled Rachel's fingers from my shirt. "Go back to the mausoleum now, Rachel. You'll be safe if you do as I say."

Her eyes went wide, and she got a crazed look on her face. Then, she took off sprinting toward her car, parked in the middle of the cemetery road.

"Great. She picks now to grow a spine," Race said, taking off to catch her.

I couldn't waste time on this and let my Speaker get out of

physical striking range. Vivienne and Smith had stopped to watch Race chasing Rachel down like a lion pursuing a gazelle. Race caught up with her easily and wrapped his arms around her upper body, holding her back tight against him, arms pinned against her sides, while she kicked and flailed madly.

Race hauled her to the mausoleum, and Smith and Vivienne continued toward the monument with the weeping angel on top.

Feeling for her soul's transmissions that would indicate fear, I watched Vivienne and Smith talking as if they were friends. As if our very lives were not in danger. As if he had not brutally murdered Lenzi hours before.

Vivienne laughed and took Cinda's hand.

"Okay, now it's just getting weird," Race said, joining me again. "If they start kissing, I'm out."

I didn't answer, but remained focused on Vivienne's emotions. She wasn't afraid. In fact, she flipped between anxiety and excitement. I wished I could hear what they were talking about, but with the steady wind and their distance, I couldn't.

"So, Alden's going to go back in his own body," Race whispered.

"That leaves Rachel open. She's a human. We can't do that."

Race shook his head. "Maddi was given authority to make decisions by Vivienne, remember? She decided that Vivienne's grandmother was not a target for obvious reasons, so she's going to leave her unprotected while she covers Rachel. I'll remain on Cinda."

I hated losing coverage of Tibby, but Maddi's logic was sound, and it was safer for Alden to return to his body in case the injury was worse than anticipated.

"What in the hell is she doing?" Race said, shaking his head. "Usually, Smith possesses someone and starts killing people. He never just talks."

I closed my eyes and focused on Vivienne's transmissions. Her anxiety was lessening. "He seems to be intrigued by her. She didn't react as he expected. I think she's going to pull this off."

Smith and Vivienne sat down on the stoop of a different mausoleum that looked ready to crumble apart. Plants and ferns grew from the cracks in the brick mortar, and plywood boarded up the opening instead of its original marble door, which had fallen away years ago and broken into the large pieces still littering the area in front of the structure. The moonlight leached color out of everything, making the scene even more surreal.

I shuffled closer and could hear bits and pieces of their conversation. Smith told her about a dog he'd had as a boy, and Vivienne described her cat.

"Are you ready?" Vivienne asked him.

"For what?"

She put her hand over Cinda's. Unlike Protectors, Hindered and Malevolents had access to all the host Vessel's senses. Smith could feel Vivienne's touch. How long had it been since he had felt someone's gentle touch? Probably since before 1863—possibly never.

"To move on to whatever comes after this," Vivienne said. No fear. No taunting. No hate or need for revenge. Just an invitation.

"No." Smith shook Cinda's head violently. "Talk to me."

Vivienne added her other hand to her first, enfolding Cinda's completely. "Every ghost I've met wants something specific. What do you really want? I can help you."

"Revenge."

She shook her head. "No, no. That's circular and getting us right back to where we were. Go back to *why* you want revenge."

"Everything she said—everything she did was a lie."

"Ah, Rose."

"Yes. She said she loved me. That we would be together." He slammed Cinda's hand down so hard on the concrete, it bled. "It was all a lie."

She took Cinda's hand in hers. "I'm sorry you were hurt. I wish I had known you when you were alive. I think we would have been friends."

"You lie! You're tricking me. That's all Speakers do."

"I will never lie to you." She reached over and tucked Cinda's hair behind her ear. "I think I know what you want, but you've been at this demon gig so long, you don't remember it yourself."

Smith shook Cinda's head. "I want revenge."

"Yes. I wanted revenge too. But it is a secondary desire—a byproduct of having lost what I really want. I really want my mom back. I want my aunt back. I want their love. But revenge won't get me that, will it?"

Vivienne moved slowly, like I had done with the tiny bird all those years ago to earn its trust, and she gently put her hand on the side of Cinda's face. "You don't want revenge. What you really want is for someone to care enough to see the real you. For someone to listen. Just like me, you want love."

Smith didn't respond.

I felt a pulse of anxiety from Vivienne. It was almost time. Race had felt it too and appeared ready to pounce if something physical happened.

This was it. I had no idea how it would go down, but I knew my responsibility was to wait for her command, then force Smith's soul out of Cinda's body. If he was weak enough or ready to leave voluntarily, he would be forced to resolution. If not, and he still had enough energy to linger in this world noncorporeally, we'd be doing this again in the future. I moved closer.

And then all hell broke loose.

Smith saw the Suburbans pulling in before we did, because our backs were to the entrance. Vivienne cried out in pain right after Cinda groaned. I could do nothing without a command from Vivienne.

Cinda scrambled to her feet and looked around in horror. Vivienne rolled over onto her side on the stoop of the mausoleum and screamed. Then she writhed as if she were having some kind of seizure.

Eyes huge, Cinda backed away from Vivienne. Race grabbed her by the arm and yanked her several yards away. "Is he out?" he asked.

Cinda just stared at him, uncomprehending.

"Is Smith out of your body?" Race shouted.

Vivienne got on her hands and knees and stared over at me. Her lips moved, but no sound came out.

"Yes," Cinda said. "He's out."

"Can I come in?" Race asked.

"Wha . . . I don't understand." Cinda swayed on her feet as if she were going to faint.

Race shook her by the shoulders. "Shit, girl. Just say yes!"

"Yes?"

Still standing, Race's body went still, and Cinda shouted out as he put his soul in her body to keep Smith from possessing her again. At least she was safe now.

Vivienne doubled over and curled into a ball. "No," she groaned, covering her head with her arms.

I'd never been so helpless in my life. I'd seen videos, I'd read accounts, but nothing could have prepared me for this. She was literally fighting Smith for control of her own body. But I had to wait for her prompt to come in. If I went in too early, she might be the weaker soul and I would evict her instead of Smith, killing her.

Her shaking hands clawed at the bricks of the structure as she pulled her way up the wall to stand, gasping for breath, cheek against the rough surface.

"Fight, Vivienne," I said, moving closer. "You can do this."

She charged past me, slamming into Race's body, which fell over, head clipping the edge of a tombstone.

Her eyes darted around, and in jerky movements, she ran to where Smith had left the knife balanced on top of the tombstone. By the time I realized what she was doing, she had already grabbed it and held it by both hands out in front of her, as if to plunge it into her own chest.

"Smith, no," I said. "Please, don't do it. I beg of you."

In a strange mechanical jerk, Smith turned her head and looked out at me through her eyes, knife still pointed at her chest. "You beg."

"Yes. I beg. I plead." I fell to my knees. "I offer you my life for hers. Whatever you want, just . . . not her."

Her brow furrowed as Smith continued to consider me, knife lowering a little. "No one has ever begged me before. You would let me kill you right now to save her."

"Right now."

And I would have, if I'd thought it would really work. He lowered the knife from her chest and approached me where I was still on my knees in the grass. There was no way to enforce this exchange. I'd be dead, and he was the least trustworthy entity on the planet. But at least he had lowered the knife. Now I needed to make him doubt his actions so he would be weakened and she could fight back.

"She cares," I said. "You know that. You talked to her. She's special."

"Yes. I thought she was. But she's not. She's just like Rose. She lied!" he shouted. He pointed with the knife to the two Suburbans parked on the road running through the cemetery. "She told me they would not come!"

"What difference does it make? They aren't approaching, and they won't until given the signal."

He appeared confused. "She lied. She knew they would come."

I shook my head. "She didn't lie. I dialed them earlier, and they heard that girl screaming. Vivienne didn't know."

If I could keep him talking, he would use energy simply by possessing yet another body. Most Malevolents were good only for one, but he had been in three today, plus he'd summoned enough power to kill Lenzi. He had to be losing strength.

"Do you know that in her spare time, she teaches little kids how to read?" I remained in a subservient position on my knees, so he'd feel he still had control. "She does. She also loves history and classical literature."

He blinked rapidly, then shook his head. "Why are you telling me this?"

"Because it's important."

He scowled but made no effort to shut me up. I needed to keep him listening and stay calm so he would stick around but not become enraged and hurt Vivienne.

"And the first time I met her, she had hot pink hair. Pink like the color of azaleas. Do you remember what azaleas are?" He looked completely baffled. "They're flowers that grow on bushes all over the South in the spring." I slowly rose to my feet, and he didn't react. "They're beautiful and vivid, like her." I walked to within a foot of where he stood in Vivienne's body. "You know it too. You felt it, didn't you? She's special. And she cares about people. She cares about you."

Tears spilled from Vivienne's eyes. "Yes," Smith's voice whispered.

"Let her go."

"I can't. It's . . . I . . . I can't."

Slowly, smoothly, palm up, I reached for the knife in his hand. Vivienne's fingers loosened on the handle as mine wrapped around it. I pulled the knife away, almost fainting from relief.

Violent trembling started in the hands and moved its way up Vivienne's arms until she shook all over, then crumpled into the grass.

She whimpered in her own voice, and every muscle in my body tensed as she rose to her knees, gasping for air, face contorted with pain. She bit her lip and reached around to her back pocket as if every inch she moved was excruciating. She pulled a card out of her pocket.

She took a breath and stared down at it. "The Death card," she said, in her own lovely voice. She was quiet for a while, then she nodded her head. "Yes, Smith. My favorite. Do you remember what it represents?" She nodded again and sat back on her heels, meeting my eyes. "Yes, the transition to the next level of life."

I couldn't believe it. She had overpowered Smith, had retaken control of her body.

She held the card back up before her eyes. "It's a good card for both of us. We both need to transition now. Leave revenge and hate behind."

She shuddered and closed her eyes. "I can't let you have my body again." Another, more violent tremor racked her slender frame. "I said no." She took a deep breath and let it out slowly. "I'm scared too, but I'll be here with you the whole time. You won't be alone." Her voice was so low I could barely hear her.

Her pale skin glowed blue in the moonlight, making her look like an angel among the tombstones. Another gust of wind blasted from the east, whipping her hair around. Then a funny look crossed her face, and she laughed, startling me.

"Well, not yet, but I'm working on it," she said. Eyes closed, she appeared to be listening. "Shhhh. Be still," she said. Then, she opened her eyes and looked directly into mine. "Now, Paul," she whispered.

"Out," I commanded my soul, ready to battle Smith and rid her body of him. Since we weren't touching, it was going to hurt. "In," I ordered, regretting her groan.

I'd been told that evicting a Malevolent was like lifting a heavy weight made of fire. And it was a perfect comparison. Crushing pressure and searing heat pounded me on all sides when my soul entered Vivienne's body. I pressed against the foreign soul pushing against me. It was sickening and dark and utterly terrifying.

"It's over, Smith," I heard Vivienne say. "Just let go."

I couldn't hear Smith, but I felt his response. He wasn't going without a fight. I resisted a hard blast of energy from him, knowing that it would extinguish my soul to be pushed out.

I had to be strong and fight for Vivienne.

"Come on, Paul," she said. "I know you can do it." She stifled a groan as Smith gave another hard shove.

I gathered as much energy as I could scrape together to ram full force into Smith's soul, and Vivienne screamed. And then I did it again, and again, and again. The burning stopped, and for a moment it felt as though my soul had expanded, but I realized that it had simply stretched to fill the space that Smith had emptied.

TWENTY-FOUR

I could see nothing. Vivienne's eyes were closed.

Open your eyes, I told her.

"I can't look," she whispered, sorrow flooding her body.

Behind us, car doors slammed, and footsteps approached.

Open your eyes, Vivienne. We have to see it. We need to confirm the outcome.

Her eyes cracked open, and standing right in front of her, flickering like a blue hologram, was Nicaragua Smith.

He looked nothing like I'd imagined—nothing like a demon at all. Small in stature, with a full beard, he wore tattered black clothes, and his hands were bound behind his back. He stared at Vivienne for several moments, then he gave her a sad, slight smile and bowed at the waist. She nodded back. As he straightened, a black swirl rose up around him until he was no longer visible. Then, the cloud dissipated, Smith along with it.

"Game over," she breathed.

Somewhere behind us, Cinda cried out and Race whooped. "Yeah, buddy! That's how it's done!" Vivienne turned, and through her eyes, I watched Race shake his backside and dance in a circle. Charles was there with six or so guys in medical clothes.

"Fatalities?" Charles asked.

"Only Smith," Vivienne answered. Her eyes shot to the mausoleum and concern consumed her body. "But Alden was hurt pretty bad." She struck out running toward the white-washed stone structure.

The heavy footsteps of the others racing through the dry grass behind us filled her ears.

Vivienne ducked under the archway of the mausoleum, scanning the room. The candle had burned down to a nub, its flame flickering wildly in the puddle of wax remaining in the candlestick, causing a strobe-light effect. Rachel hunkered in the corner just to the left inside the door. Maddi's empty body faced straight forward in the middle of the left coffin slab. Tibby appeared to be asleep on the bench in the back, where Smith had left her. And Alden sat on the right coffin slab, his leg elevated and bound with the teal scarf that had been draped over the table earlier.

His eyes searched Vivienne's face.

He doesn't know, I said.

"It's over," Vivienne whispered.

"She and Junior kicked Smith's ass!" Race shouted from outside.

The light from the candle flickered in Alden's tear-filled eyes. "Thank you."

Charles ducked in next, followed by two medics. He assessed the room quickly, nodded to Alden, and stuck his head back out the opening, instructing the medics outside to retrieve a wheelchair.

Rachel whimpered, and Maddi's body gasped to life.

"If you are ambulatory, please wait outside with me," Charles said.

He stopped in an empty plot close to the mausoleum, and two men escorted Rachel to the cars. I knew they wouldn't let her just go home. They would debrief her first, then make sure she wouldn't go to the media or reveal us, possibly by offering her a plush paperwork job at headquarters. Many of the civilian employees at IC headquarters were past resolution witnesses.

"Go take care of Paul," Charles instructed Vivienne.

While Charles questioned Maddi, Vivienne walked back to my body and placed both hands on my shoulders. "Go ahead," she said.

I didn't want to exit, because no one else could hear me when I spoke from inside and I had so many things to say that didn't bear an audience—so many new things I'd discovered.

Vivienne, I—

"Get moving, Protector 993," Charles ordered.

Her flush of frustration matched my own. It would have to wait until we were alone.

After my soul was reunited with my body, we rejoined the others. That amazing, warm emotion that I felt from Vivienne when we kissed transmitted from her, flooding my body, making it hard to concentrate on anything else while Charles wrote Race's account on a sheet of paper fastened to a clipboard.

It was Maddi's turn next. Cinda sat on a tombstone in a nearby plot, shivering, while Maddi recounted what had happened. When Charles called on Cinda to report, she only shook her head and whispered, "Can't."

"Why did you come to the scene when instructed not to do so?" Charles asked.

She shrugged, staring at the grave at her feet.

Charles looked up from his clipboard. "You showed reckless disregard for the mission, and you compromised the lives of multiple people, including a civilian and the family member of a Speaker."

Cinda didn't meet his eyes. "I'm . . . I didn't . . ." She shook her head. "I can't do this."

Charles made a note on his clipboard. "I agree."

Two medics escorted Tibby out of the mausoleum, one on each arm, and led her toward the cars. Vivienne ran after them and caught her up in a huge hug. Tibby grinned. "I'll see you at home after these two handsome young men get my blood sugar all undiscombobulated."

Vivienne shook her head and chuckled. "Behave yourself."

Alden emerged in a wheelchair pushed by a guy in a lab

coat next. His eyes shot directly to us as the man rolled him over the rough ground. Then Alden gasped as if he had just reanimated. He did it again and grabbed his chest. The man pushing the wheelchair stopped.

Charles's phone rang, and he put it to his ear. "Yes, I know," he said with a smile. His eyes locked on Alden, who looked like he had seen a ghost, which was funny if you really thought about it. "And her Protector knows too. Thank you for the call. Keep me updated on her progress." He put the phone in his pocket and waited for Alden to catch his breath.

"She's back," Alden choked out. "She died, but she's back." He thumped his chest. "I feel her!"

"She was never dead. She had a complicated surgery, and she's recovering now," Charles explained, walking toward him.

He shook his head in disbelief. "She was *dead*. I felt her die."

Charles patted his shoulder. "General anesthesia is new to you this cycle. Before this lifetime, I don't think Rose ever underwent any kind of surgery requiring she be unconscious. I imagine it would feel like she had died."

Alden looked as though he were going to launch out of the chair. "I have to see her. Now!"

"Treat him at the same facility," Charles instructed the medics. "Go ahead and take the two patients and the civilian girl."

Race cleared his throat and fidgeted. Charles smiled. "And Race and Maddi can follow you in the civilian's car."

"What about me?" Cinda asked.

Charles sighed. "You'll ride with me, Paul, and Vivienne in the second vehicle."

The emotional pulses coming from Vivienne intensified, and it was all I could do to not grab her and kiss her right there. Instead, I took a step away so that the scent of candles and incense weakened. I fought hard to focus on Charles as he spoke. "I'll interview the two of you after you have had some time to relax, since your reports will take the longest. I have enough to do a preliminary write-up for now. That doesn't mean you're off the hook on your own report, Paul."

"No, sir," I said.

The moment he turned his back, Vivienne grabbed me and made good on what I'd been wanting to do myself. She wrapped around me like her life depended on it, and stayed that way until Charles cleared his throat. I ended the kiss, but she didn't release my neck, creating the most awkward situation ever. I met Charles's eyes.

He lifted a finger at Vivienne. "I do need one thing clarified, though, Speaker 961. Race told me you said something unusual to Smith immediately before Protector 993 entered the Vessel. Do you recall your last words with Smith?"

"Of course I do."

In the moonlight, I couldn't make out Charles's expression clearly, but I could hear the amusement in his voice. "What was it he asked you?"

She turned loose of my neck and grinned. "Oh. He asked me if Paul was in love with me."

Leaving me dumbstruck, she strode toward the cars while I racked my brain for her response. What had she said? What had she said . . . ?

Turning to look over her shoulder at Charles and me, she winked. "I told him I was working on it."

TWENTY-FIVE

21st-Century Cycle, Journal Entry 7:

The resolution and exorcism of a Malevolent was executed without incident, resulting in a positive conclusion including no fatalities. ~~The Speaker is assuming her role effectively. The working relationship between Speaker and Protector is satisfactory.~~ The Speaker kicks ass, and the relationship between Speaker and Protector is mind-blowing.

Paul Blackwell—Protector 993

Because of records and the probability of exposure, the IC didn't use regular hospitals. They housed patients in luxury hotels owned by the IC under the care of its own physicians, most of whom were Protectors and Speakers themselves.

Sunlight streamed into the huge hotel suite, making the gold silk brocade on the chairs and bedcovers shimmer. Lenzi's head was wrapped in bandages. A tall neck brace came up to her chin, and what flesh I could see on her face was swollen and bruised. I wouldn't have been able to identify her, were it not for the fact Alden was sleeping in a chair next to the bed and the nurse confirmed I had the right room when I knocked.

"At least Alden's getting some sleep now," Maddi whispered from a chair in the corner of the bedroom.

"His neck's gonna hurt like blazes if he stays like that," Race said.

Maddi glared at Race over the top of her magazine. "Well, if you weren't hogging the spare bed, maybe he could get in it."

Race sat up. "Hey. He wasn't using it."

"Shhhhh!" the nurse hissed from the sitting room behind me. "Do not raise your voices above a whisper, please. The patients need to rest."

Maddi flipped a page with a flourish. "So are you two going to just stand there in the doorway, or what?"

Vivienne plopped in a chair next to Maddi, and I took the one closest to Race, who had his muddy cowboy boots on the bedcovers.

Race cocked an eyebrow at me. "So, where have you guys been, Junior? Cinda said you didn't come home last night."

"Charles interviewed us about the resolution," I answered.

Race smirked. "All night long?"

"Shut up, Race," Maddi scolded.

I glanced over at Vivienne, and she blushed.

The nurse bustled in, checked on one of the pieces of medical equipment, gave us all warning glares, and then went back into the adjoining sitting room.

Maddi put her magazine on the table next to her. "How's your grandmother, Vivienne?"

"She's good. She was eating breakfast in front of the TV, watching a *Spirit Seekers* episode when we left."

Alden groaned and shifted in his chair. The nurse came back in and touched his arm. "Do you need some painkillers?"

Alden opened his eyes and squinted at her, then looked around the room. He straightened his leg and winced. "Uh, yeah. That'd be great."

Maddi stood and stretched. "How's the leg?" She walked to a bureau near Alden and poured a glass of water from a pitcher.

"Hurts like hell." He touched Lenzi's hand. "Could be worse, though."

Race scooted up in the bed and leaned against the headboard. "Charles told us that Lenzi is going to be fine."

"Yeah," Alden said. "Thanks to Vivienne and Paul."

Maddi held up the glass of water in salute.

"How did you do it?" Alden asked. "I didn't really think it was possible to resolve Smith."

Race snorted. "She came up with a strategy all her own— she talked him to death."

Vivienne smiled. "No, actually, I figured out what to do because of something Paul said the first day we met."

My mind filed through the conversations we had had that

first day, but I couldn't think of anything that would've given her a strategy for taking Smith down.

The nurse returned with a tiny paper cup and a glass of water. Alden took the cup, tilted the pills into his mouth, then swallowed them down while she watched. She took the paper cup and left.

Vivienne continued. "See, I figured out right away Smith was making his grand finale. He went to a lot of trouble to impress us, which I doubt he usually did."

"No, he just killed people," Alden said.

"And then he was offended when I didn't pay enough attention. So he kept trying to get noticed by being flashy. Showy." She looked right at me. "Toxic."

I lowered my eyes and studied the swirl pattern in the hotel carpet. Being her inspiration may not have been a good thing.

"At dinner that first night, Paul told me that he thought I was like a beautiful, toxic flower. I lashed out and dressed in an unconventional way to hide my vulnerability. He was right."

Maddi sat back in her chair.

"I believed that Smith was doing the same thing," Vivienne said. "He was using flash to cover his desires and vulnerability. Paul had also told me that revenge wasn't a primary desire. It was a byproduct. Kind of a symptom, I guess. I just had to figure out what Smith really wanted."

"What was it?" Alden asked.

"I think he'd been demonic so long, he didn't know anymore. He just needed to be reminded of why he wanted revenge so badly."

Race threw his legs over the side of the bed. "Well, that clears it right up, Dr. Viv."

Vivienne laughed. "Smith longed for what Rose had denied him in the 1860s. A human connection—a personal relationship. Sounds stupid, I know, but that was it. The card thing is the perfect example. The minute I started talking to him like he wasn't a demon, he responded. He almost forgot what he was supposed to be. What he *wanted* to be: evil."

"He *was* evil," Alden said.

"Yes, he was," Vivienne agreed. "Through and through."

I knew that for a fact. My soul still felt scorched from dealing with him.

Vivienne leaned forward in her chair. "But he wanted to interact and be heard so badly he was willing to lose power to achieve it. I knew if I could keep him engaged enough, he would weaken enough for Paul to force him out, and he'd be too used up to stay."

"And it worked," Maddi said.

"It did. It also helped that Cinda came along, because possessing her and then me took a ton of his energy."

Race rolled his eyes.

"Where *is* Cinda?" I asked.

"Charles decided she needs to serve out this cycle at the administration office instead of in the field," Race said. "Some folks just aren't cut out for this, regardless of their gifts. Cinda is smart enough to know she's not ready."

"Does that mean she won't ever be your Speaker?" Vivienne asked.

Race offered Maddi his hand and helped her to her feet. "We'll see how she feels next cycle," he said.

Maddi grinned.

The nurse came into the room and put a blanket over Alden, who had drifted off to sleep in the chair again. "All of you should leave now so that they can rest."

Maddi tugged Race toward the door. "You owe me breakfast."

"You guys wanna join us?" Race asked over his shoulder as Maddi pulled him down the hallway by the hand.

"Nah. We're good," Vivienne said.

And we were.

We stepped out into the long hotel hallway, and the nurse closed the door behind us. "What do you want to do now?" I asked.

She struck out toward the elevators and paused outside a door with a brass plaque that said LINENS. She opened the door, peeked in, then turned to me and arched an eyebrow. With both hands, she pulled me into the closet full of clean, folded towels and bedsheets and pushed the door closed with her foot. "How about some physical therapy?"

"Game on," I said.

ACKNOWLEDGMENTS

Thank you to all the great folks at Philomel for making it possible for me to go back into the world of the Intercessor Council one more time.

As always, Jill Santopolo, your guidance was spot-on. Thanks to Brian Geffen, Ana Deboo, Cindy Howle, Linda McCarthy, Amy Wu, Tony Sahara, and the whole gang at Penguin for making my work shine.

Ammi-Joan Paquette, agent extraordinaire—you rock. That is all.

Big hugs to Leah Clifford and Kari Olson for emergency reads and input.

I love you, Laine, Hannah, Robert, and Emily. I am nothing without my amazing husband and kids, who endure dirty dishes, plot discussions, and incoherent mumblings.

Special gratitude to my little Emily-Bee-Bug, who decided Paul needed his own book. I'm glad I agreed. He's pretty cool.

Most of all, thank you to my fantastic, supportive readers. You are what it's all about.